States of Mind

Patrice & Emilie Guillon
Writers

Sebastien Samson
Artist

•

Montana Kane
Translator

•

Fabrice Sapolsky
Alex Donoghue
US Edition Editors

Amanda Lucido
Assistant Editor

Vincent Henry
Original Edition Editor

Jerry Frissen
Senior Art Director

Fabrice Giger
Publisher

Rights and Licensing - licensing@humanoids.com
Press and Social Media - pr@humanoids.com

STATES OF MIND
This title is a publication of Humanoids, Inc. 8033 Sunset Blvd. #628, Los Angeles, CA 90046.
Copyright © 2019 Humanoids, Inc., Los Angeles (USA). All rights reserved. Humanoids and its logos are ® and © 2019 Humanoids, Inc.
Library of Congress Control Number: 2018966992

Life Drawn is an imprint of Humanoids, Inc.

First published in France under the title "Journal d'une Bipolaire"
Copyright © 2010 La Boîte à Bulles, Patrice Guillon, Emilie Guillon, Sebastien Samson. All rights reserved.
All characters, the distinctive likenesses thereof and all related indicia are trademarks
of La Boîte à Bulles Sarl and/or of Patrice Guillon, Emilie Guillon, Sebastien Samson.

States of Mind

EMILIE GUILLON • PATRICE GUILLON • SEBASTIEN SAMSON

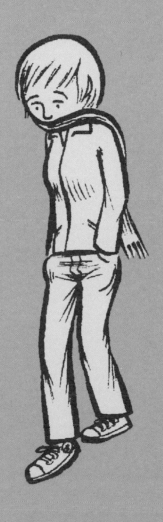

Life Drawn

To Marylène and Jean-Marie…
Special thanks to Rosalie for her support.
Sebastien Samson

To my mother.
Emilie Guillon

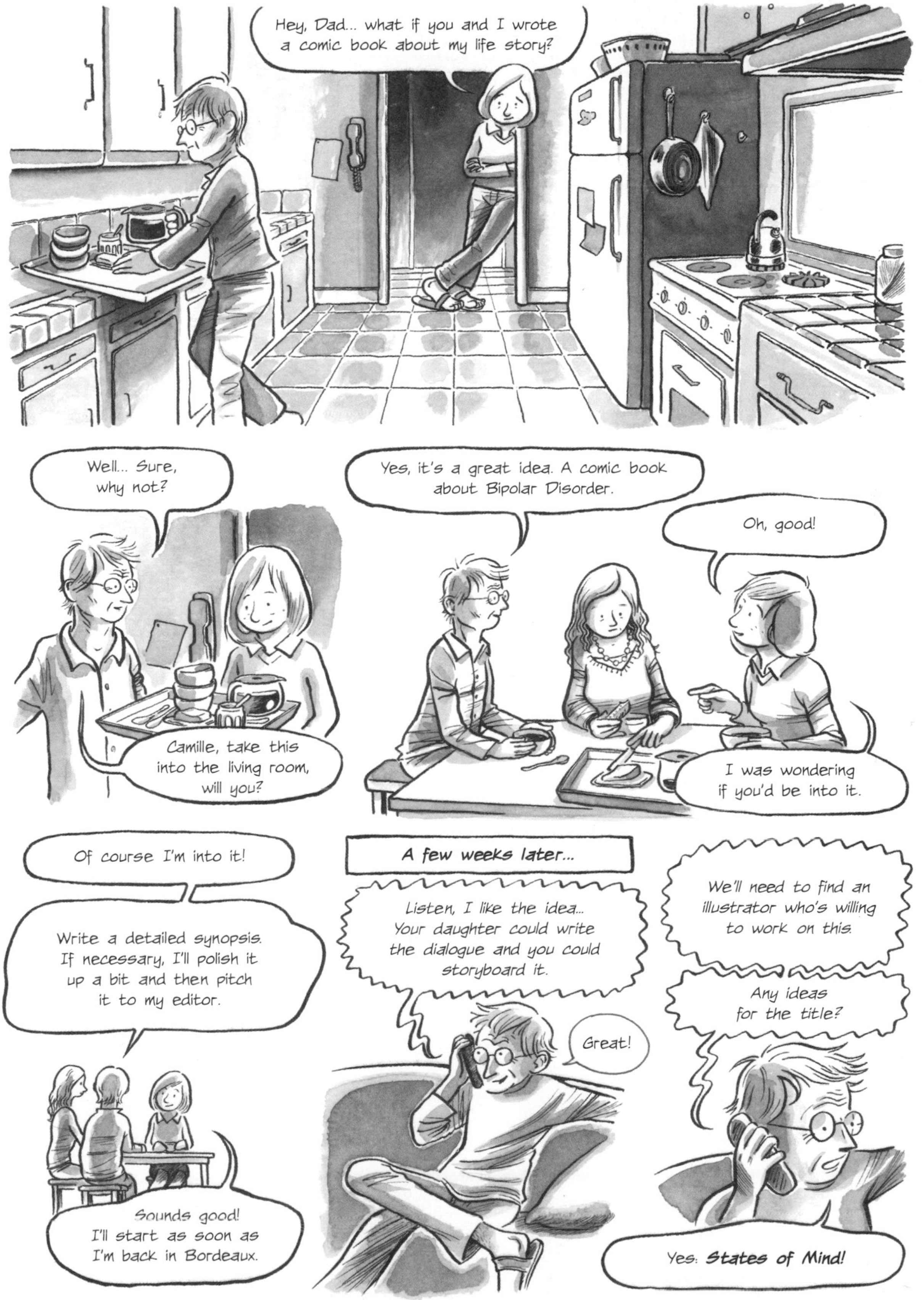
Hey, Dad... what if you and I wrote a comic book about my life story?
Well... Sure, why not?
Camille, take this into the living room, will you?
Yes, it's a great idea. A comic book about Bipolar Disorder.
Oh, good!
I was wondering if you'd be into it.
Of course I'm into it!
Write a detailed synopsis. If necessary, I'll polish it up a bit and then pitch it to my editor.
Sounds good! I'll start as soon as I'm back in Bordeaux.
A few weeks later...
Listen, I like the idea... Your daughter could write the dialogue and you could storyboard it.
Great!
We'll need to find an illustrator who's willing to work on this.
Any ideas for the title?
Yes: States of Mind!

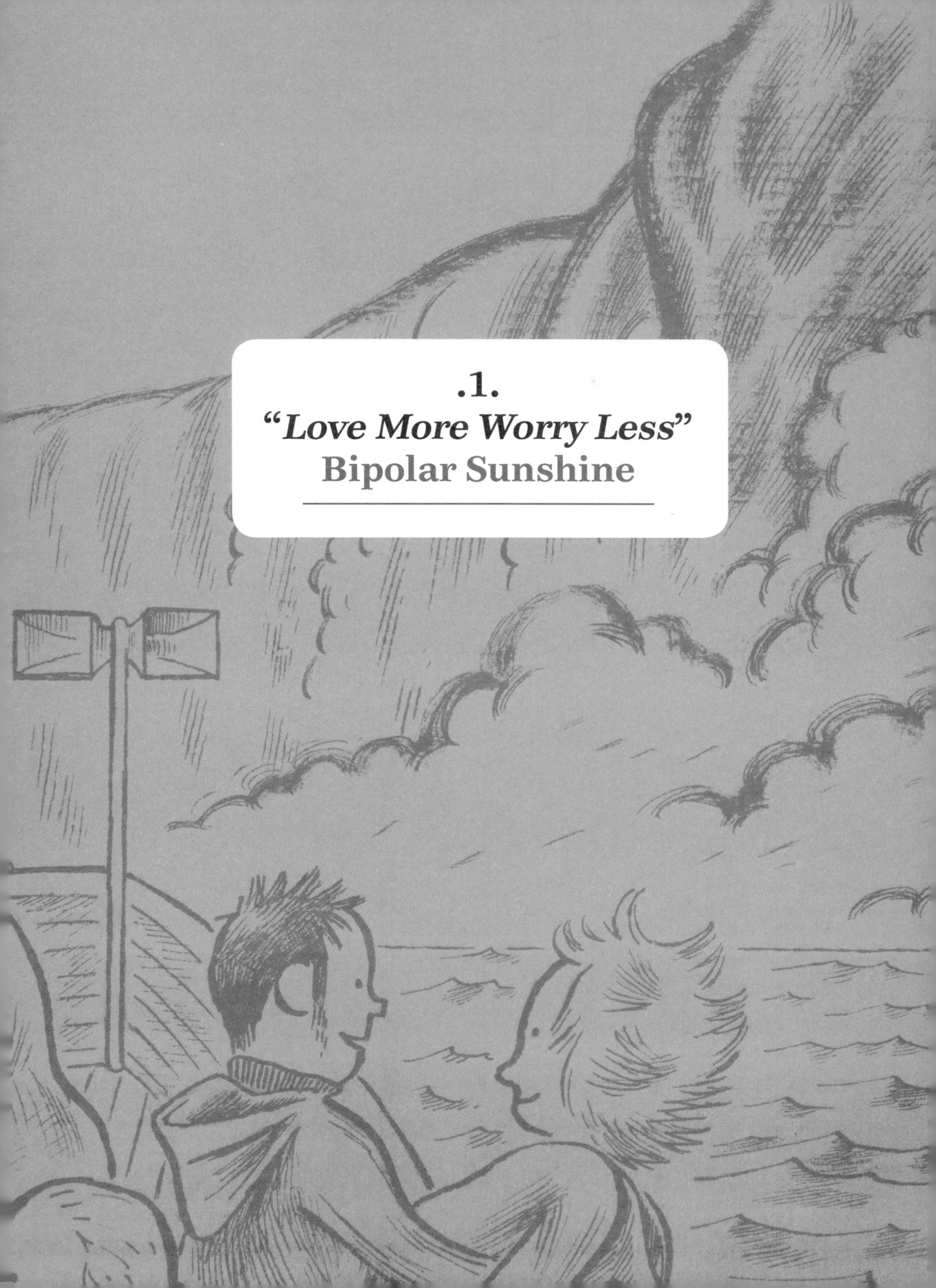

.1.
"Love More Worry Less"
Bipolar Sunshine

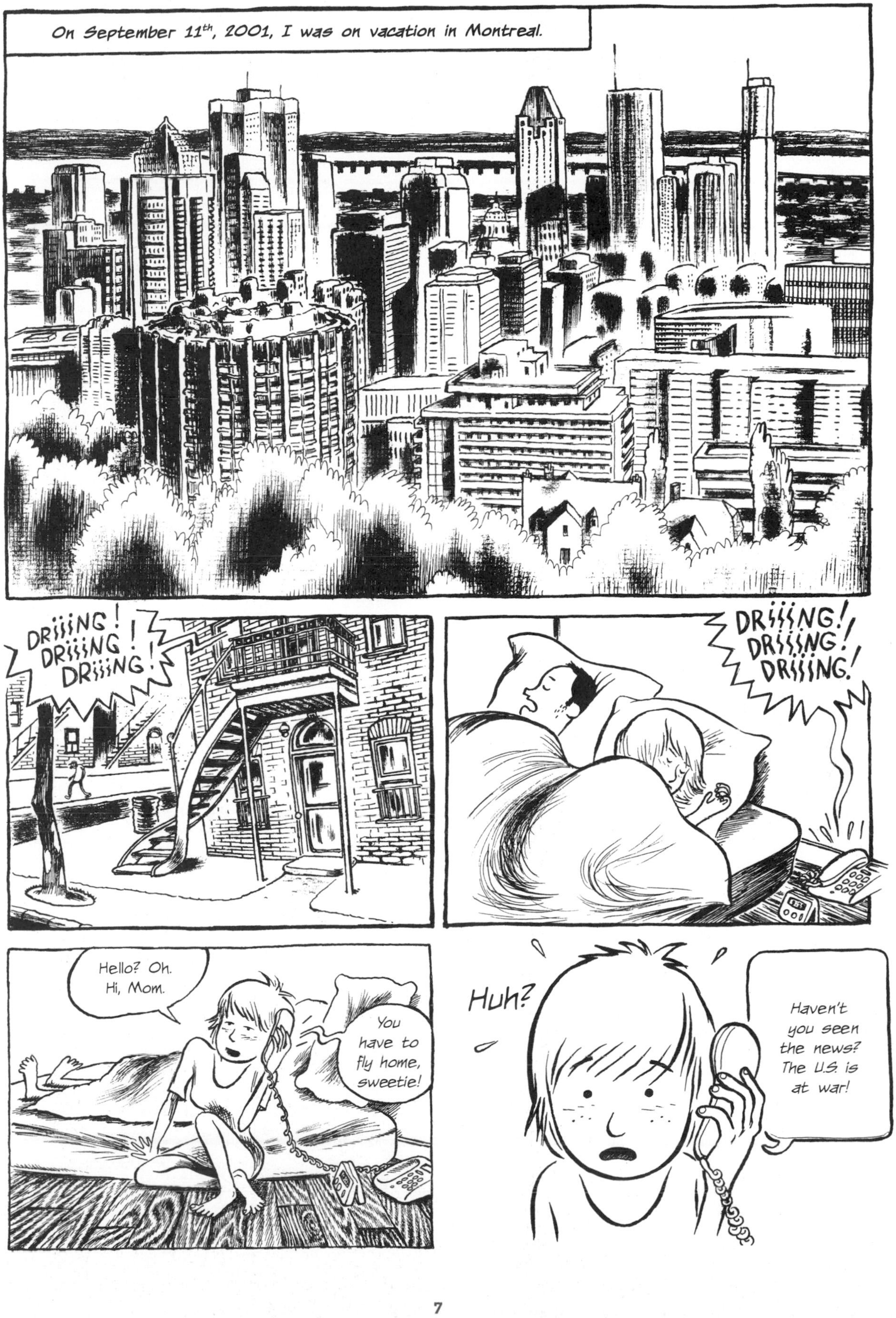
On September 11th, 2001, I was on vacation in Montreal.
DRiiiNG! DRiiiNG! DRiiiNG!
DRiiiNG! DRiiiNG! DRiiiNG!
Hello? Oh. Hi, Mom.
You have to fly home, sweetie!
Huh?
Haven't you seen the news? The U.S. is at war!

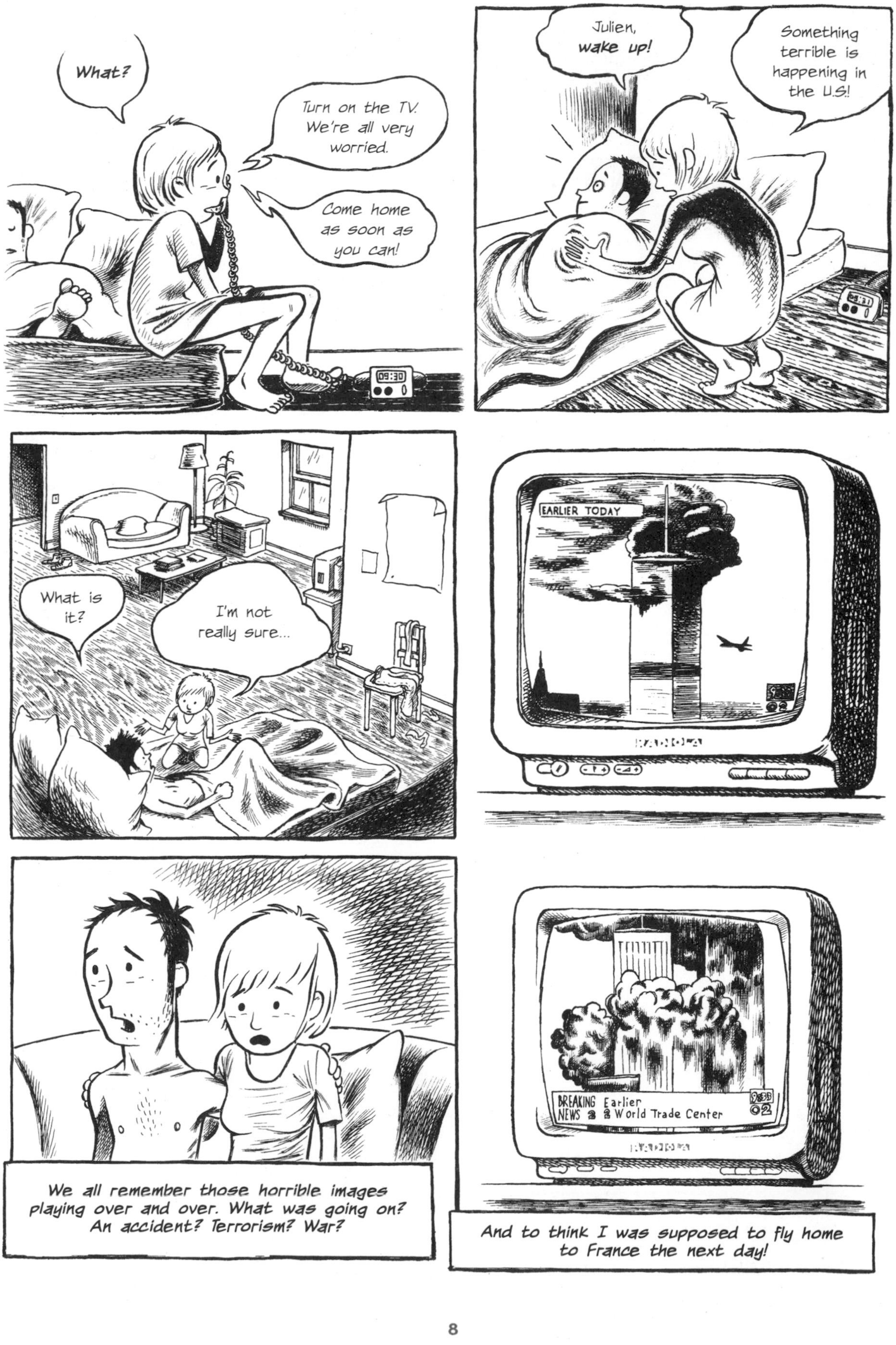
What?
Turn on the TV. We're all very worried.
Come home as soon as you can!
Julien, wake up!
Something terrible is happening in the U.S!
What is it?
I'm not really sure...
EARLIER TODAY
We all remember those horrible images playing over and over. What was going on? An accident? Terrorism? War?
BREAKING NEWS
Earlier
World Trade Center
And to think I was supposed to fly home to France the next day!

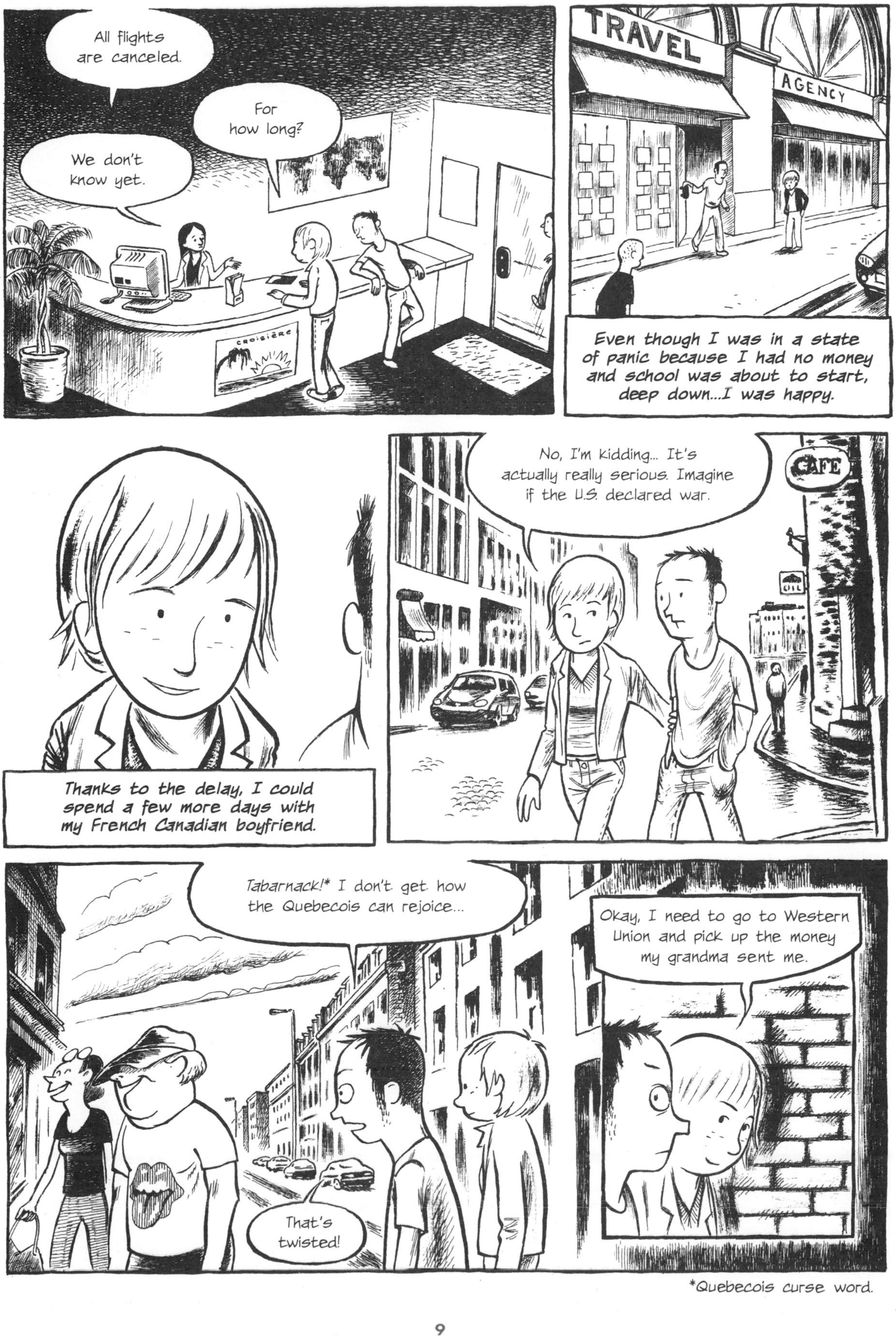
All flights are canceled.
For how long?
We don't know yet.
CROISIÈRE
TRAVEL
AGENCY
Even though I was in a state of panic because I had no money and school was about to start, deep down...I was happy.
Thanks to the delay, I could spend a few more days with my French Canadian boyfriend.
No, I'm kidding... It's actually really serious. Imagine if the U.S. declared war.
CAFE
Tabarnack!* I don't get how the Quebecois can rejoice...
That's twisted!
Okay, I need to go to Western Union and pick up the money my grandma sent me.

*Quebecois curse word.

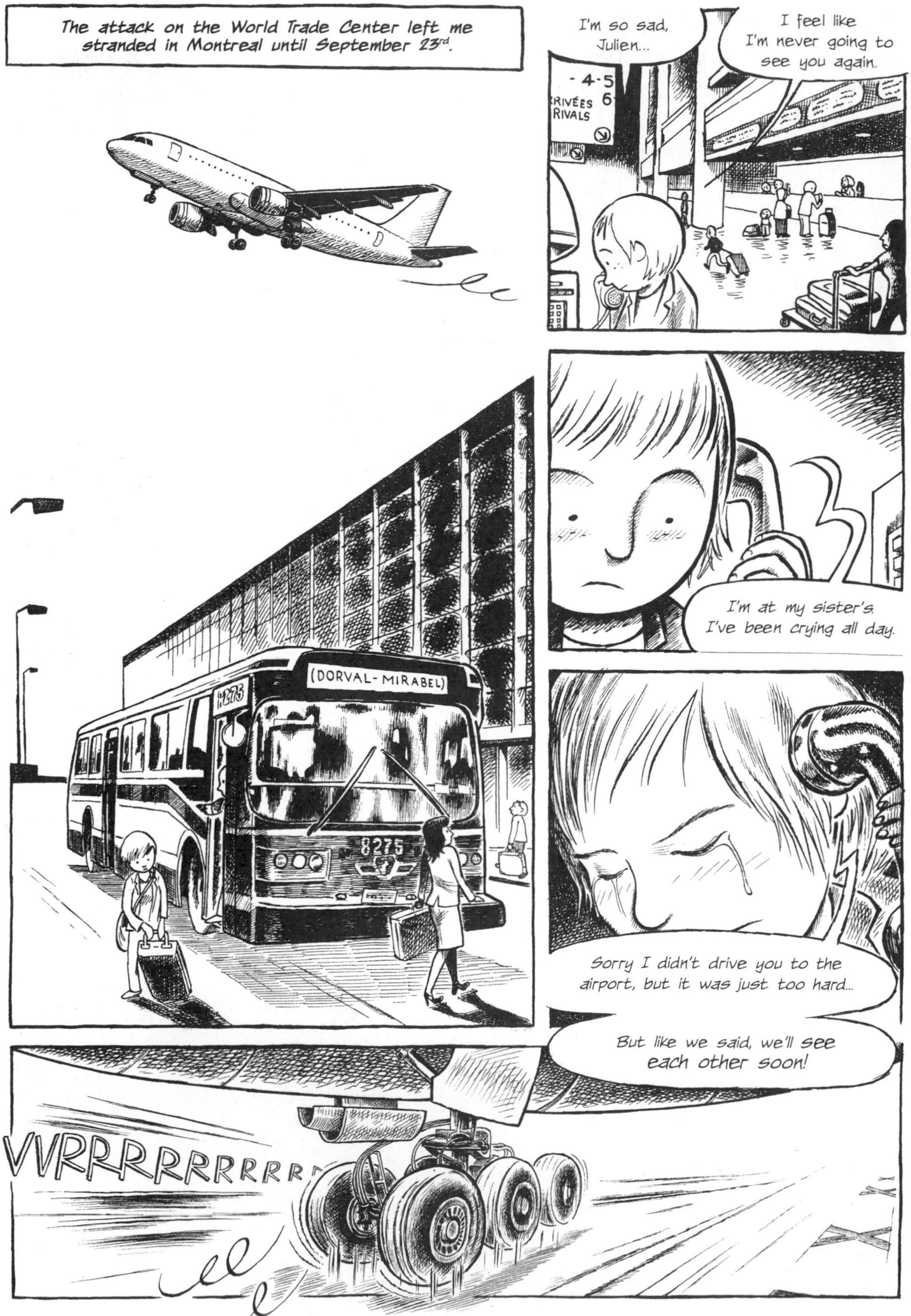
The attack on the World Trade Center left me stranded in Montreal until September 23rd.
I'm so sad, Julien...
I feel like I'm never going to see you again.
4-5
6
RIVÉES
RIVALS
I'm at my sister's. I've been crying all day.
(DORVAL-MIRABEL)
8275
Sorry I didn't drive you to the airport, but it was just too hard...
But like we said, we'll see each other soon!
VVRRRRRRRRRRR

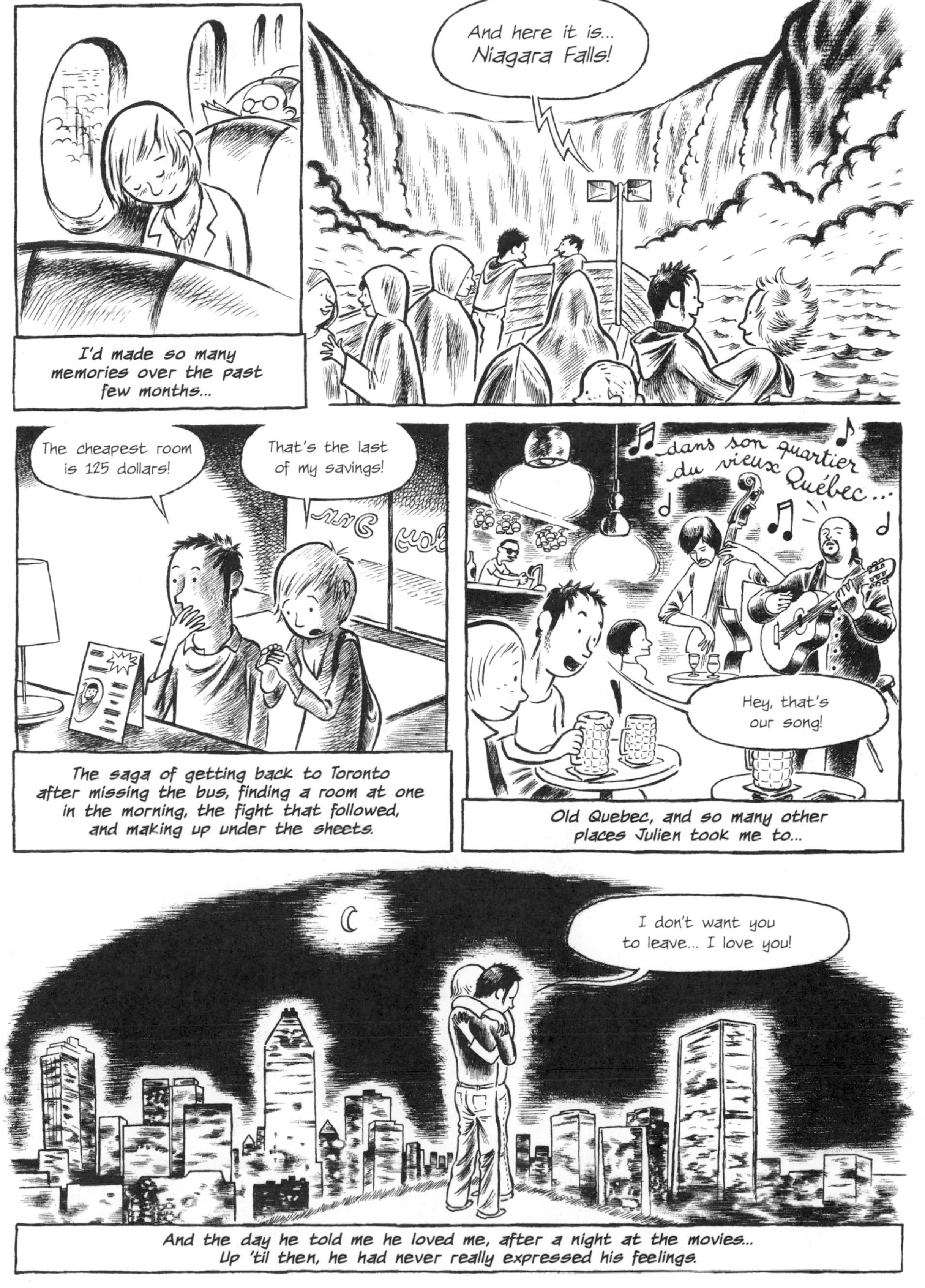
I'd made so many memories over the past few months...
And here it is... Niagara Falls!
The cheapest room is 125 dollars!
That's the last of my savings!
The saga of getting back to Toronto after missing the bus, finding a room at one in the morning, the fight that followed, and making up under the sheets.
dans son quartier du vieux Québec...
Hey, that's our song!
Old Quebec, and so many other places Julien took me to...
I don't want you to leave... I love you!
And the day he told me he loved me, after a night at the movies...
Up 'til then, he had never really expressed his feelings.

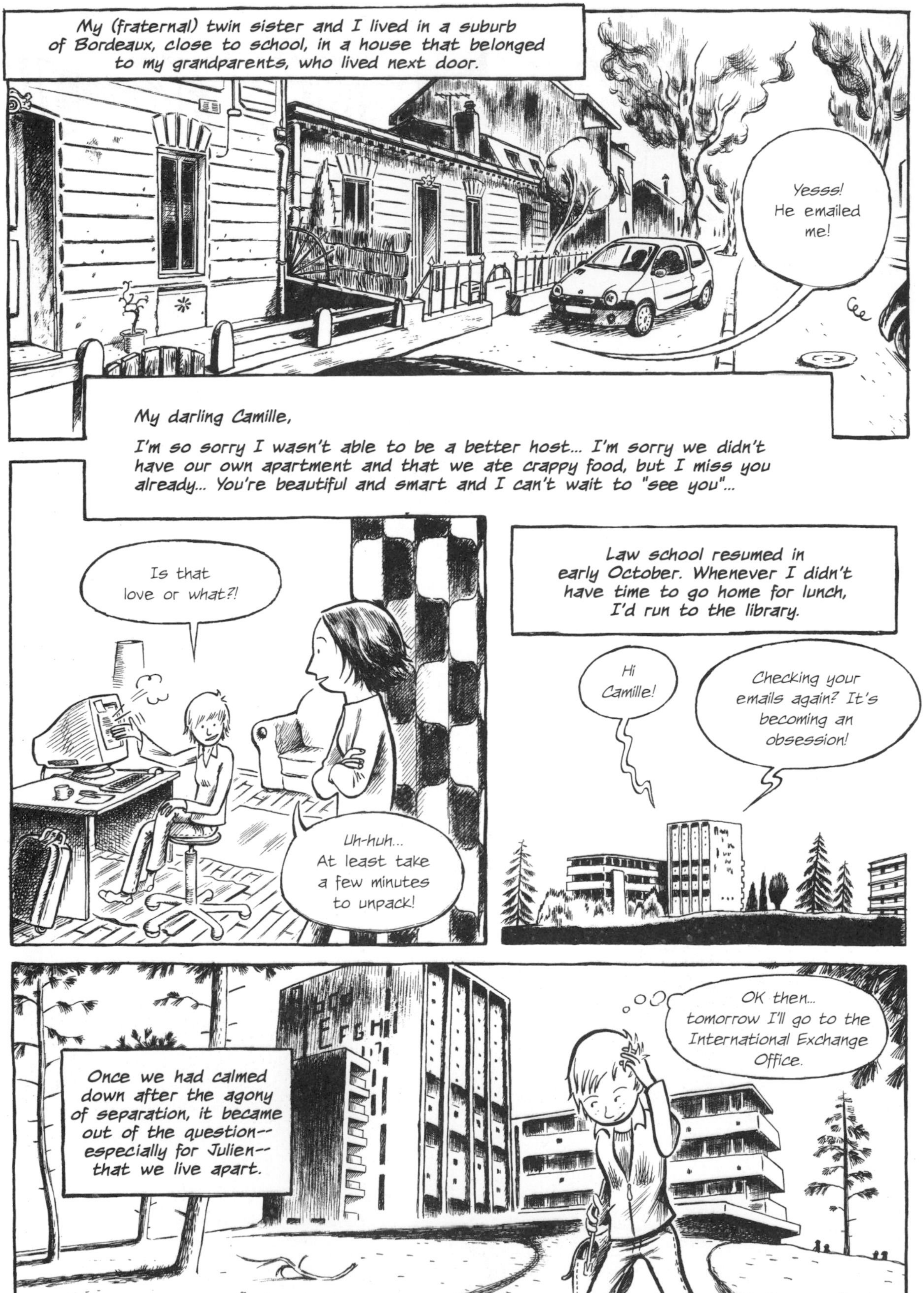

My (fraternal) twin sister and I lived in a suburb of Bordeaux, close to school, in a house that belonged to my grandparents, who lived next door.
Yesss! He emailed me!
My darling Camille,
I'm so sorry I wasn't able to be a better host... I'm sorry we didn't have our own apartment and that we ate crappy food, but I miss you already... You're beautiful and smart and I can't wait to "see you"...
Is that love or what?!
Uh-huh... At least take a few minutes to unpack!
Law school resumed in early October. Whenever I didn't have time to go home for lunch, I'd run to the library.
Hi Camille!
Checking your emails again? It's becoming an obsession!
Once we had calmed down after the agony of separation, it became out of the question-- especially for Julien-- that we live apart.
OK then... tomorrow I'll go to the International Exchange Office.

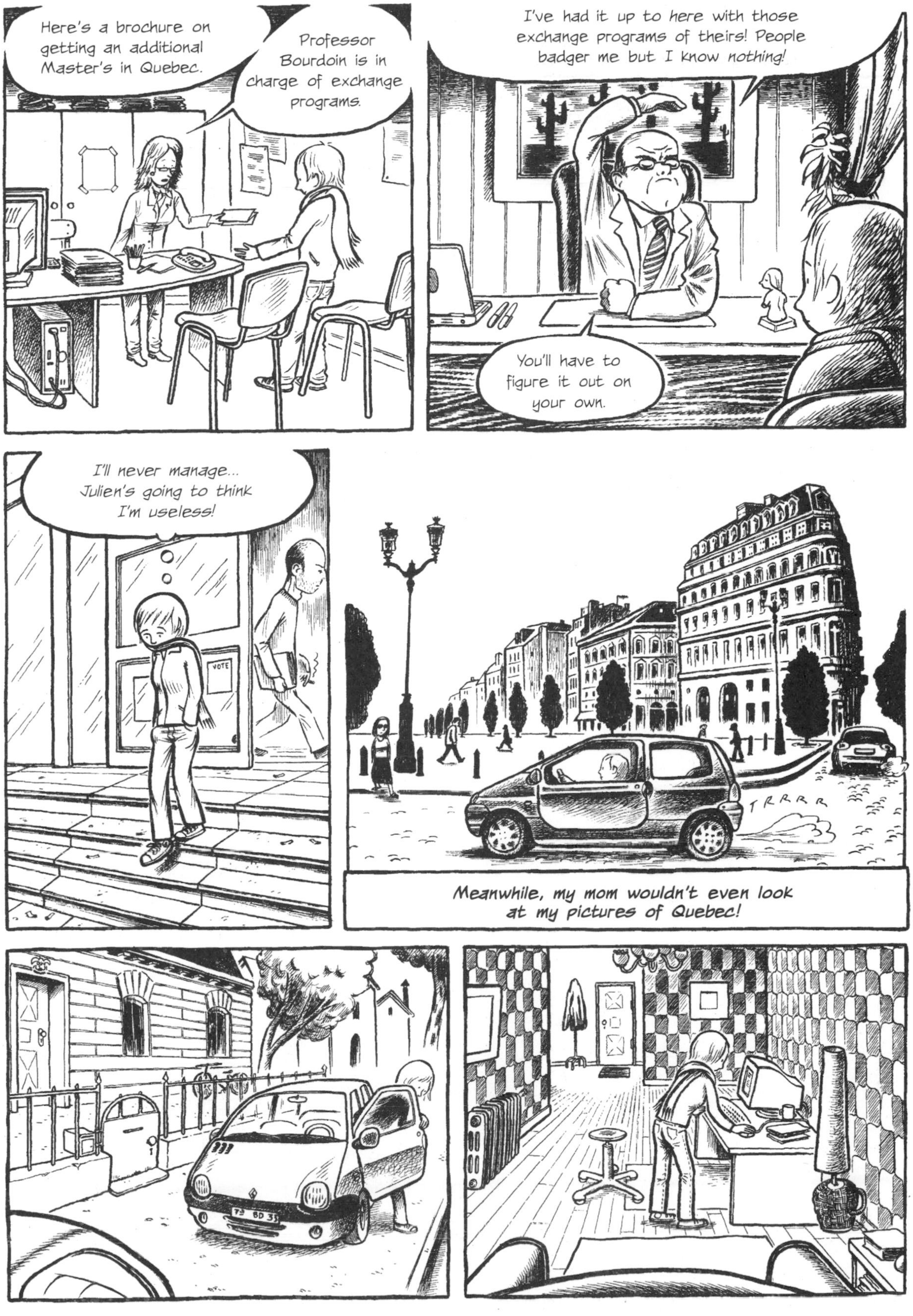
Here's a brochure on getting an additional Master's in Quebec.
Professor Bourdoin is in charge of exchange programs.
I've had it up to here with those exchange programs of theirs! People badger me but I know nothing!
You'll have to figure it out on your own.
I'll never manage... Julien's going to think I'm useless!
VOTE
TRRRR
Meanwhile, my mom wouldn't even look at my pictures of Quebec!

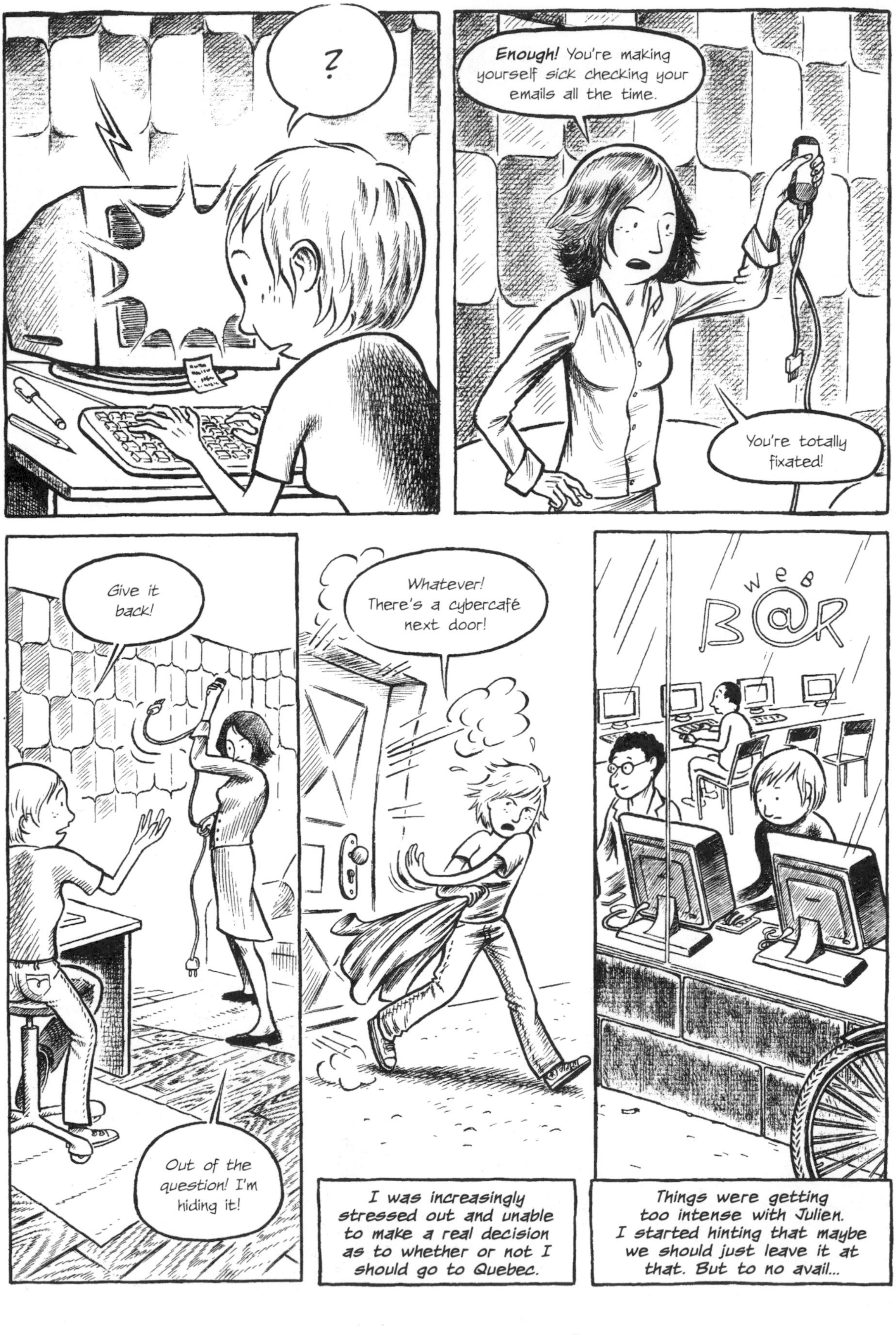
?
Enough! You're making yourself sick checking your emails all the time.
You're totally fixated!
Give it back!
Out of the question! I'm hiding it!
Whatever! There's a cybercafé next door!
I was increasingly stressed out and unable to make a real decision as to whether or not I should go to Quebec.
WEB B@R
Things were getting too intense with Julien. I started hinting that maybe we should just leave it at that. But to no avail...

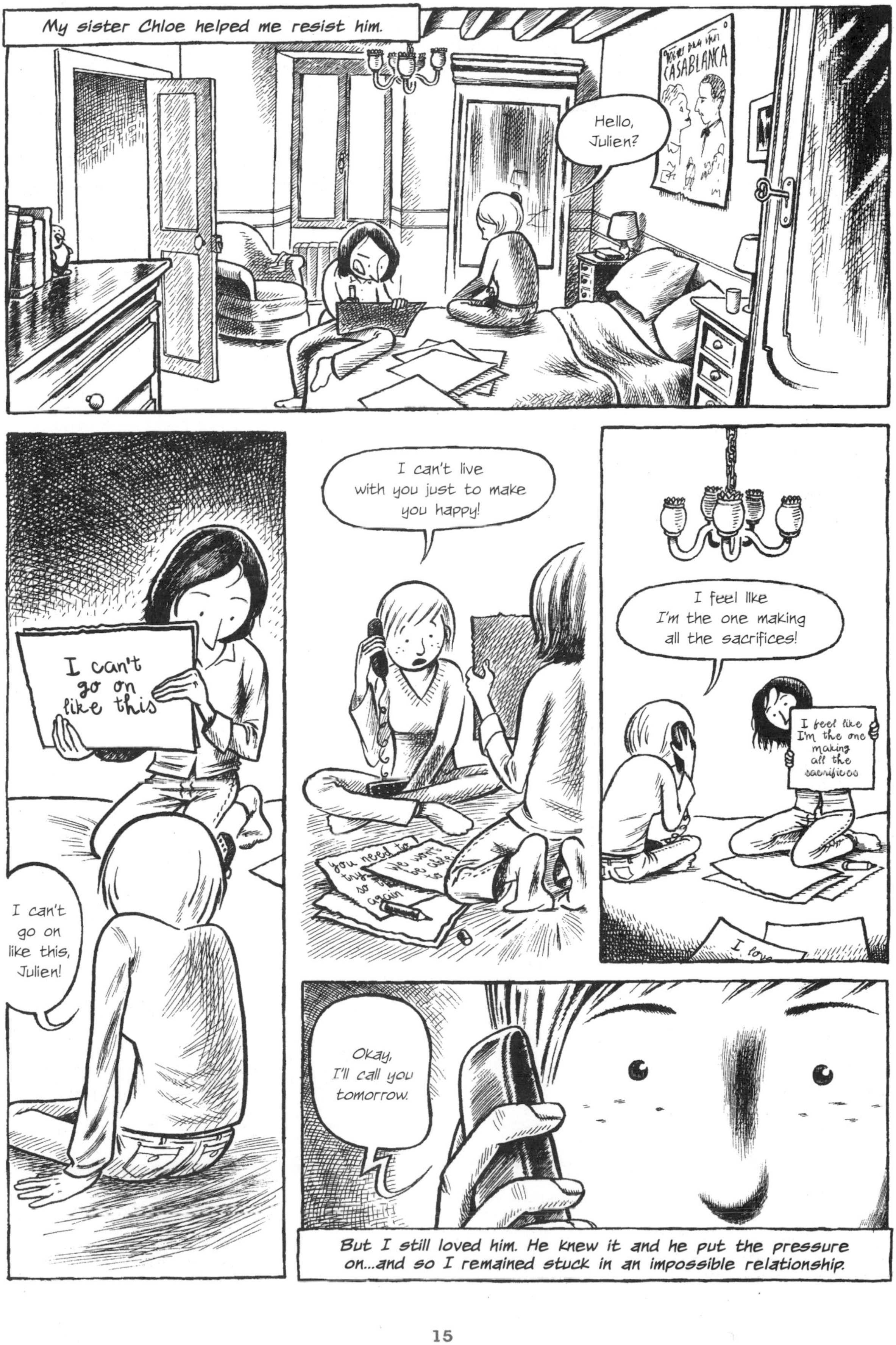
My sister Chloe helped me resist him.
Hello, Julien?
I can't go on like this
I can't go on like this, Julien!
I can't live with you just to make you happy!
I feel like I'm the one making all the sacrifices!
I feel like I'm the one making all the sacrifices
Okay, I'll call you tomorrow.
But I still loved him. He knew it and he put the pressure on...and so I remained stuck in an impossible relationship.

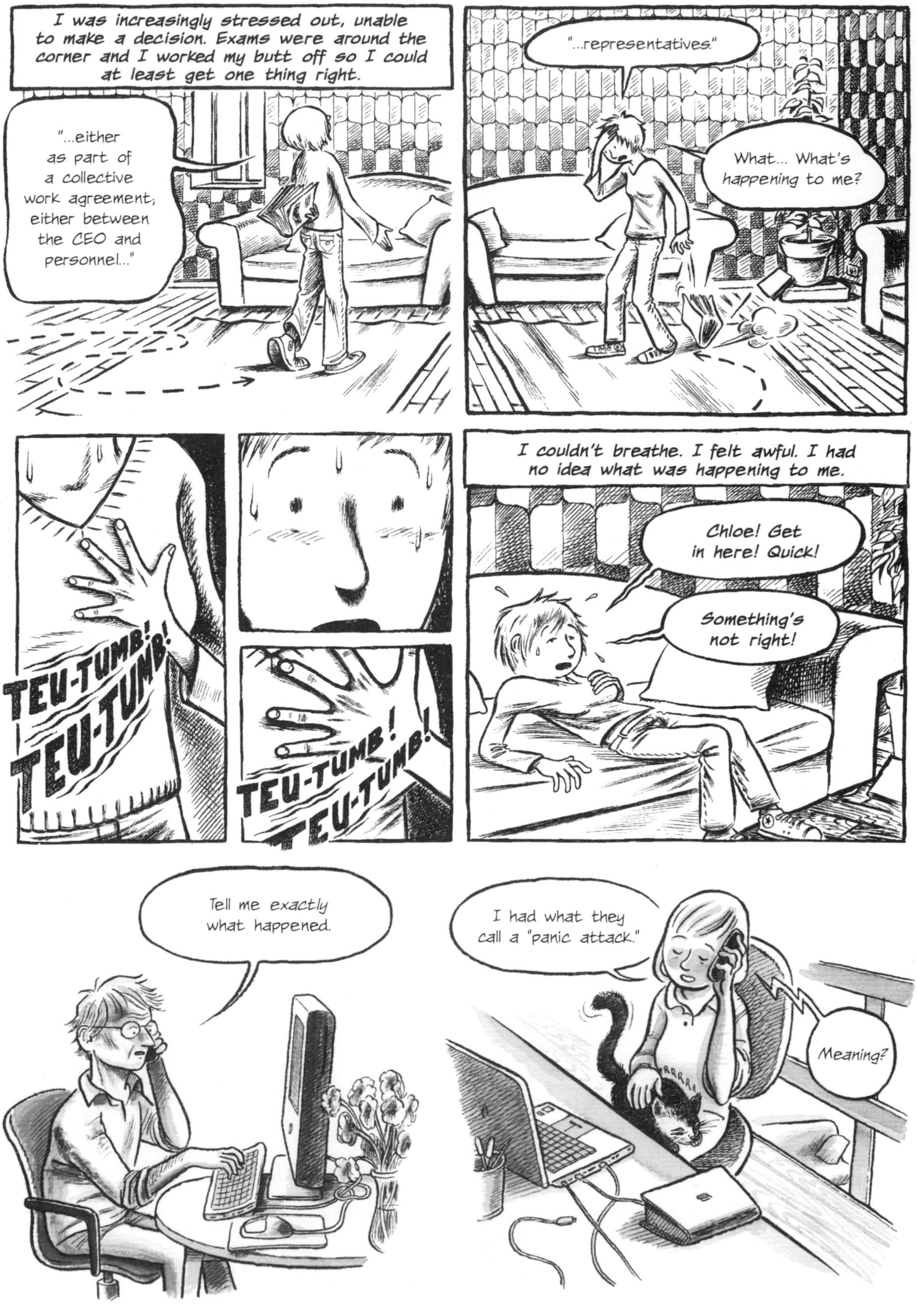
I was increasingly stressed out, unable to make a decision. Exams were around the corner and I worked my butt off so I could at least get one thing right.
"...either as part of a collective work agreement; either between the CEO and personnel..."
"...representatives."
What... What's happening to me?
TEU-TUMB! TEU-TUMB!
TEU-TUMB! TEU-TUMB!
I couldn't breathe. I felt awful. I had no idea what was happening to me.
Chloe! Get in here! Quick!
Something's not right!
Tell me exactly what happened.
I had what they call a "panic attack."
Meaning?

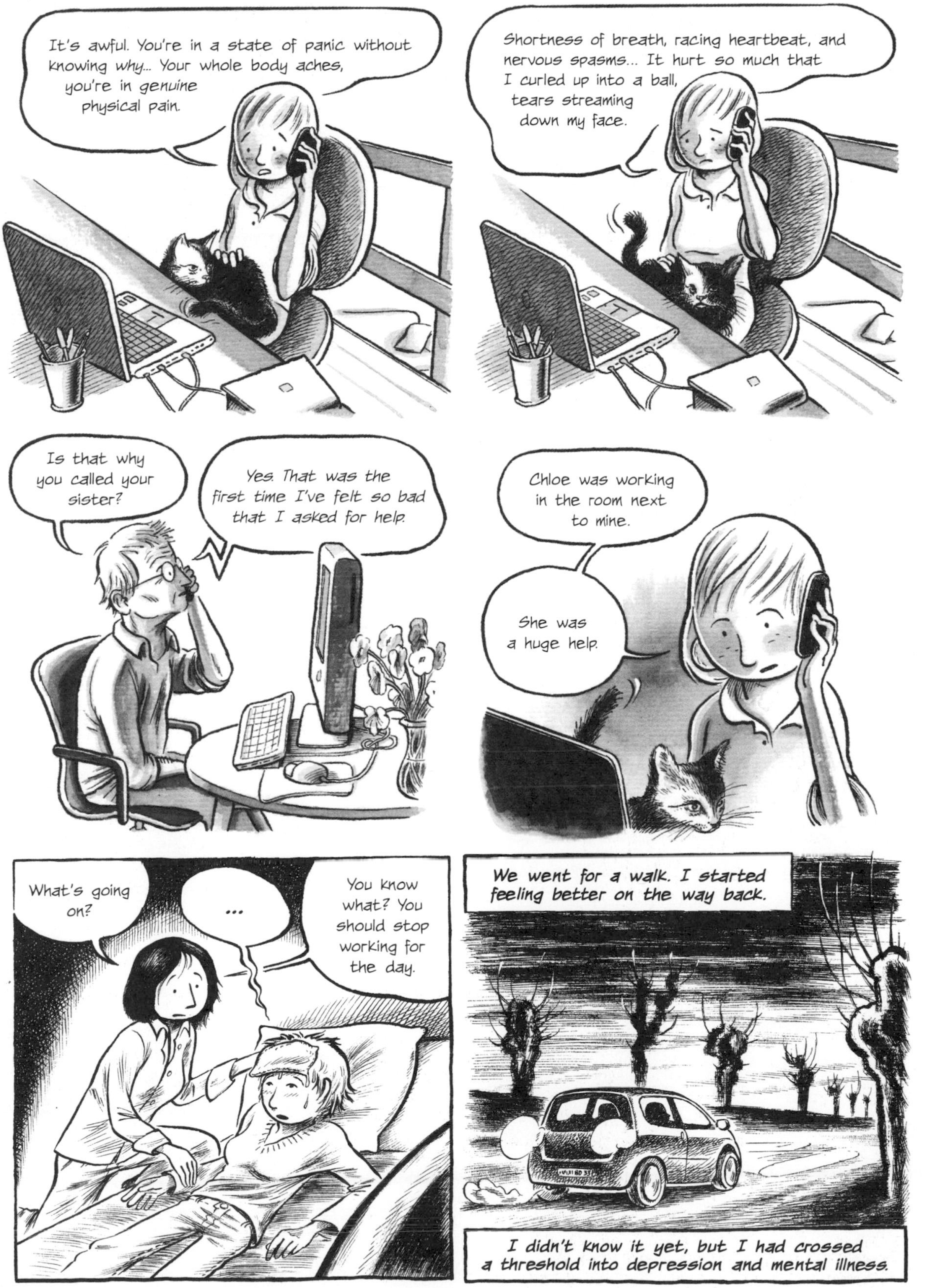
It's awful. You're in a state of panic without knowing why... Your whole body aches, you're in genuine physical pain.
Shortness of breath, racing heartbeat, and nervous spasms... It hurt so much that I curled up into a ball, tears streaming down my face.
Is that why you called your sister?
Yes. That was the first time I've felt so bad that I asked for help.
Chloe was working in the room next to mine.
She was a huge help.
What's going on?
...
You know what? You should stop working for the day.
We went for a walk. I started feeling better on the way back.
I didn't know it yet, but I had crossed a threshold into depression and mental illness.

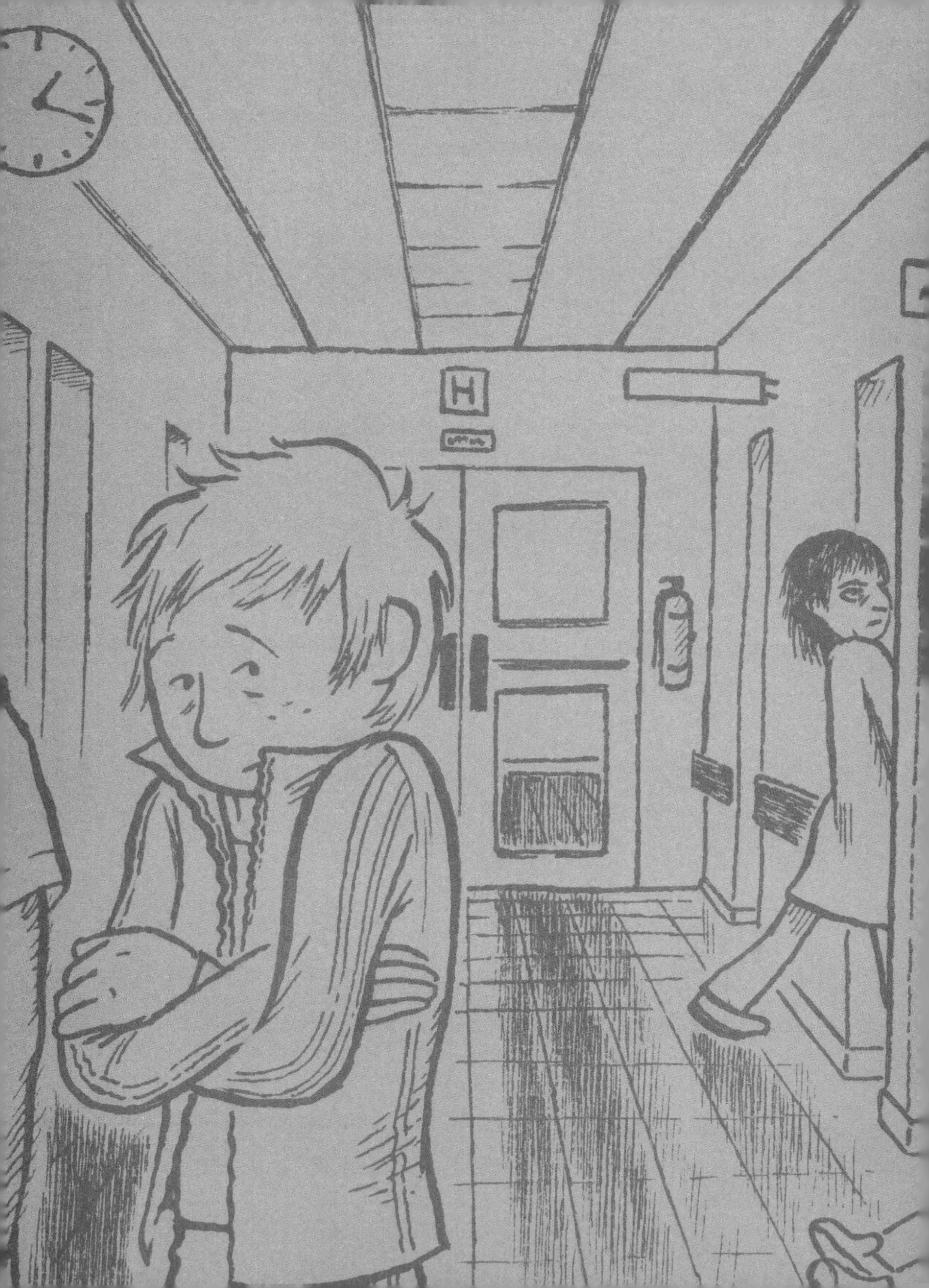
H

.2.
“*Breathe Me*”
Sia

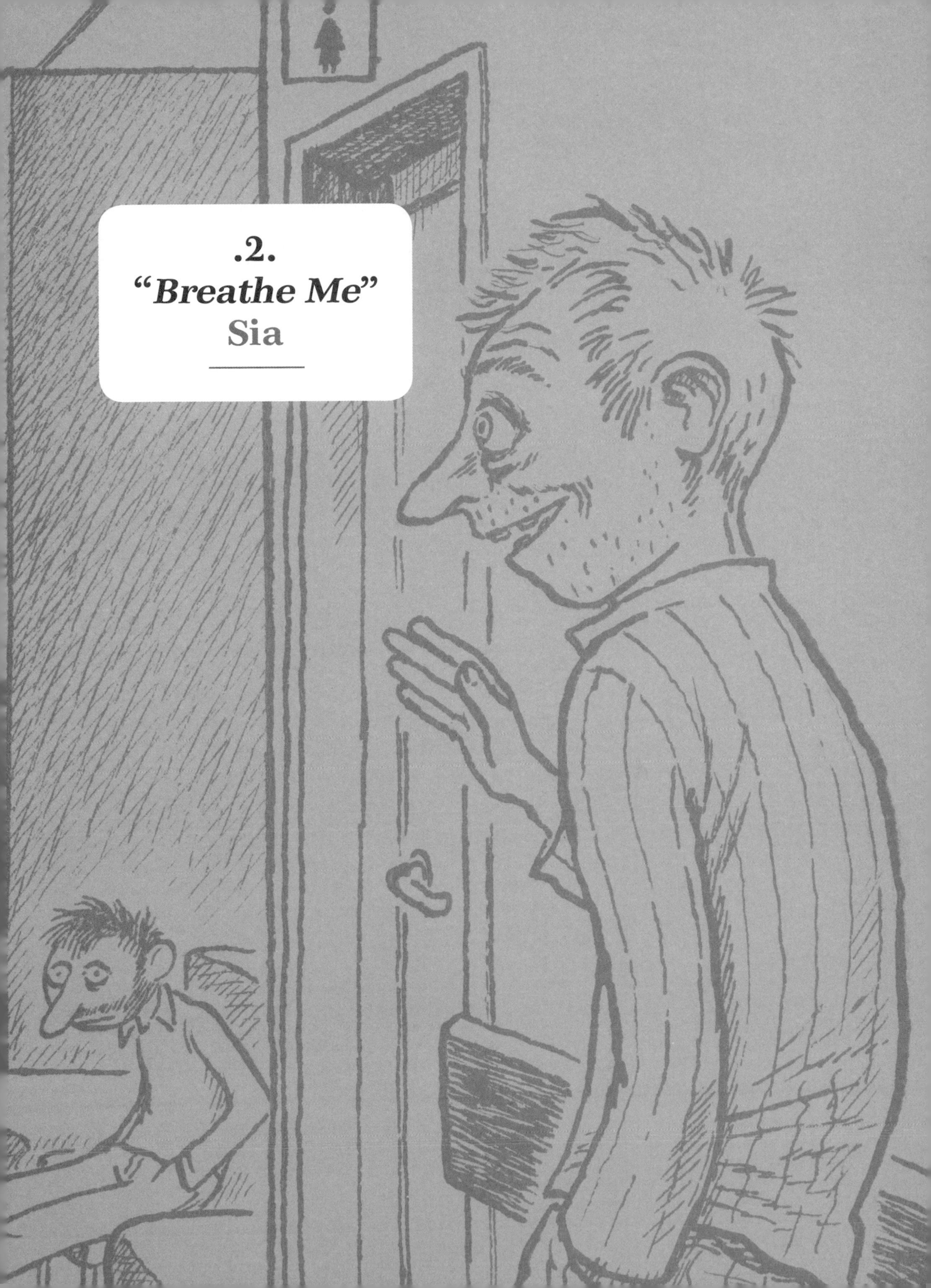

Listen, Camille, I can spend the night if you want.

THE END

♪AAAAAH!

On Valentine's Day and the day before our first term grades were posted, a friend came over, sensing that I wasn't doing too well.

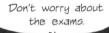

I was so stressed out about possibly failing my exams that I couldn't concentrate on the film we were watching.

No, I'll be fine. Go home.

It wouldn't change anything anyway.

PLOP

Don't worry about the exams.

You freak out every time, and every time, *you* pass!

Yeah, we'll see. Either way, I hope you aced yours.

This isn't good... This isn't good at all... I'm a loser...a total loser... I'll never make it!
Sniff
I can't go on like this...
I just can't... I need to end this!
I'm a worthless piece of shit!
Sniff!
I vaguely remembered how to tie a noose...
I just needed a place to hang it.

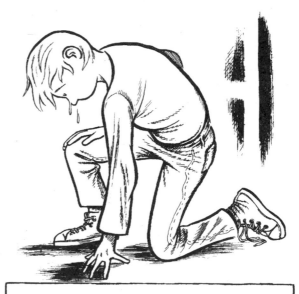

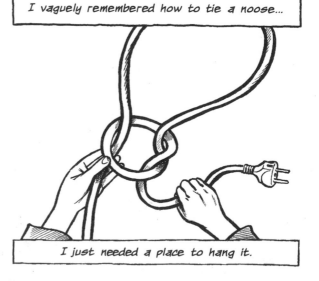

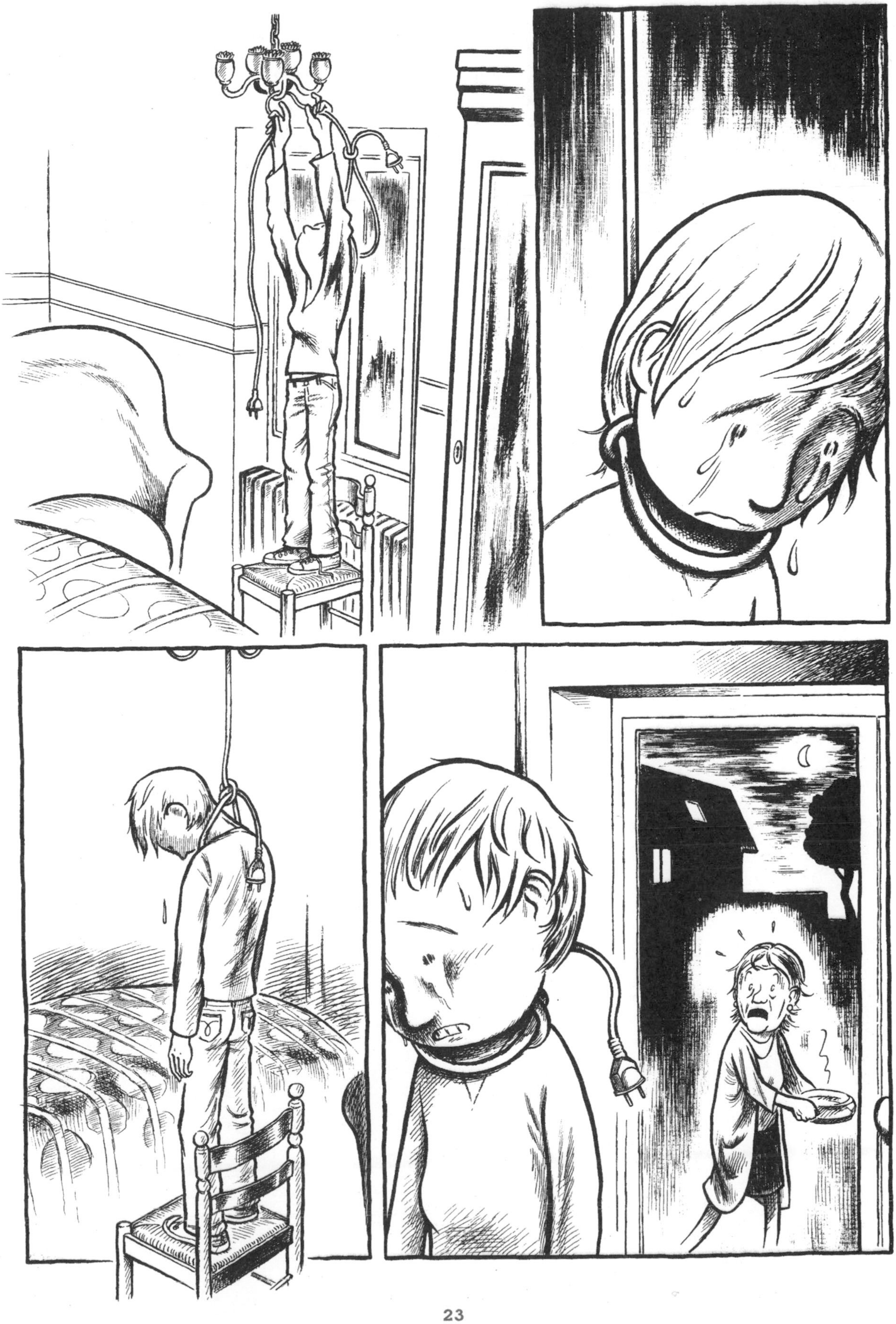

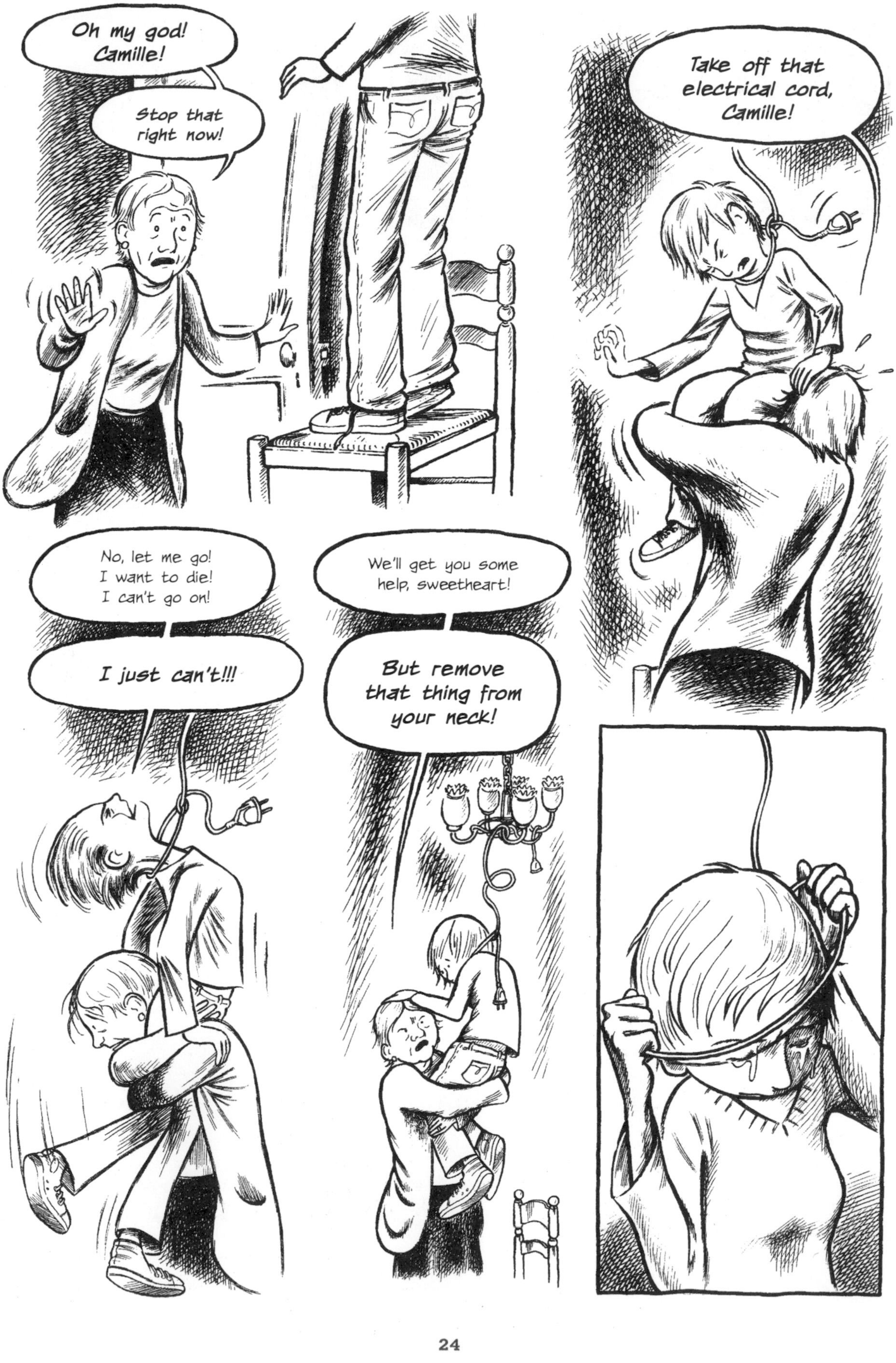
Oh my god! Camille!
Stop that right now!
Take off that electrical cord, Camille!
No, let me go! I want to die! I can't go on!
I just can't!!!
We'll get you some help, sweetheart!
But remove that thing from your neck!

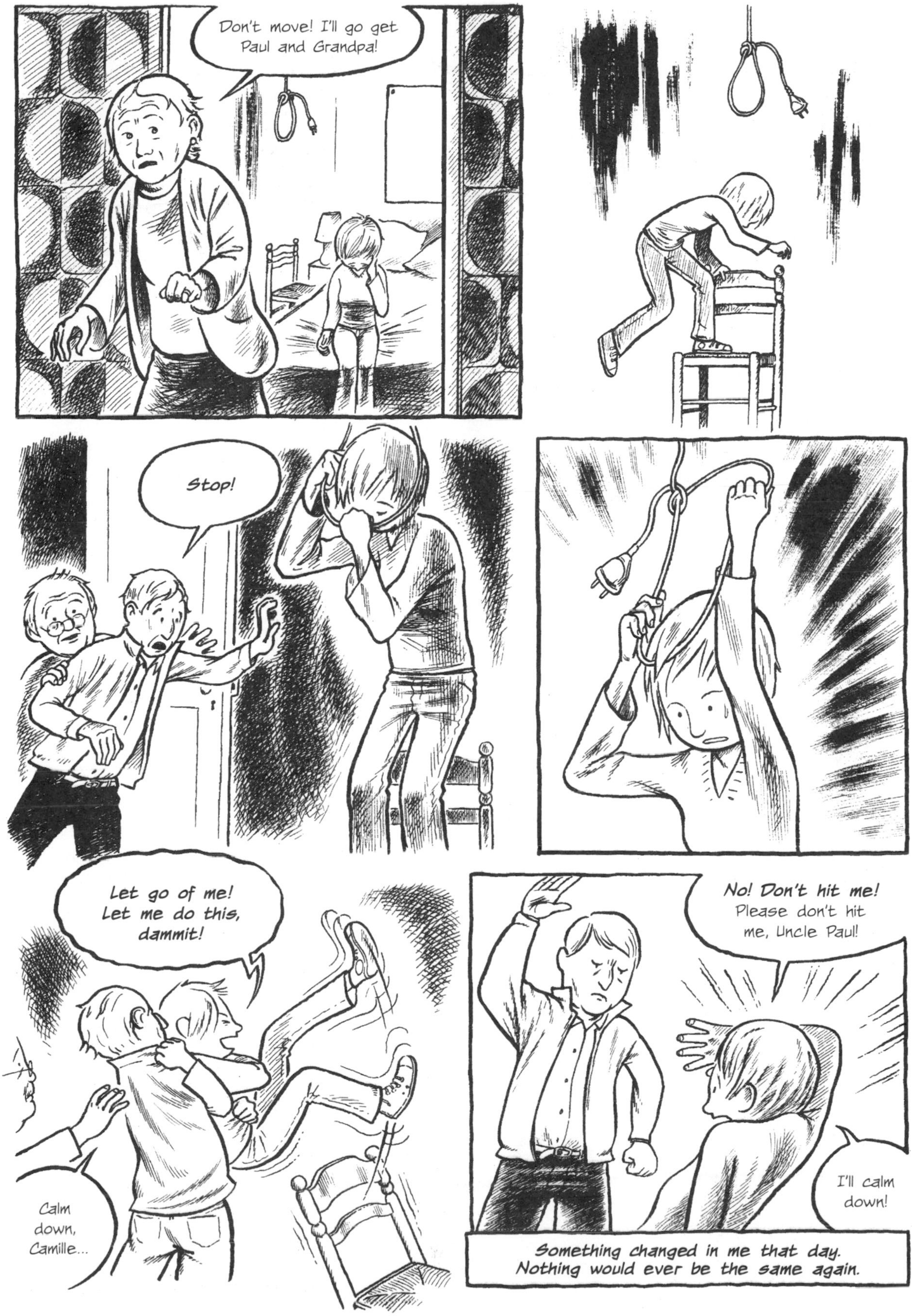

Don't move! I'll go get Paul and Grandpa!
Stop!
Let go of me! Let me do this, dammit!
Calm down, Camille...
No! Don't hit me! Please don't hit me, Uncle Paul!
I'll calm down!
Something changed in me that day. Nothing would ever be the same again.

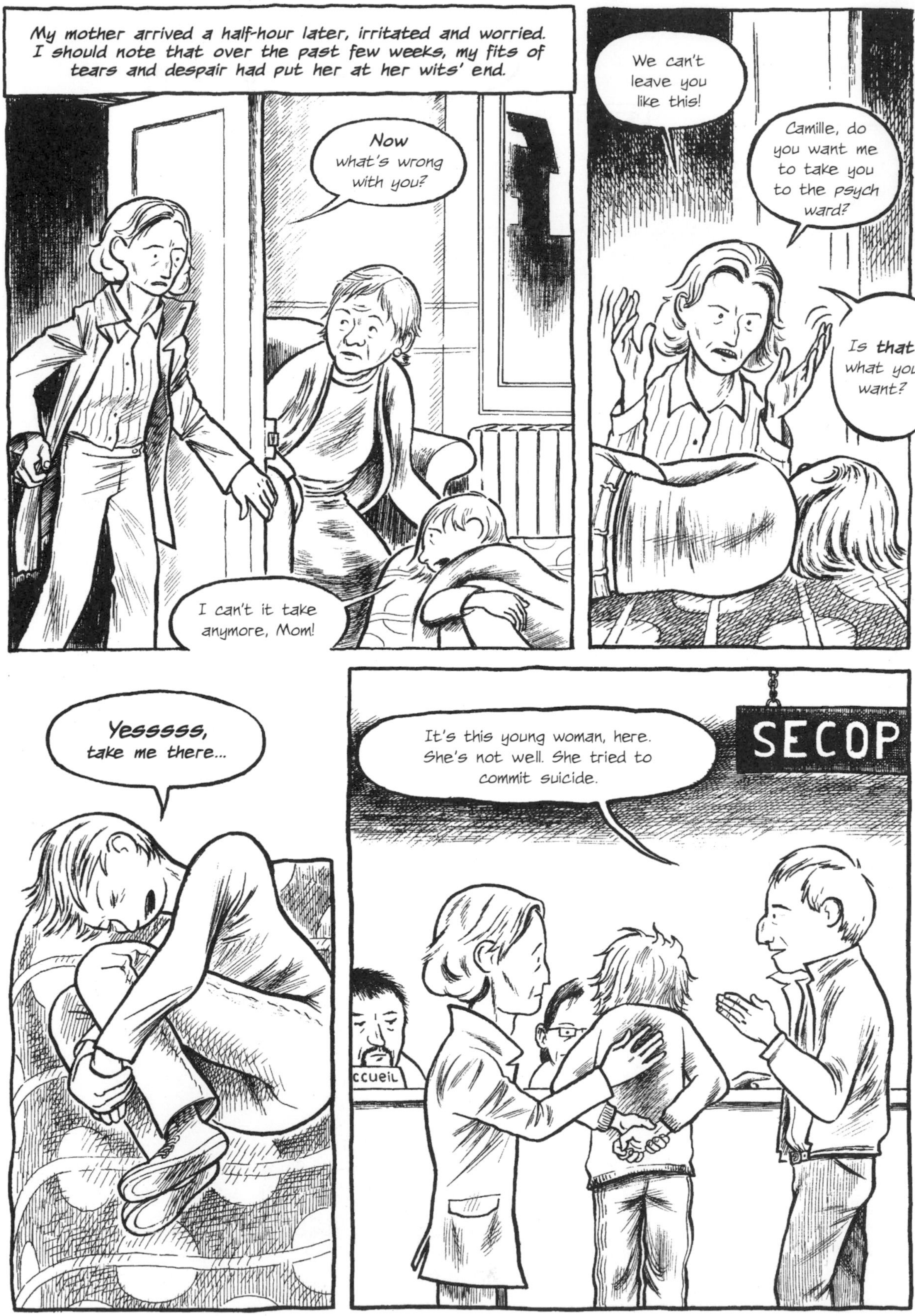
My mother arrived a half-hour later, irritated and worried. I should note that over the past few weeks, my fits of tears and despair had put her at her wits' end.
Now what's wrong with you?
I can't it take anymore, Mom!
We can't leave you like this!
Camille, do you want me to take you to the psych ward?
Is that what you want?
Yessssss, take me there...
SECOP
It's this young woman, here. She's not well. She tried to commit suicide.
ccueil

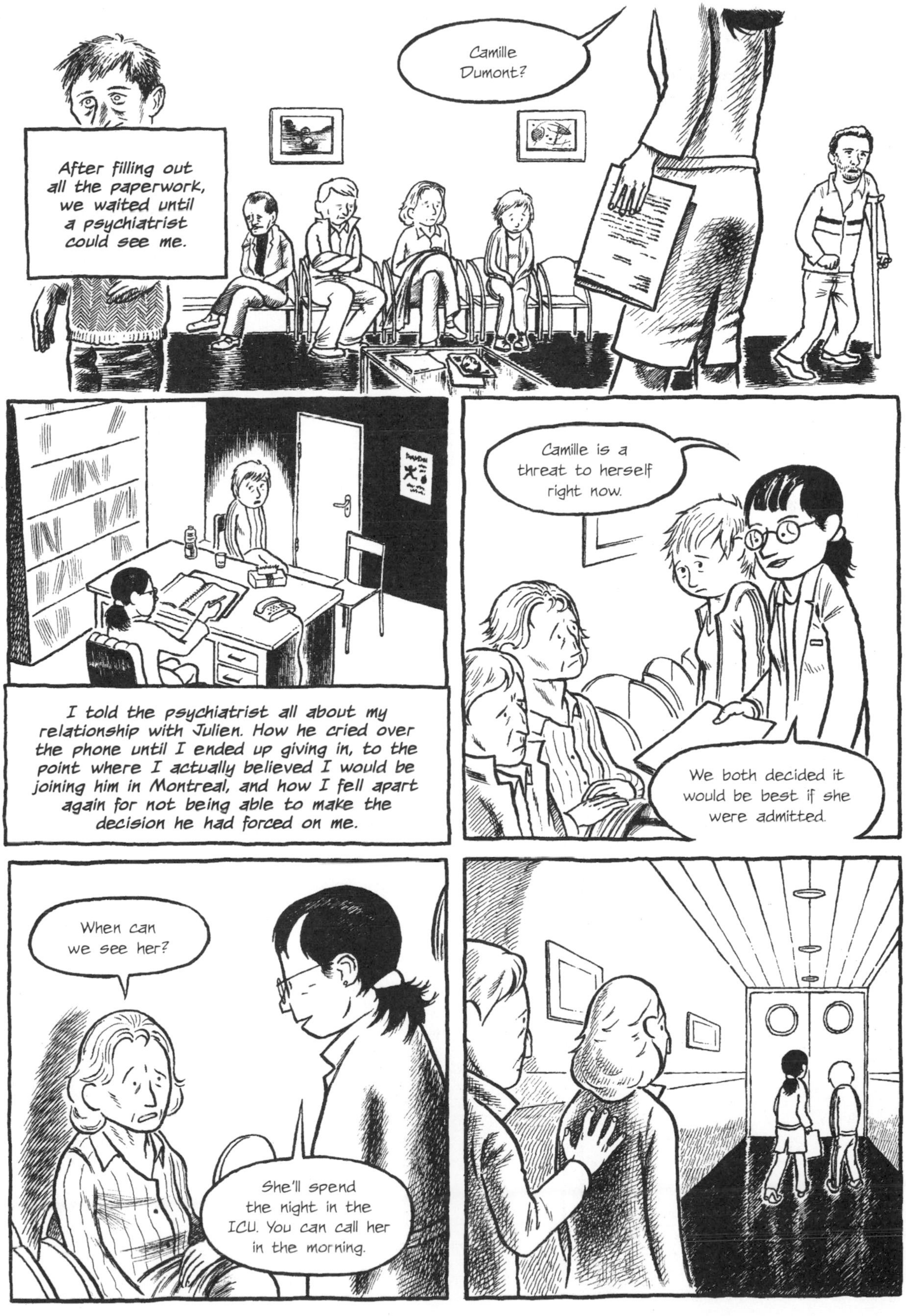

After filling out all the paperwork, we waited until a psychiatrist could see me.
Camille Dumont?
I told the psychiatrist all about my relationship with Julien. How he cried over the phone until I ended up giving in, to the point where I actually believed I would be joining him in Montreal, and how I fell apart again for not being able to make the decision he had forced on me.
Camille is a threat to herself right now.
We both decided it would be best if she were admitted.
When can we see her?
She'll spend the night in the ICU. You can call her in the morning.

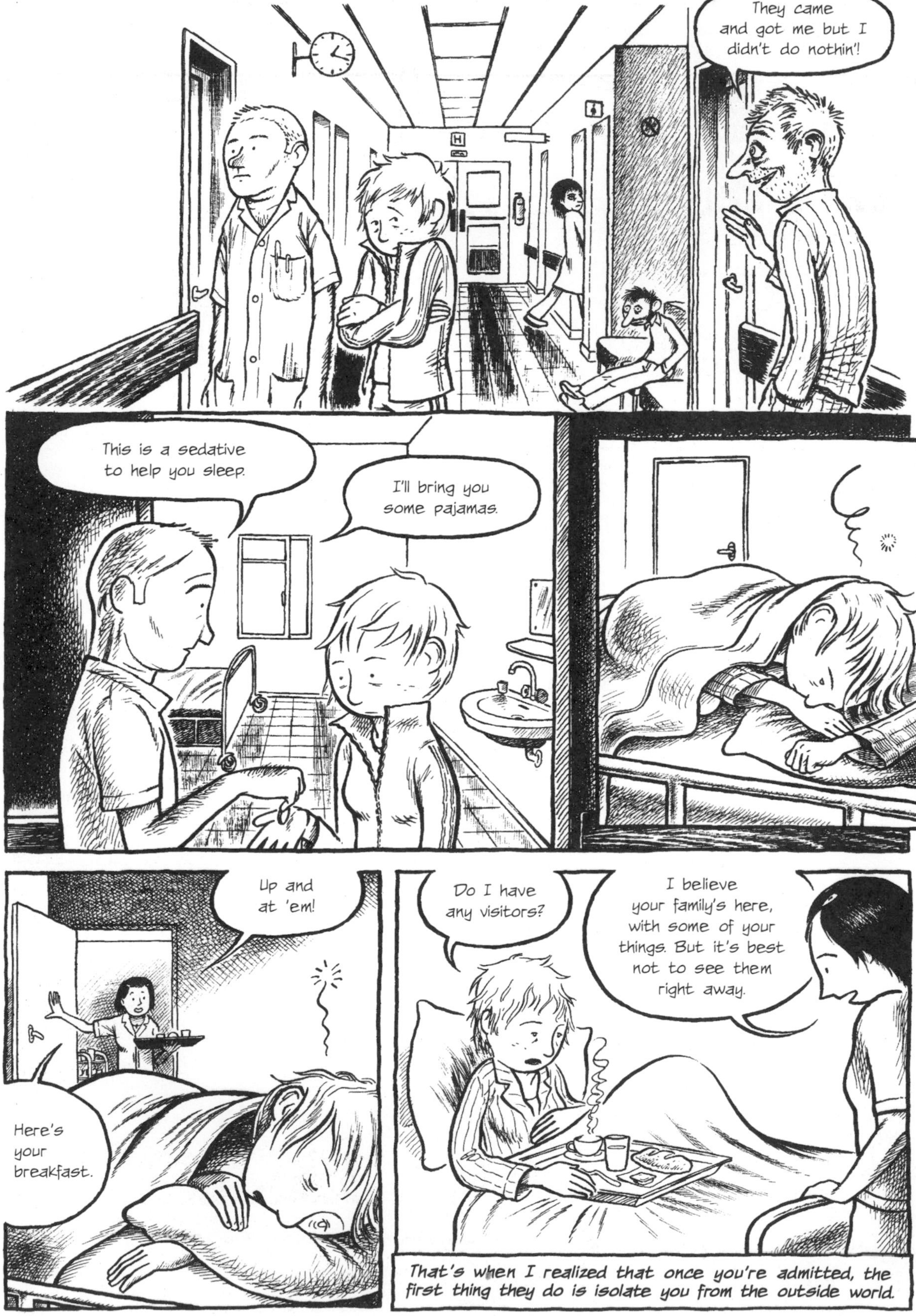
They came and got me but I didn't do nothin'!
This is a sedative to help you sleep.
I'll bring you some pajamas.
Up and at 'em!
Here's your breakfast.
Do I have any visitors?
I believe your family's here, with some of your things. But it's best not to see them right away.
That's when I realized that once you're admitted, the first thing they do is isolate you from the outside world.

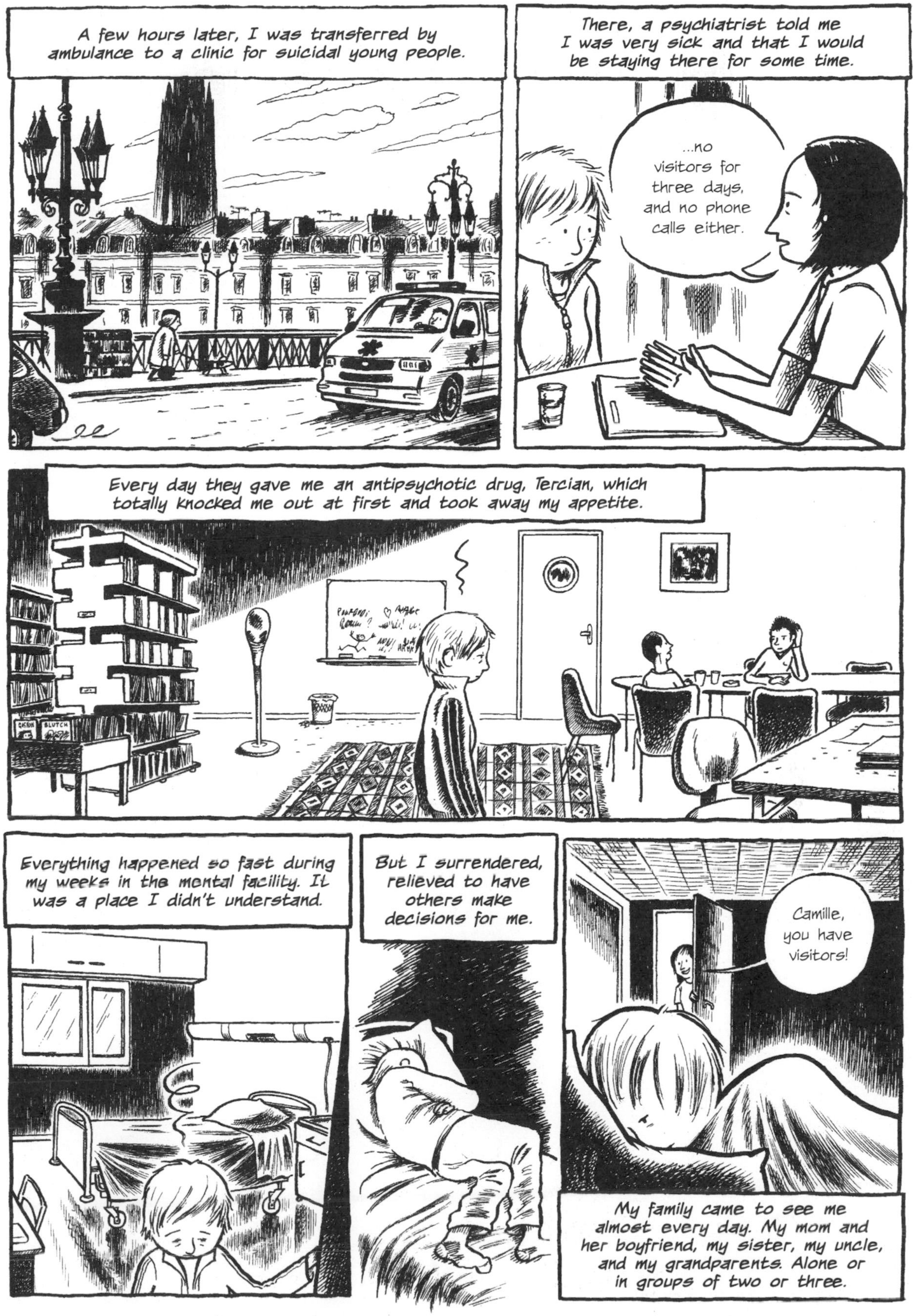
A few hours later, I was transferred by ambulance to a clinic for suicidal young people.
There, a psychiatrist told me I was very sick and that I would be staying there for some time.
...no visitors for three days, and no phone calls either.
Every day they gave me an antipsychotic drug, Tercian, which totally knocked me out at first and took away my appetite.
Everything happened so fast during my weeks in the mental facility. It was a place I didn't understand.
But I surrendered, relieved to have others make decisions for me.
Camille, you have visitors!
My family came to see me almost every day. My mom and her boyfriend, my sister, my uncle, and my grandparents. Alone or in groups of two or three.

As for my dad, who lived outside of Paris, my mom would report to him on the phone, and he would call me.

Hi, Camille!

First, we have excellent news.

You passed your exam with honors!

Really, Uncle Paul?

That news ignited a little flame in me: hope!

Well done, sweetie!

See, there was no reason to get so worked up over it!

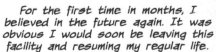
For the first time in months, I believed in the future again. It was obvious I would soon be leaving this facility and resuming my regular life.

Camille, phone call for you.

That day, I also got a phone call from Julien. He had managed to get the number from my sister.

I heard about what happened. It's all my fault. I'm so sorry.

He tearfully agreed that it was over between us.

I left the center for suicidal young people after two weeks. I had only one thing on my mind: going back to school.

But something felt wrong right off the bat...

...as well as the right to enforce punishment.

You wanna come over? We can prepare for tomorrow's lab.

No, I'm beat. I think I'll go straight home.

What is **wrong** with me?

That's it for today. See you Monday!

See you tomorrow!

Every day, in the early evening, I was exhausted and incapable of studying.

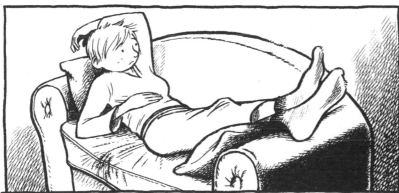

The situation was stressing me out considerably, so I decided to go see my shrink from the center.

Your body is making you feel what your mind refuses to accept... Deep down, you know you can't finish the school year.

You can't keep going like this. The exhaustion you're feeling is a sign of severe depression.

31

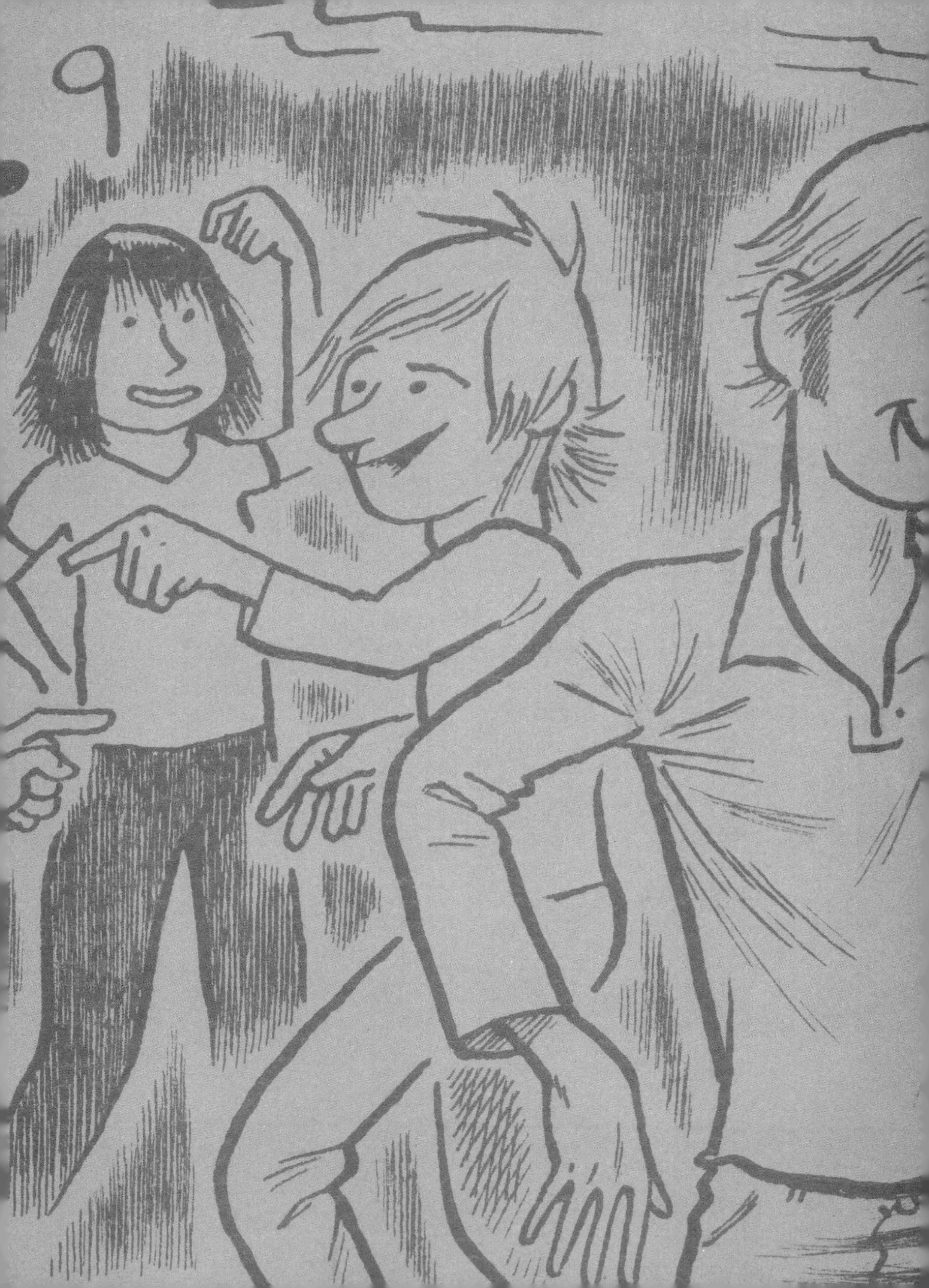

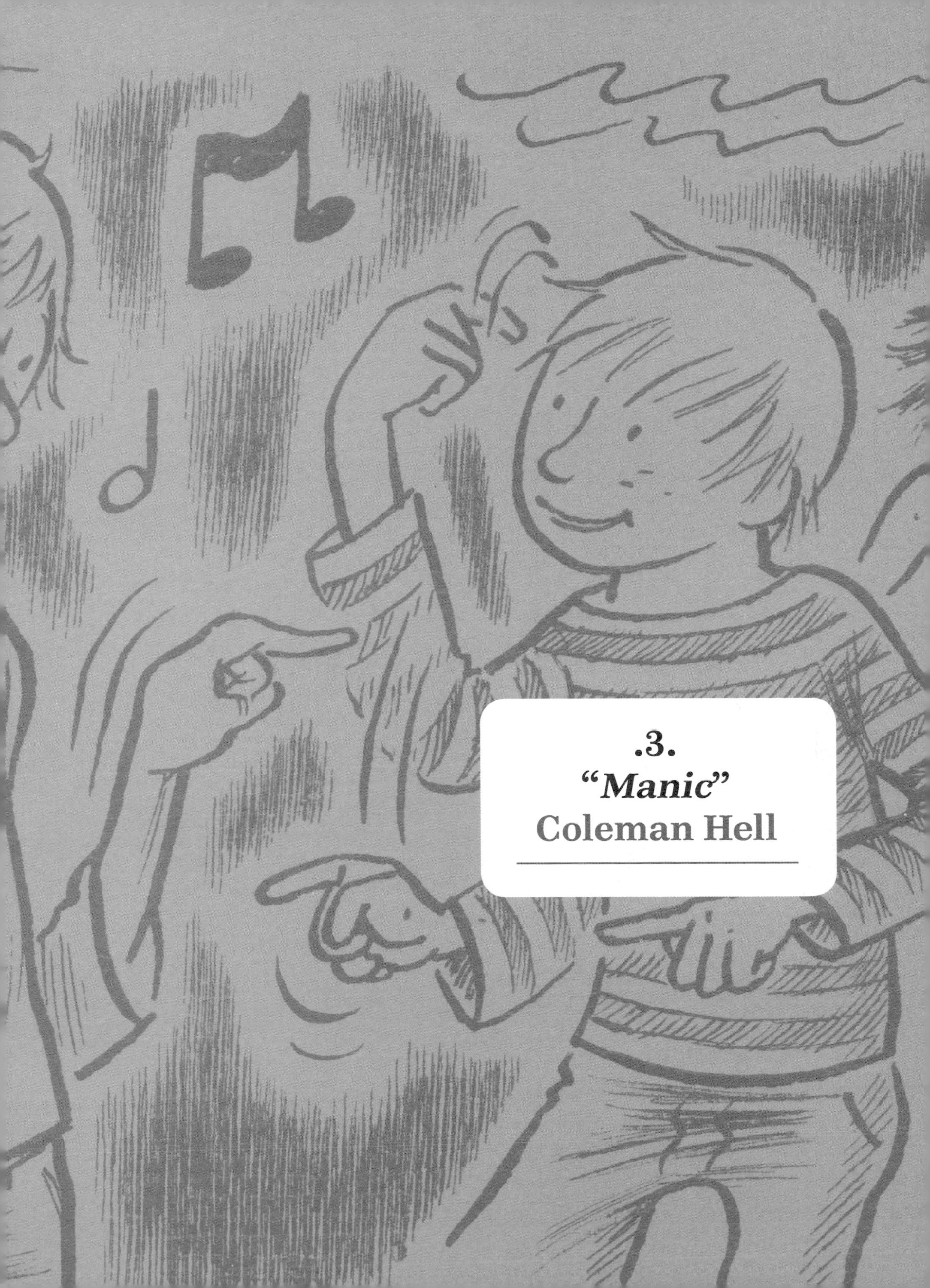

.3.

“*Manic*”

Coleman Hell

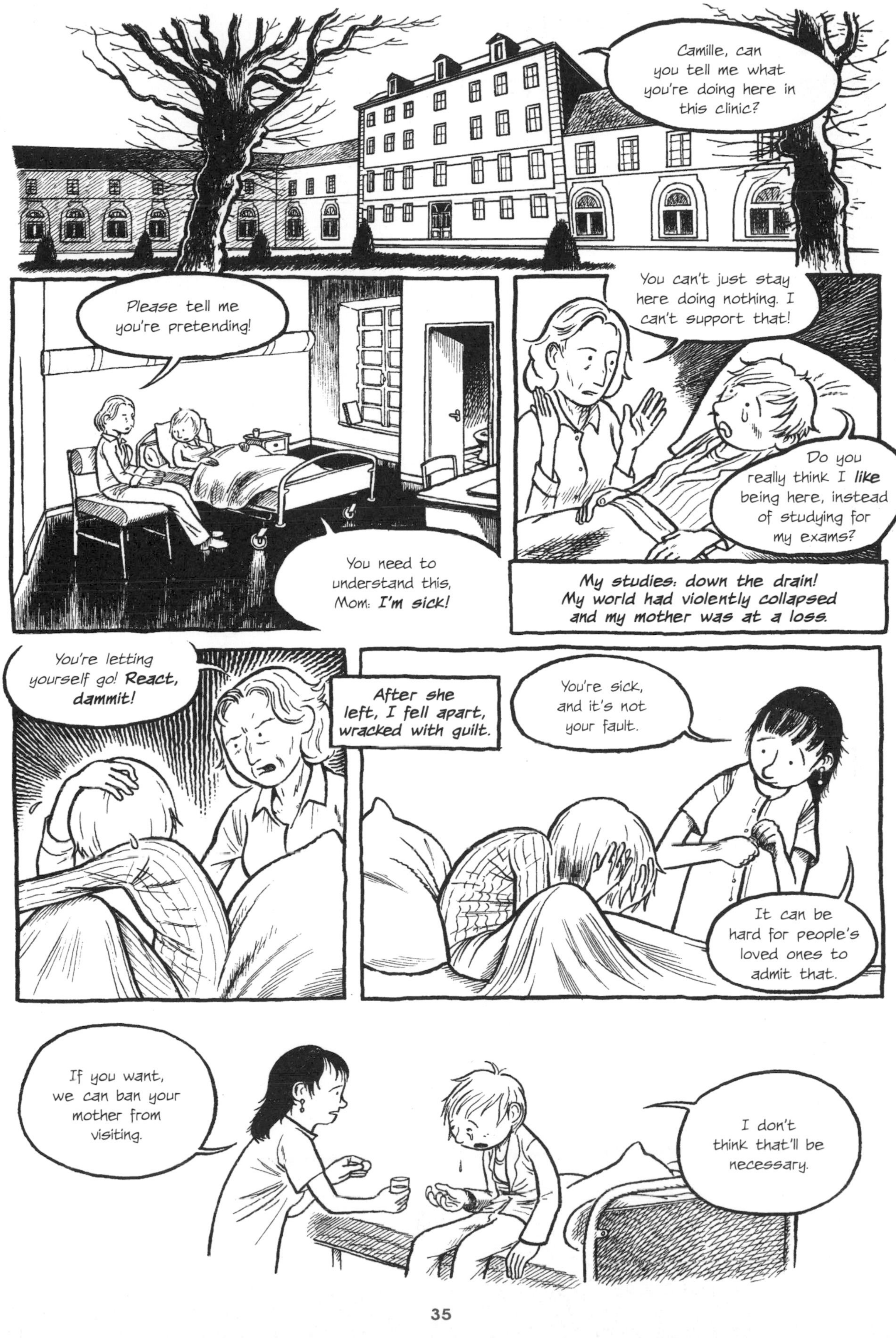
Camille, can you tell me what you're doing here in this clinic?
Please tell me you're pretending!
You need to understand this, Mom: **I'm sick!**
You can't just stay here doing nothing. I can't support that!
Do you really think I **like** being here, instead of studying for my exams?
My studies: down the drain! My world had violently collapsed and my mother was at a loss.
You're letting yourself go! **React, dammit!**
After she left, I fell apart, wracked with guilt.
You're sick, and it's not your fault.
It can be hard for people's loved ones to admit that.
If you want, we can ban your mother from visiting.
I don't think that'll be necessary.

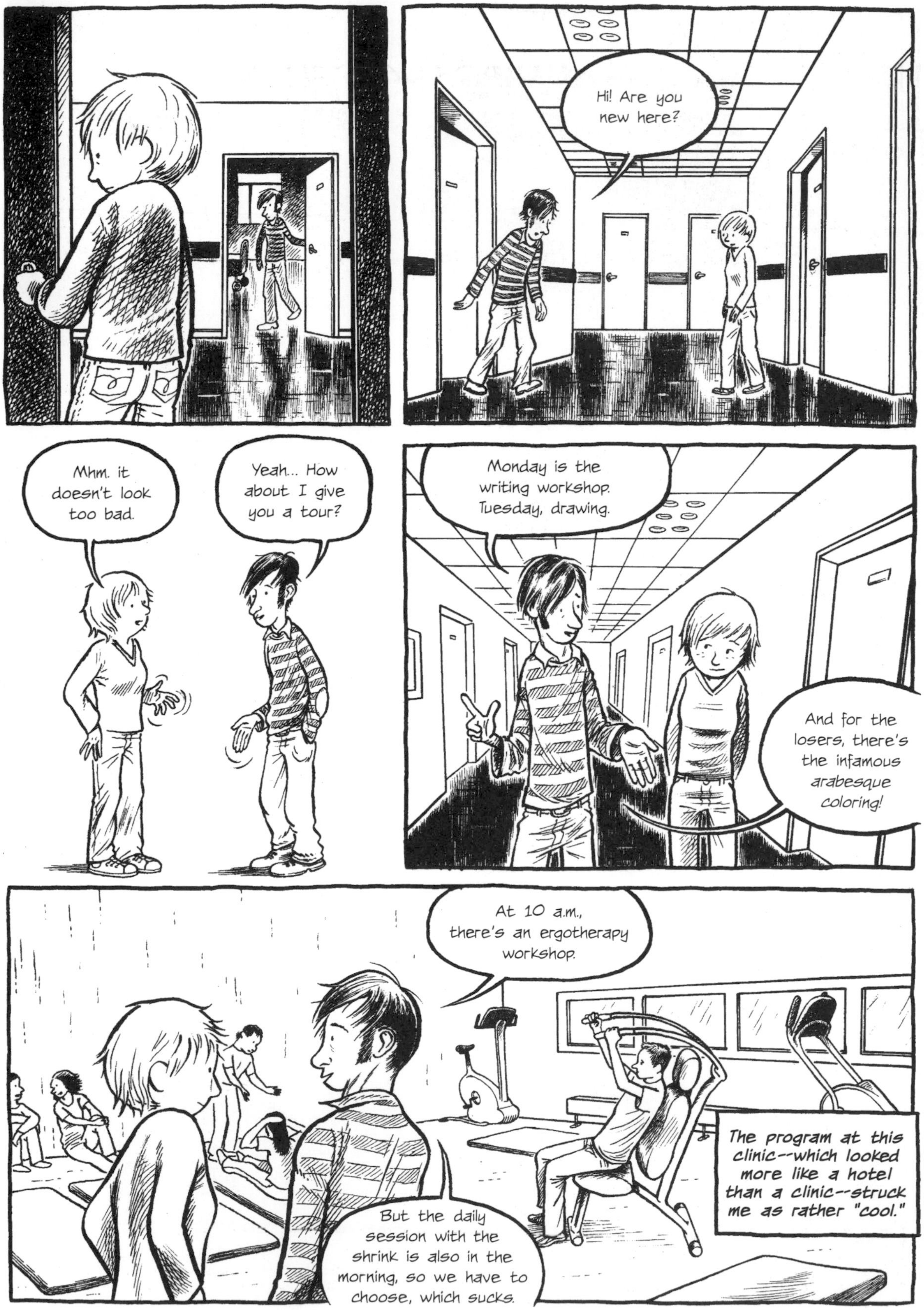
Hi! Are you new here?
Mhm. it doesn't look too bad.
Yeah... How about I give you a tour?
Monday is the writing workshop. Tuesday, drawing.
And for the losers, there's the infamous arabesque coloring!
At 10 a.m., there's an ergotherapy workshop.
The program at this clinic--which looked more like a hotel than a clinic--struck me as rather "cool."
But the daily session with the shrink is also in the morning, so we have to choose, which sucks.

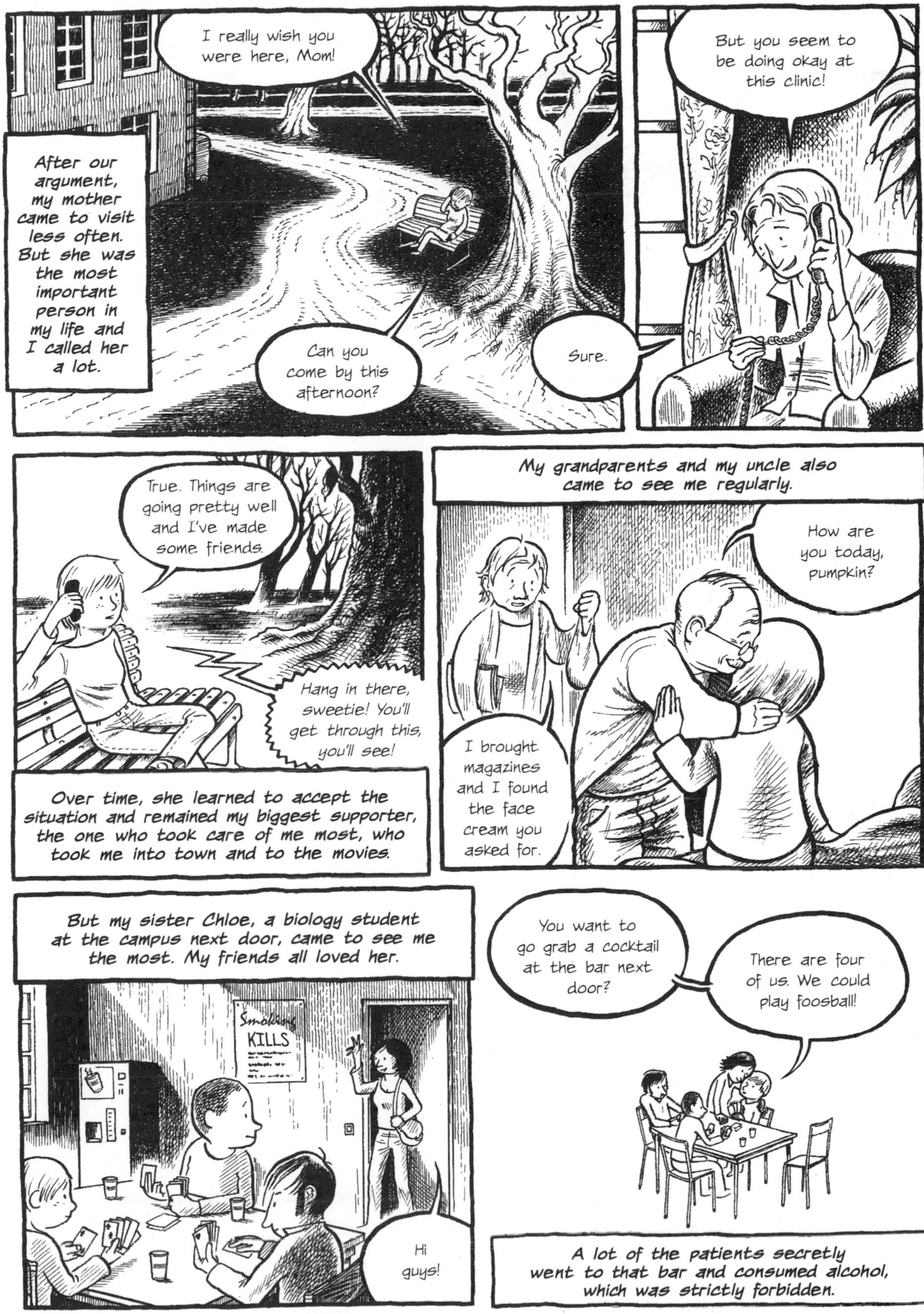
After our argument, my mother came to visit less often. But she was the most important person in my life and I called her a lot.
I really wish you were here, Mom!
Can you come by this afternoon?
But you seem to be doing okay at this clinic!
Sure.
True. Things are going pretty well and I've made some friends.
Hang in there, sweetie! You'll get through this, you'll see!
Over time, she learned to accept the situation and remained my biggest supporter, the one who took care of me most, who took me into town and to the movies.
My grandparents and my uncle also came to see me regularly.
How are you today, pumpkin?
I brought magazines and I found the face cream you asked for.
But my sister Chloe, a biology student at the campus next door, came to see me the most. My friends all loved her.
Smoking KILLS
Hi guys!
You want to go grab a cocktail at the bar next door?
There are four of us. We could play foosball!
A lot of the patients secretly went to that bar and consumed alcohol, which was strictly forbidden.

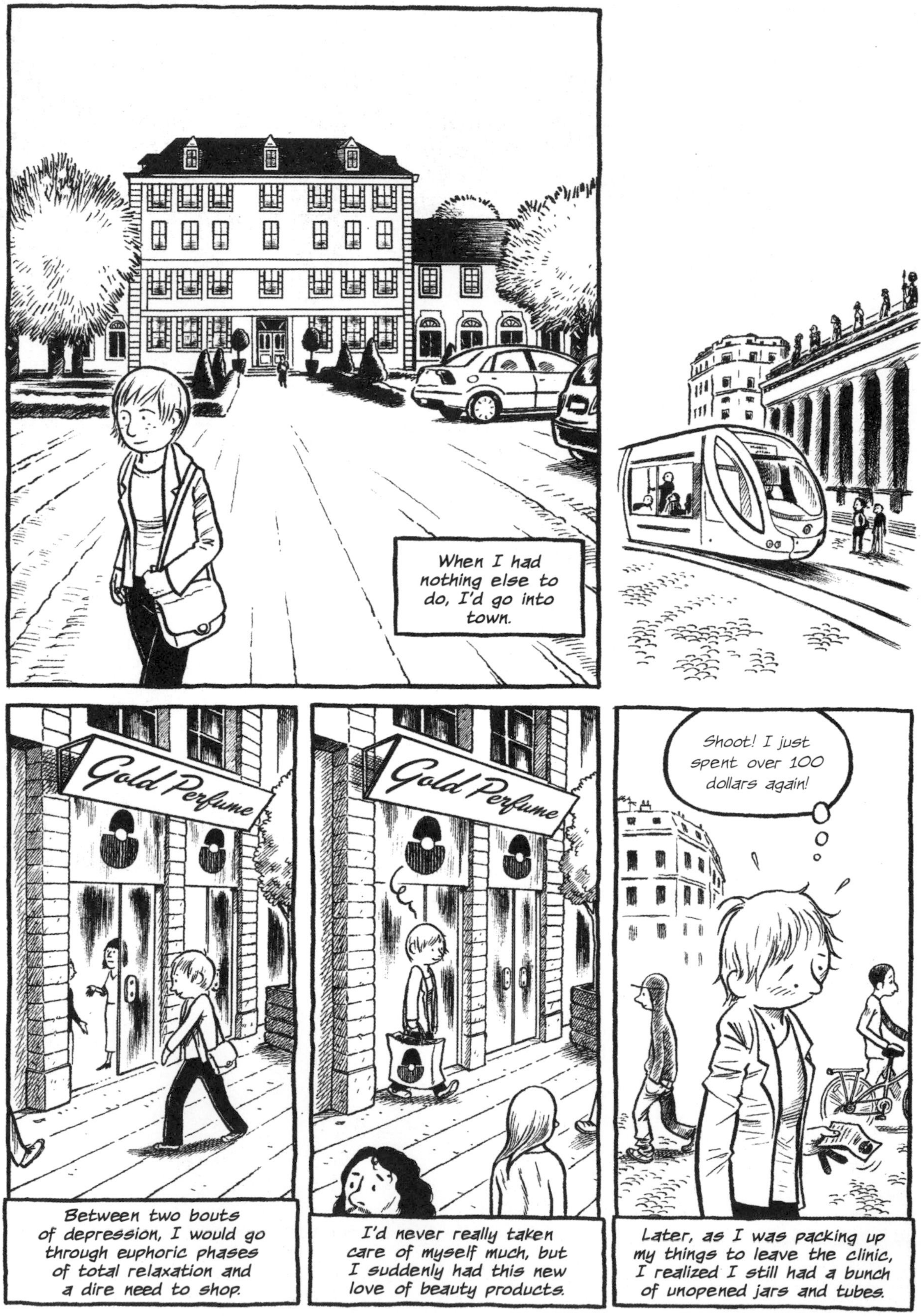
When I had nothing else to do, I'd go into town.
Gold Perfume
Between two bouts of depression, I would go through euphoric phases of total relaxation and a dire need to shop.
Gold Perfume
I'd never really taken care of myself much, but I suddenly had this new love of beauty products.
Shoot! I just spent over 100 dollars again!
Later, as I was packing up my things to leave the clinic, I realized I still had a bunch of unopened jars and tubes.

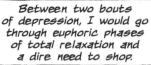

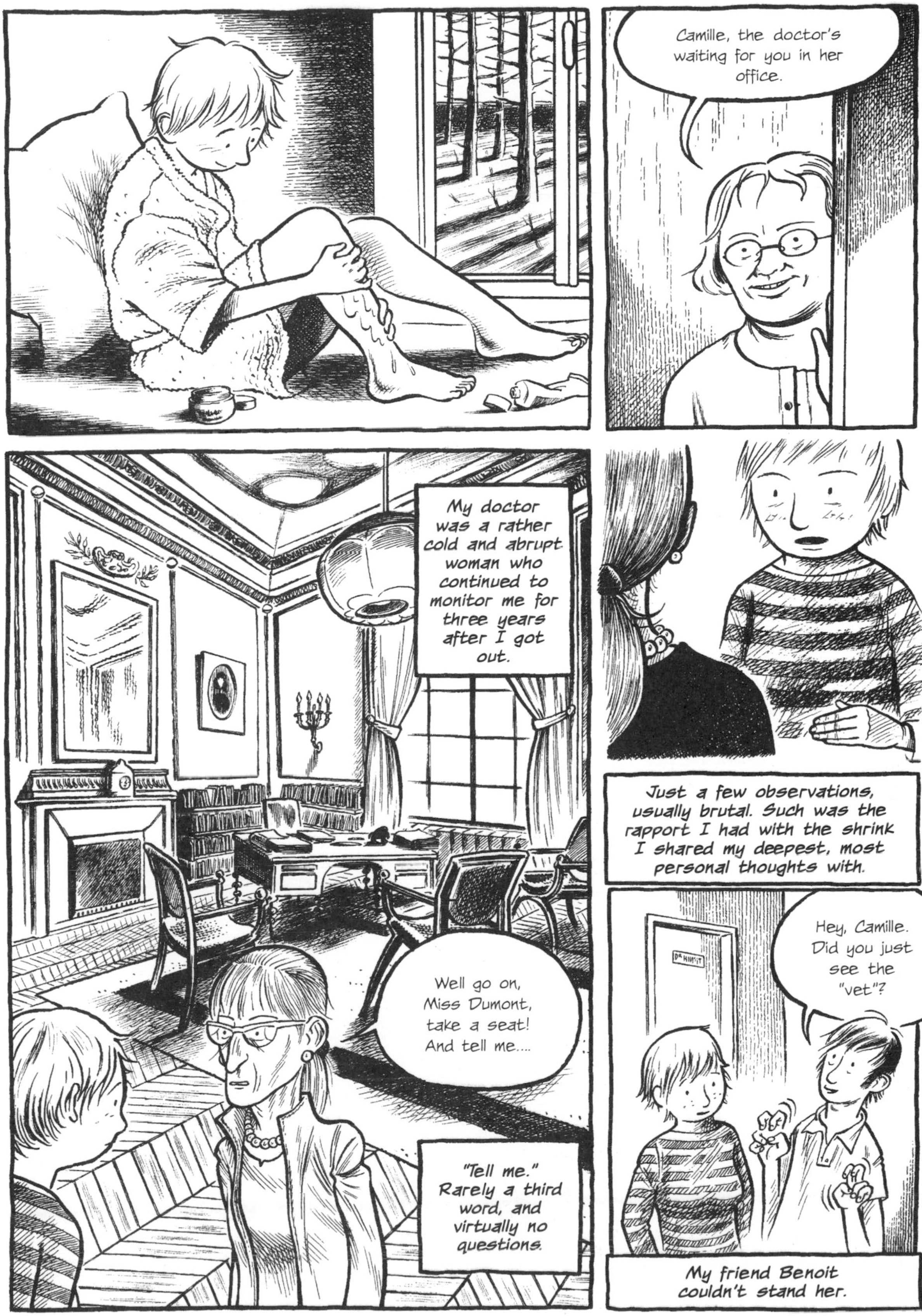
Camille, the doctor's waiting for you in her office.
My doctor was a rather cold and abrupt woman who continued to monitor me for three years after I got out.
Just a few observations, usually brutal. Such was the rapport I had with the shrink I shared my deepest, most personal thoughts with.
Well go on, Miss Dumont, take a seat! And tell me....
"Tell me." Rarely a third word, and virtually no questions.
Hey, Camille. Did you just see the "vet"?
My friend Benoit couldn't stand her.

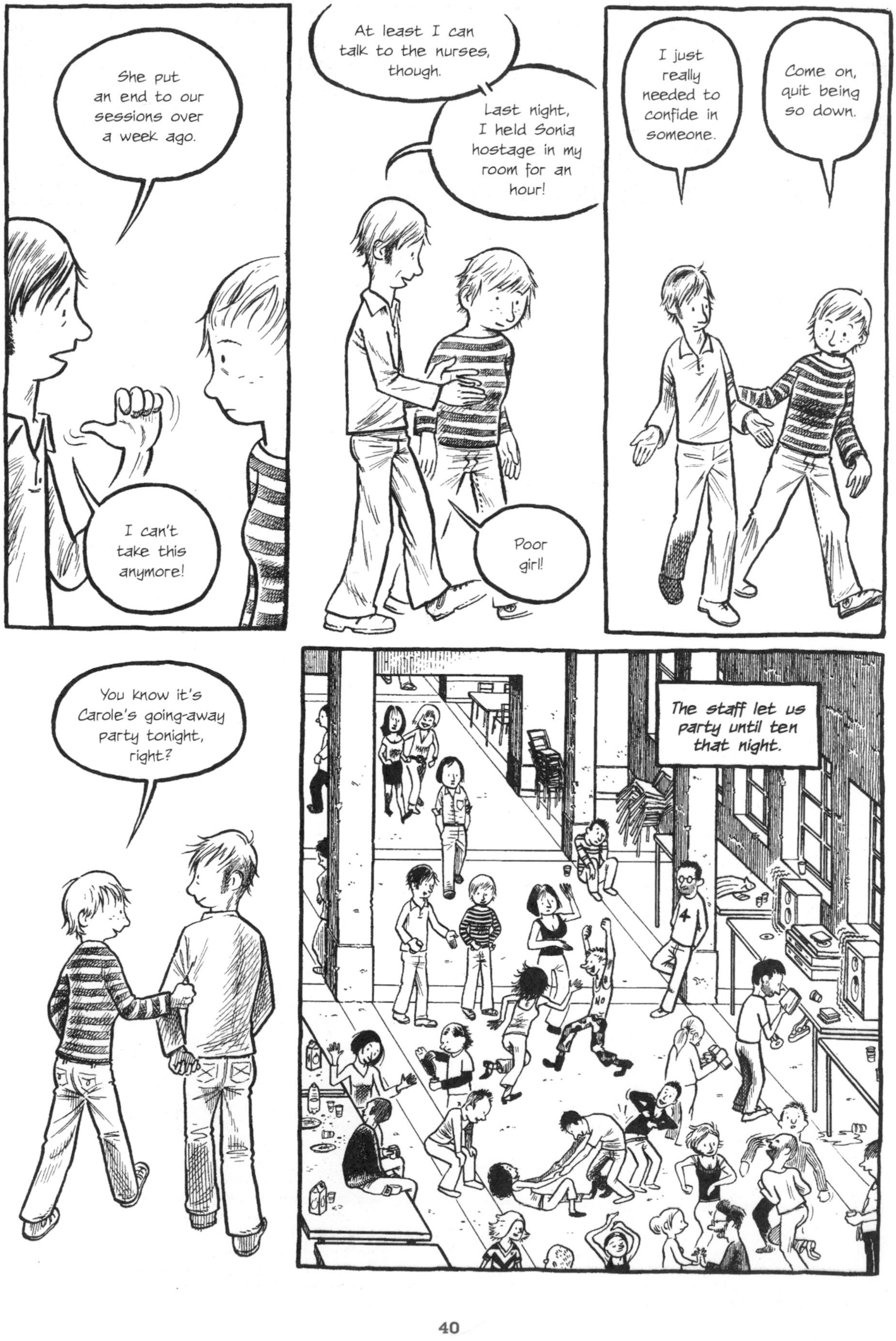
She put an end to our sessions over a week ago.
I can't take this anymore!
At least I can talk to the nurses, though.
Last night, I held Sonia hostage in my room for an hour!
Poor girl!
I just really needed to confide in someone.
Come on, quit being so down.
You know it's Carole's going-away party tonight, right?
The staff let us party until ten that night.

Hey, Camille!
Hey, Benoit!
You guys want a "whiskey"?
Let's dance, Camille, this is our song!
QUELQUE CHOSE EN TOI... NE TOURNE PAS ROOOOOND*!
At every going-away party, we played that song by the French rock band Telephone: it was sort of the clinic's anthem.
I stayed there for two months. My sister Chloe came to take me home.
Hi Camille!
Ready to go?
How are you?
Smack
Much better...
...or not!
Having been hospitalized meant I was now officially part of the group of people suffering from "a mental disorder." But that short-term treatment, necessary though it was, hadn't solved anything.

*'80s song by the French rock group Telephone that translates to: "There's something inside you that doesn't compute."

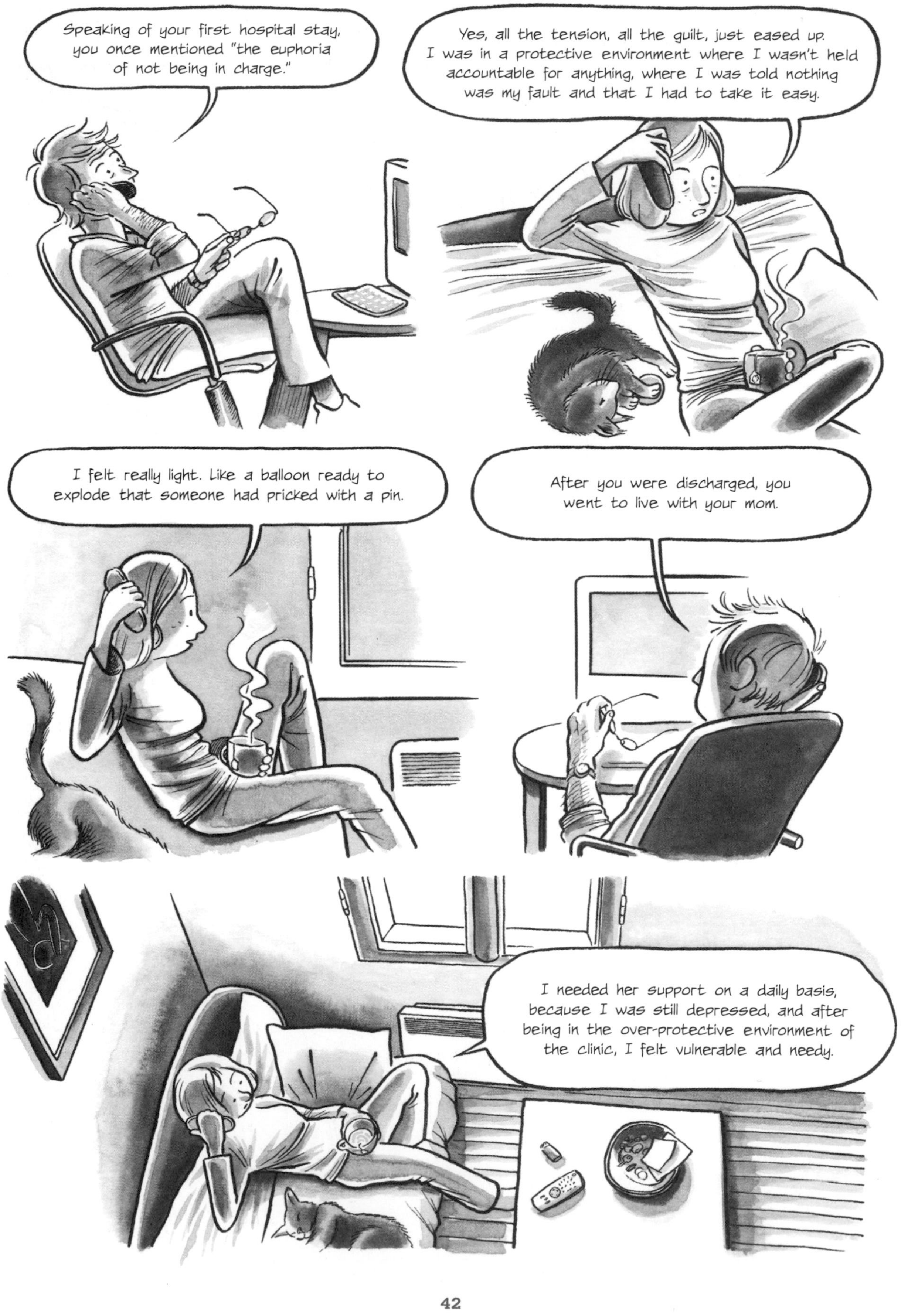
Speaking of your first hospital stay, you once mentioned "the euphoria of not being in charge."
Yes, all the tension, all the guilt, just eased up. I was in a protective environment where I wasn't held accountable for anything, where I was told nothing was my fault and that I had to take it easy.
I felt really light. Like a balloon ready to explode that someone had pricked with a pin.
After you were discharged, you went to live with your mom.
I needed her support on a daily basis, because I was still depressed, and after being in the over-protective environment of the clinic, I felt vulnerable and needy.

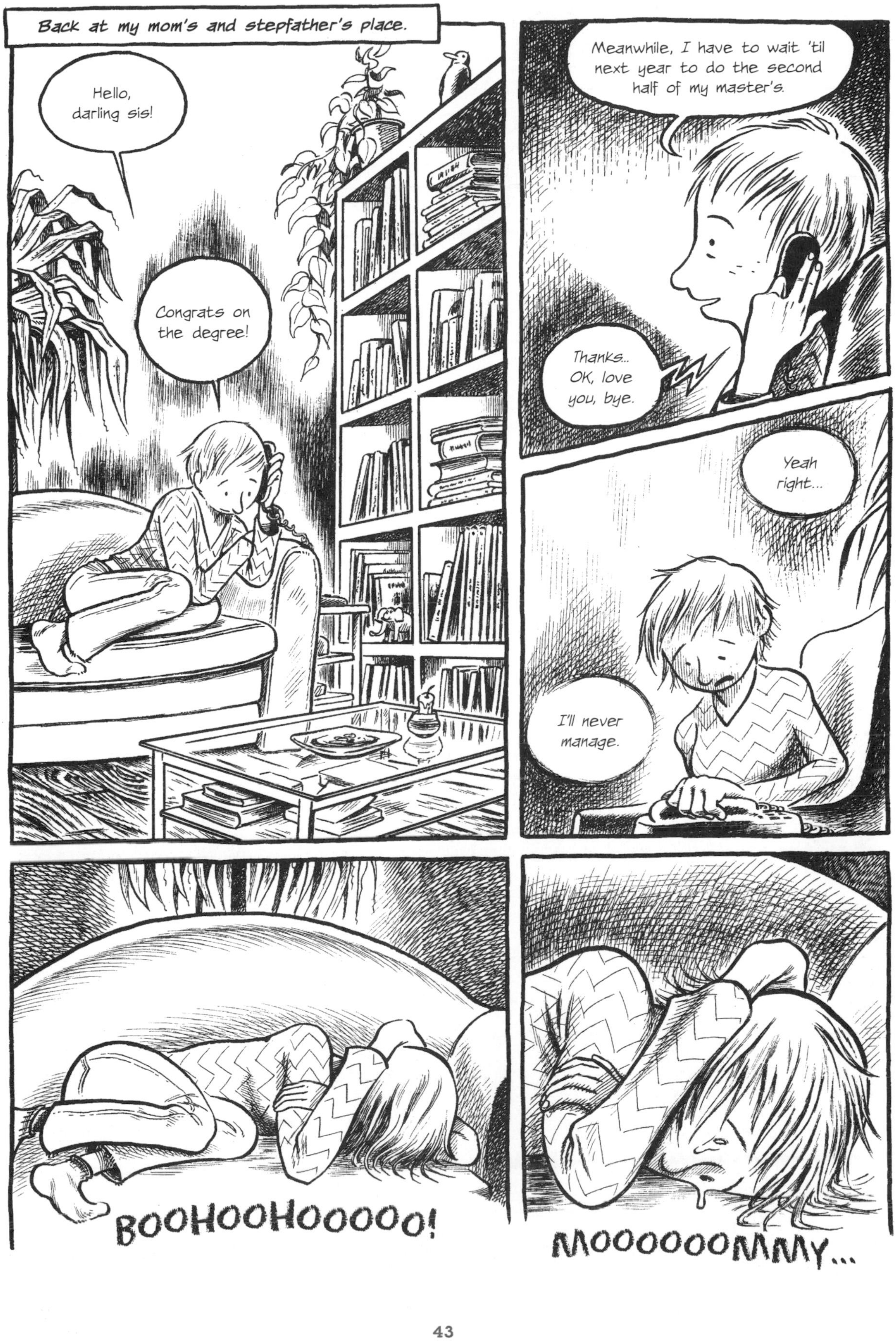

Back at my mom's and stepfather's place.
Hello, darling sis!
Congrats on the degree!
Meanwhile, I have to wait 'til next year to do the second half of my master's.
Thanks.. OK, love you, bye.
Yeah right...
I'll never manage.
BOOHOOHOOOOO!
MOOOOOOMMY...

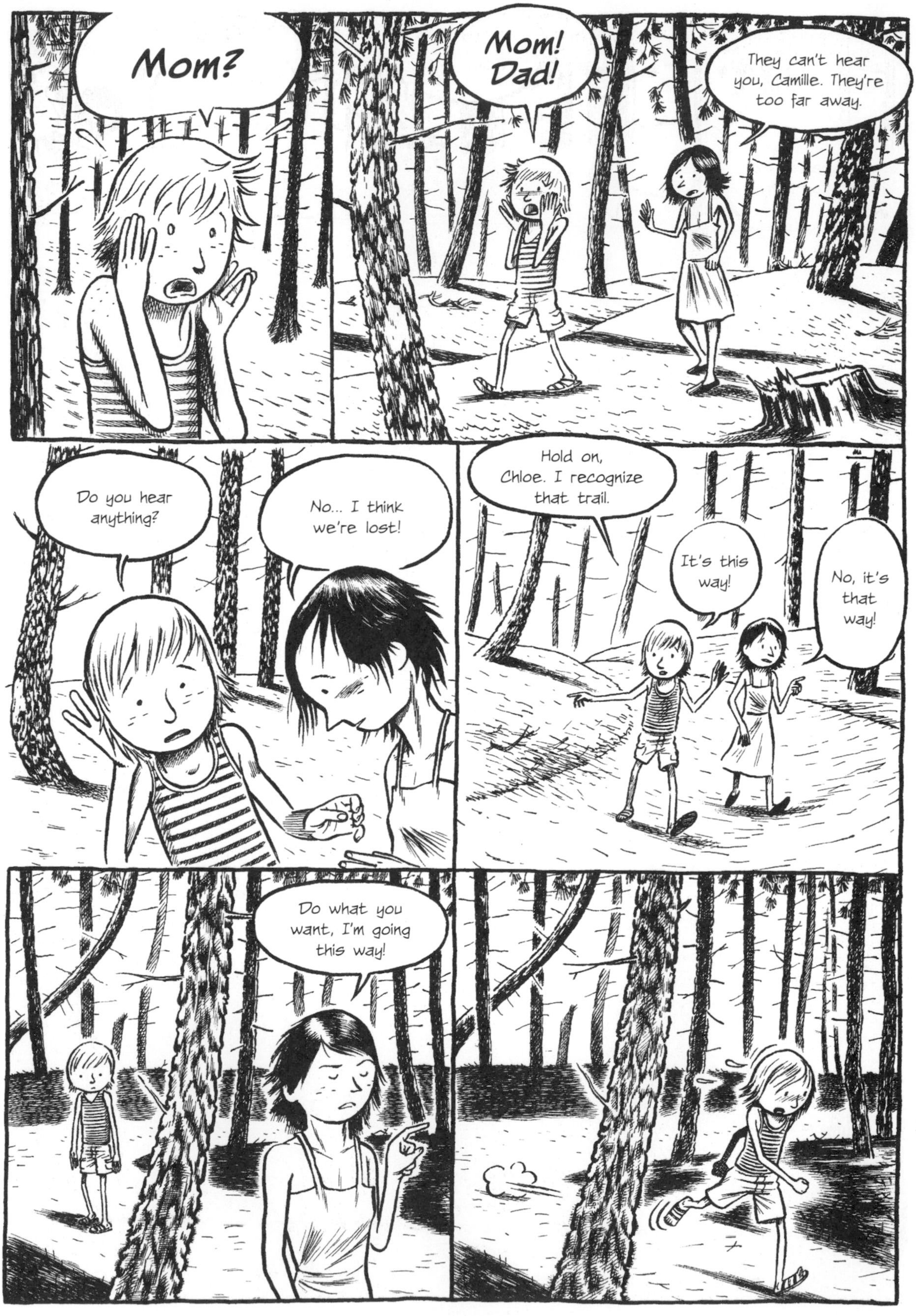
Mom?
Mom! Dad!
They can't hear you, Camille. They're too far away.
Do you hear anything?
No... I think we're lost!
Hold on, Chloe. I recognize that trail.
It's this way!
No, it's that way!
Do what you want, I'm going this way!

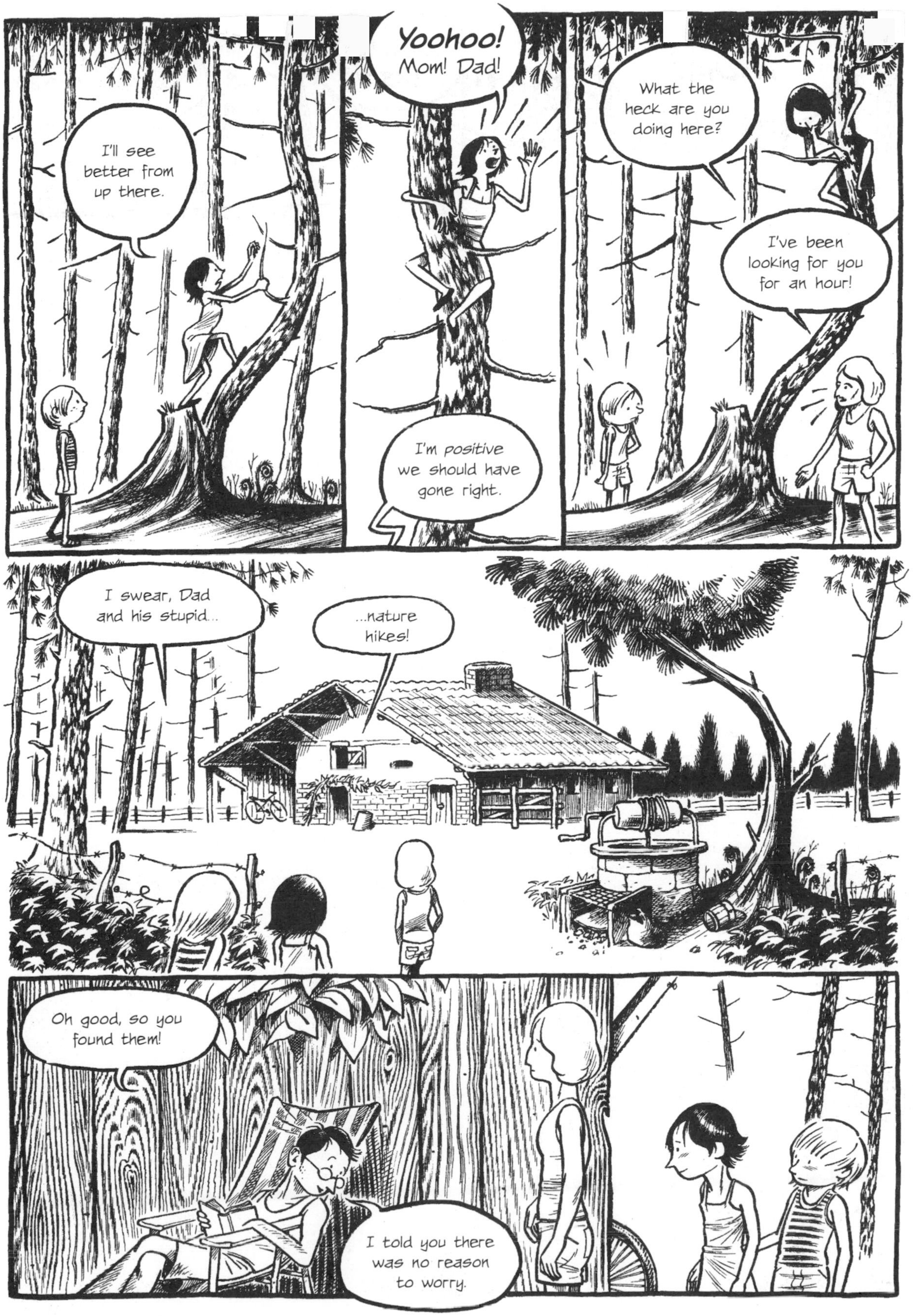
I'll see better from up there.
Yoohoo! Mom! Dad!
I'm positive we should have gone right.
What the heck are you doing here?
I've been looking for you for an hour!
I swear, Dad and his stupid...
...nature hikes!
Oh good, so you found them!
I told you there was no reason to worry.

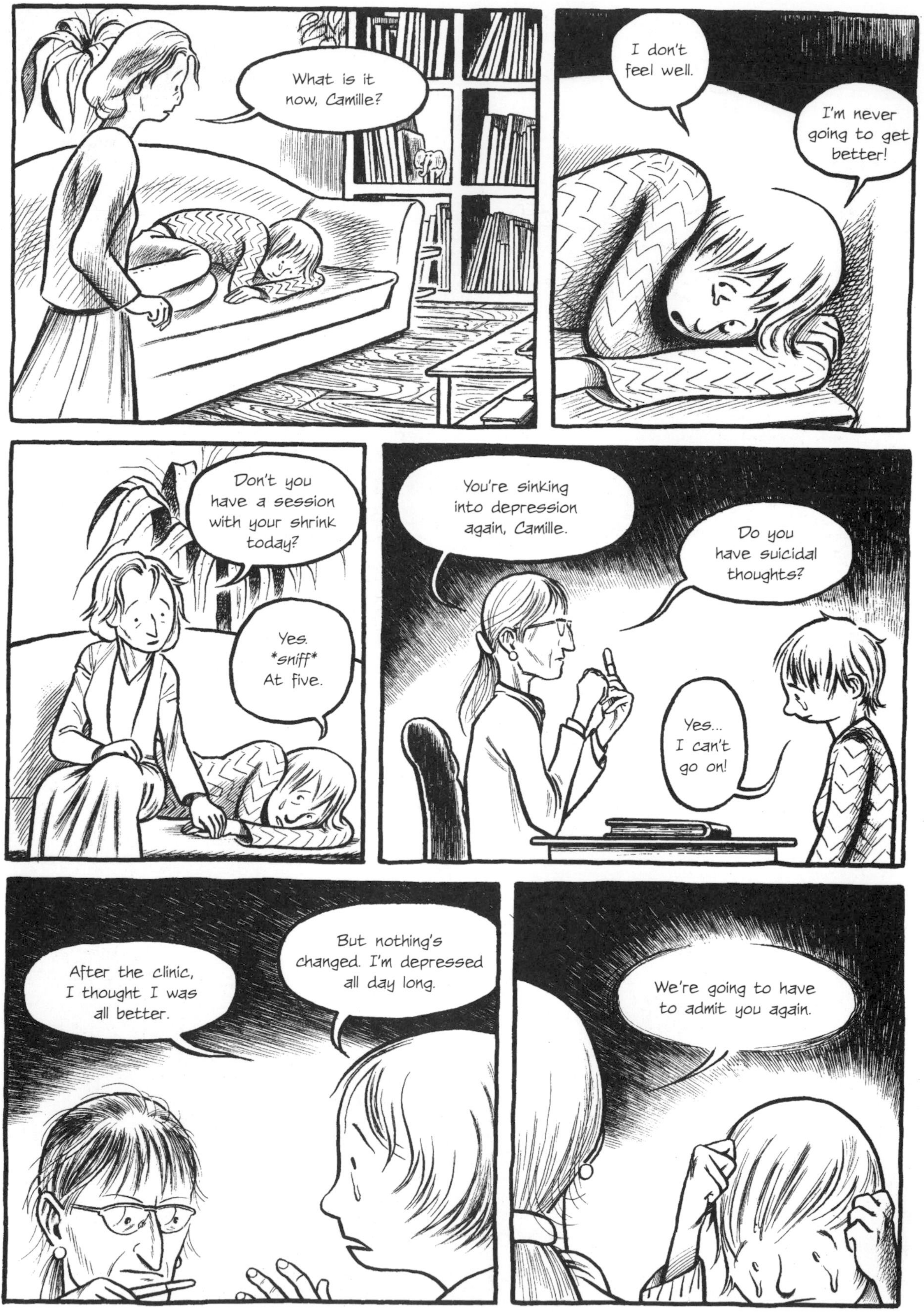
What is it now, Camille?
I don't feel well.
I'm never going to get better!
Don't you have a session with your shrink today?
Yes. *sniff* At five.
You're sinking into depression again, Camille.
Do you have suicidal thoughts?
Yes... I can't go on!
After the clinic, I thought I was all better.
But nothing's changed. I'm depressed all day long.
We're going to have to admit you again.

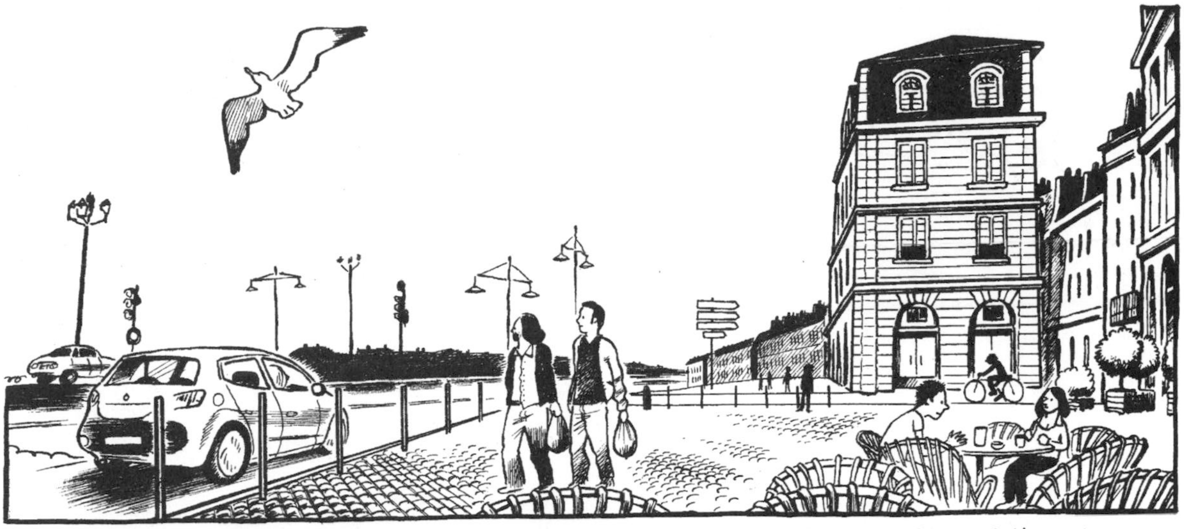

My condition hadn't improved and I started cutting my wrists. Between July and November, I was hospitalized four different times, with no hope of returning to a "normal" life anytime soon. But I couldn't very well spend the rest of my life in clinics and hospitals!

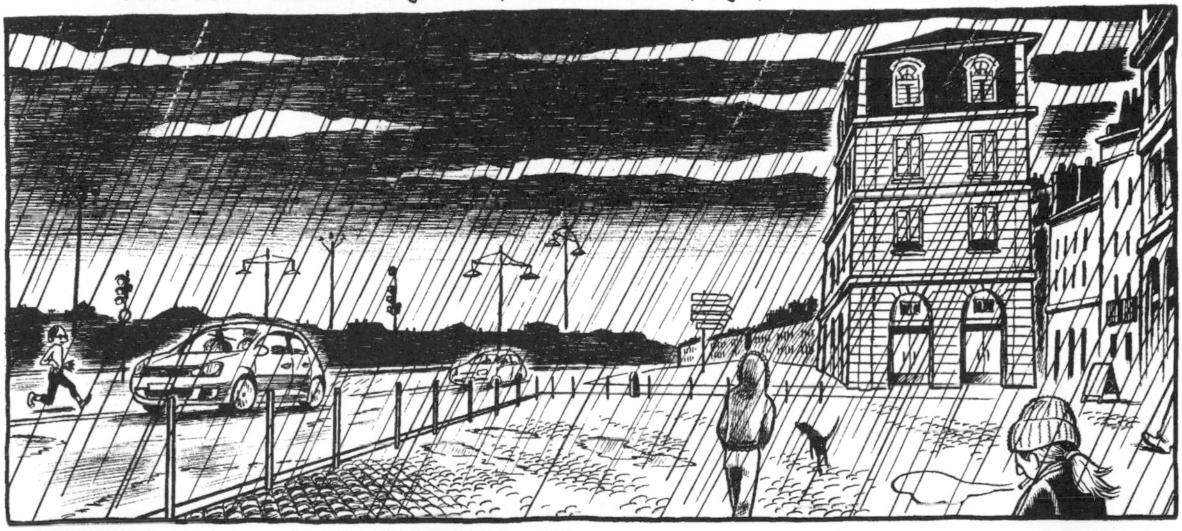

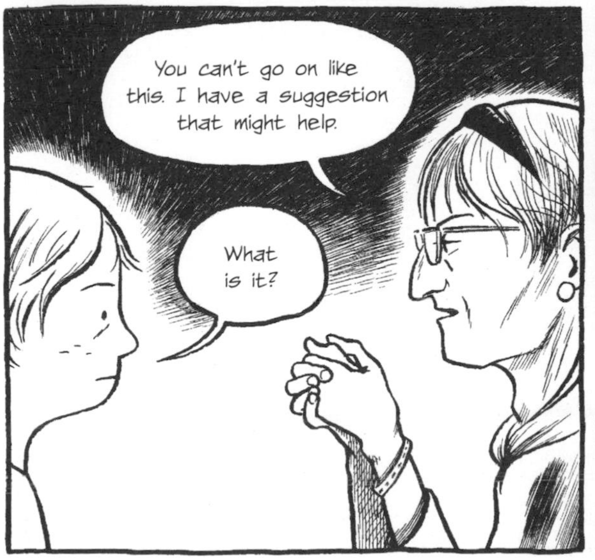
You can't go on like this. I have a suggestion that might help.
What is it?

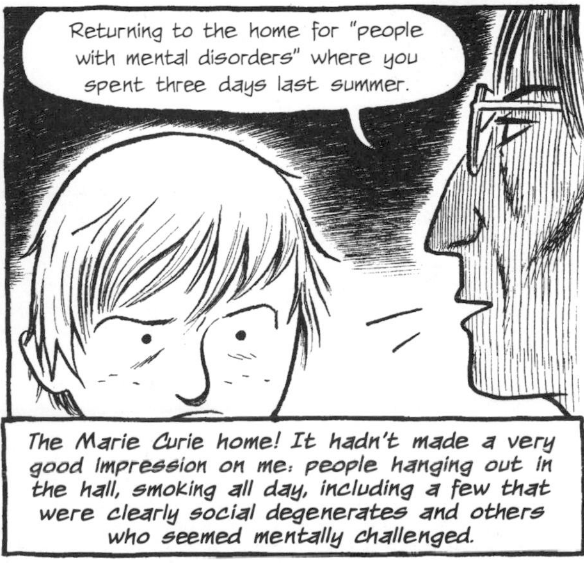
Returning to the home for "people with mental disorders" where you spent three days last summer.
The Marie Curie home! It hadn't made a very good impression on me: people hanging out in the hall, smoking all day, including a few that were clearly social degenerates and others who seemed mentally challenged.

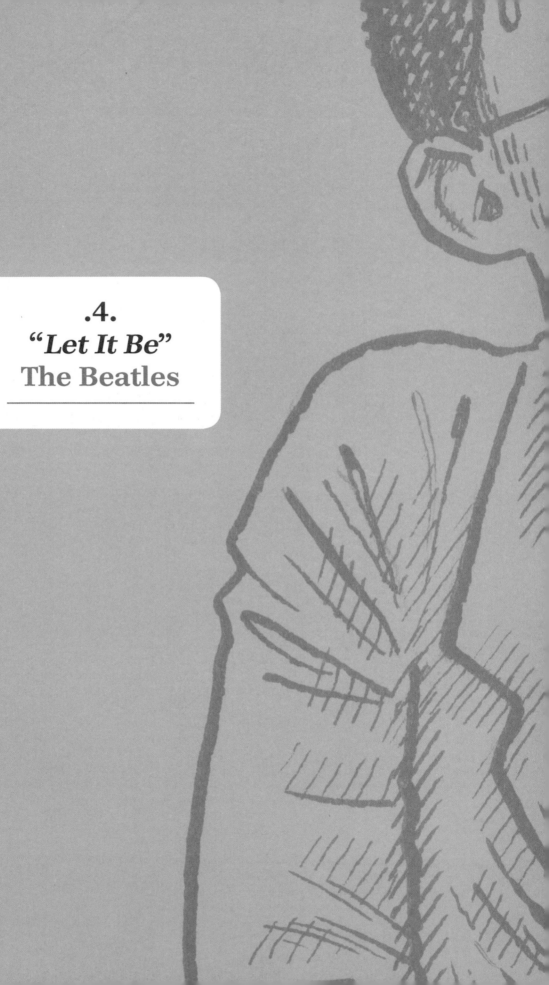

.4.

"Let It Be"

The Beatles

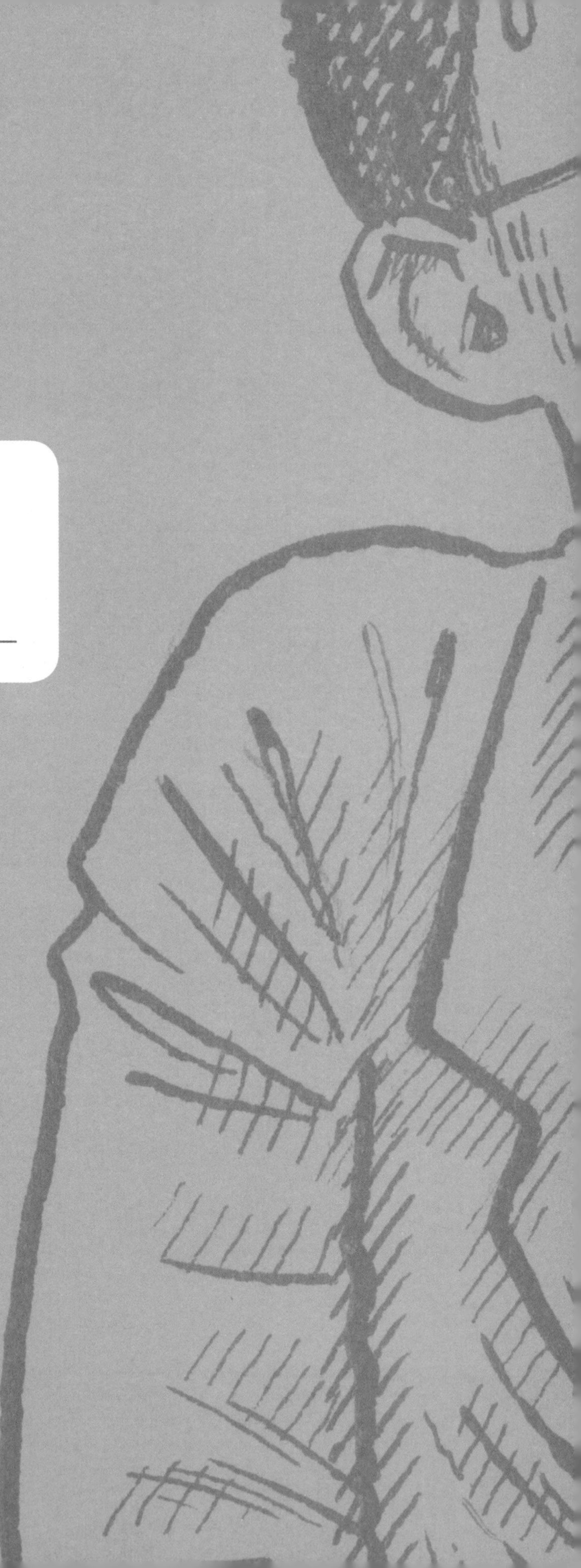

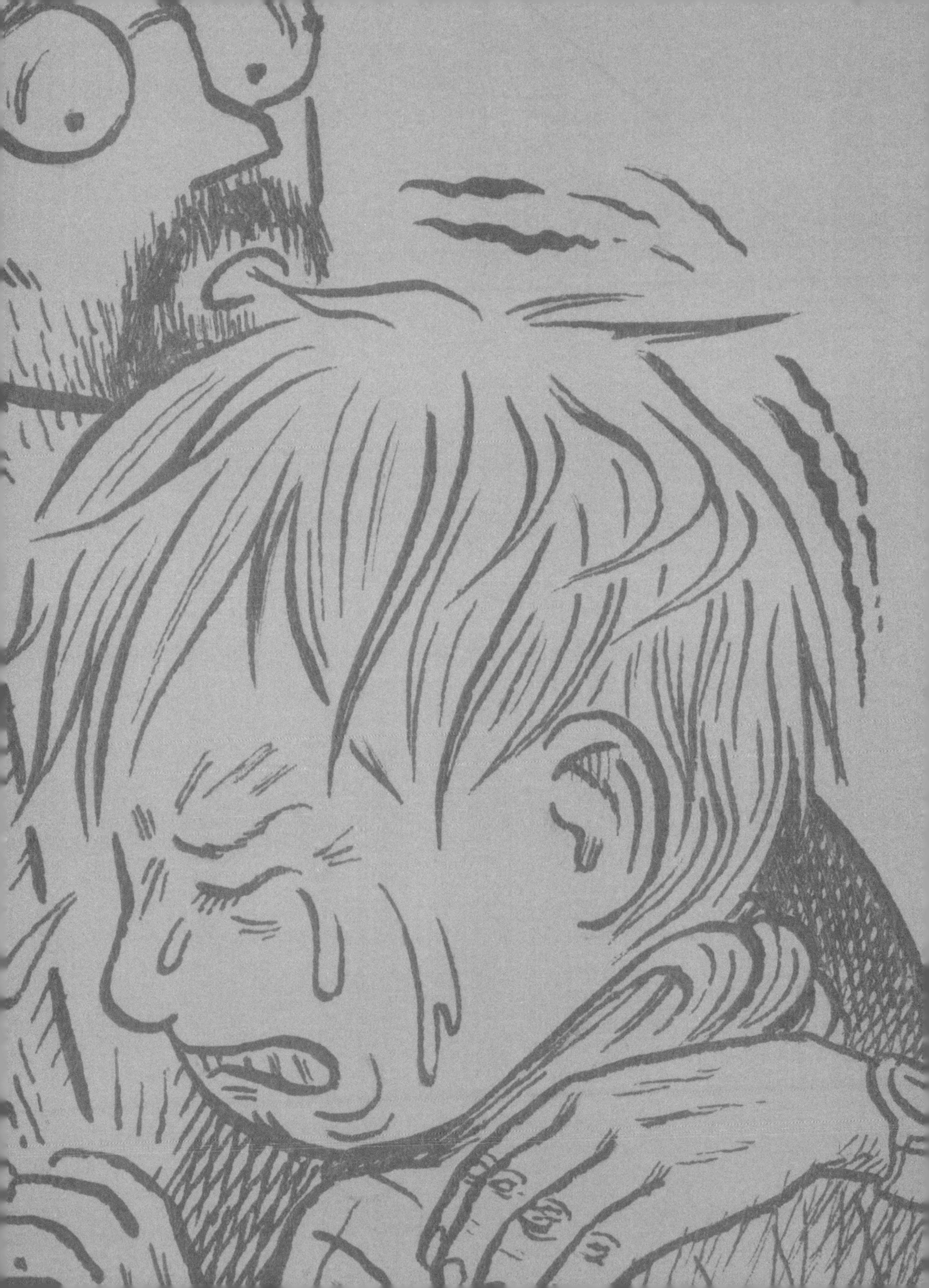

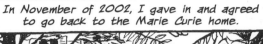

In November of 2002, I gave in and agreed to go back to the Marie Curie home.

Hello, Mom?

I'm fine. It's actually better than I thought it would be.

Little did I know I'd be staying there two and a half years!

I share a room with a girl my age.

She's reserved, but really nice. She majored in political science and history.

Same program every day. Up at nine, workshops, communal meals and lights out at eleven.

Twice a week, it was two-person dining room duty: setting the table, serving the food, clearing the table and doing the dishes.

And of course, we took our meds morning, noon and night!

At the end of these strictly regimented days, the nights were anything but!

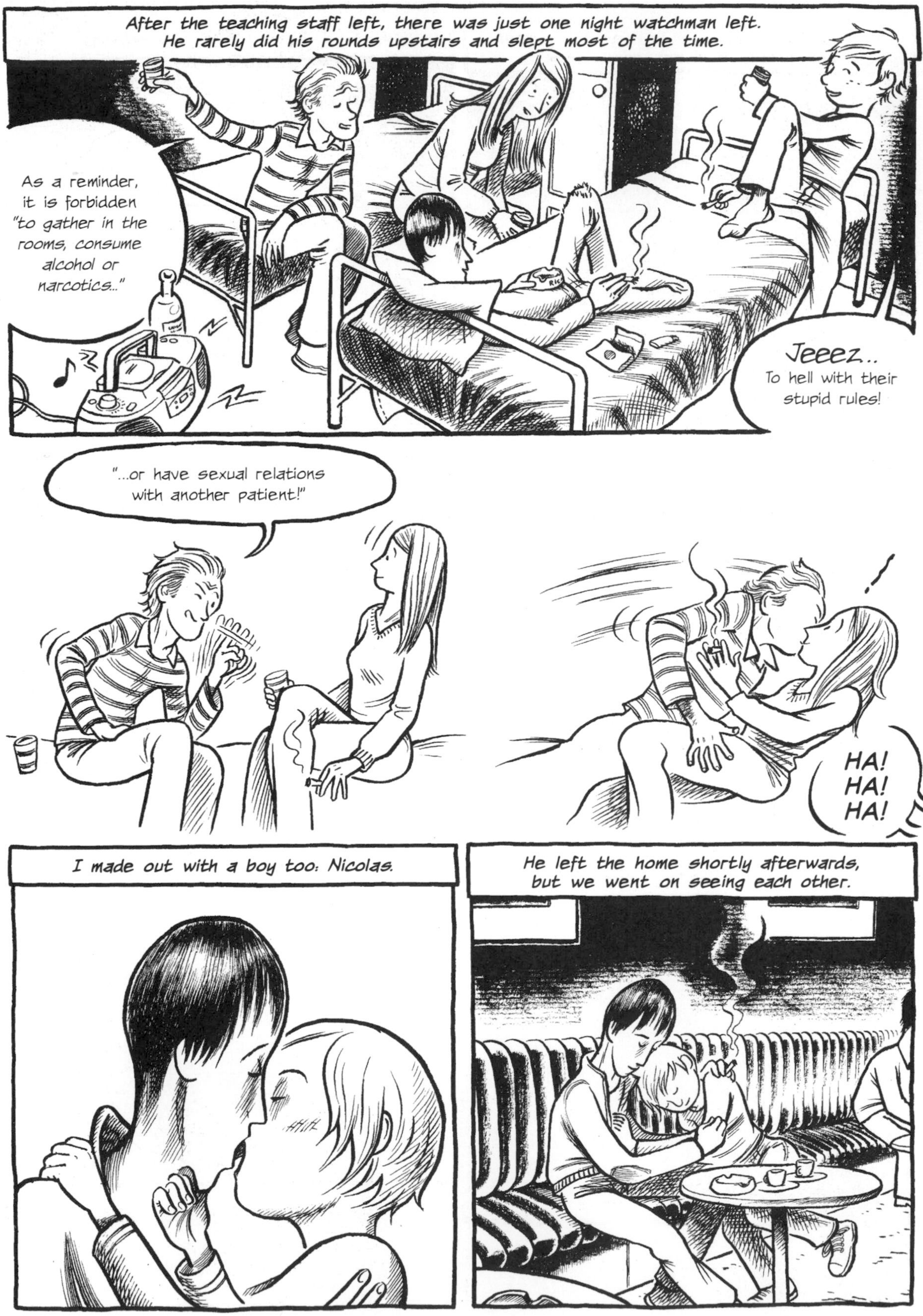
After the teaching staff left, there was just one night watchman left.
He rarely did his rounds upstairs and slept most of the time.
As a reminder, it is forbidden "to gather in the rooms, consume alcohol or narcotics..."
Jeeez.. To hell with their stupid rules!
"...or have sexual relations with another patient!"
HA! HA! HA!
I made out with a boy too: Nicolas.
He left the home shortly afterwards, but we went on seeing each other.

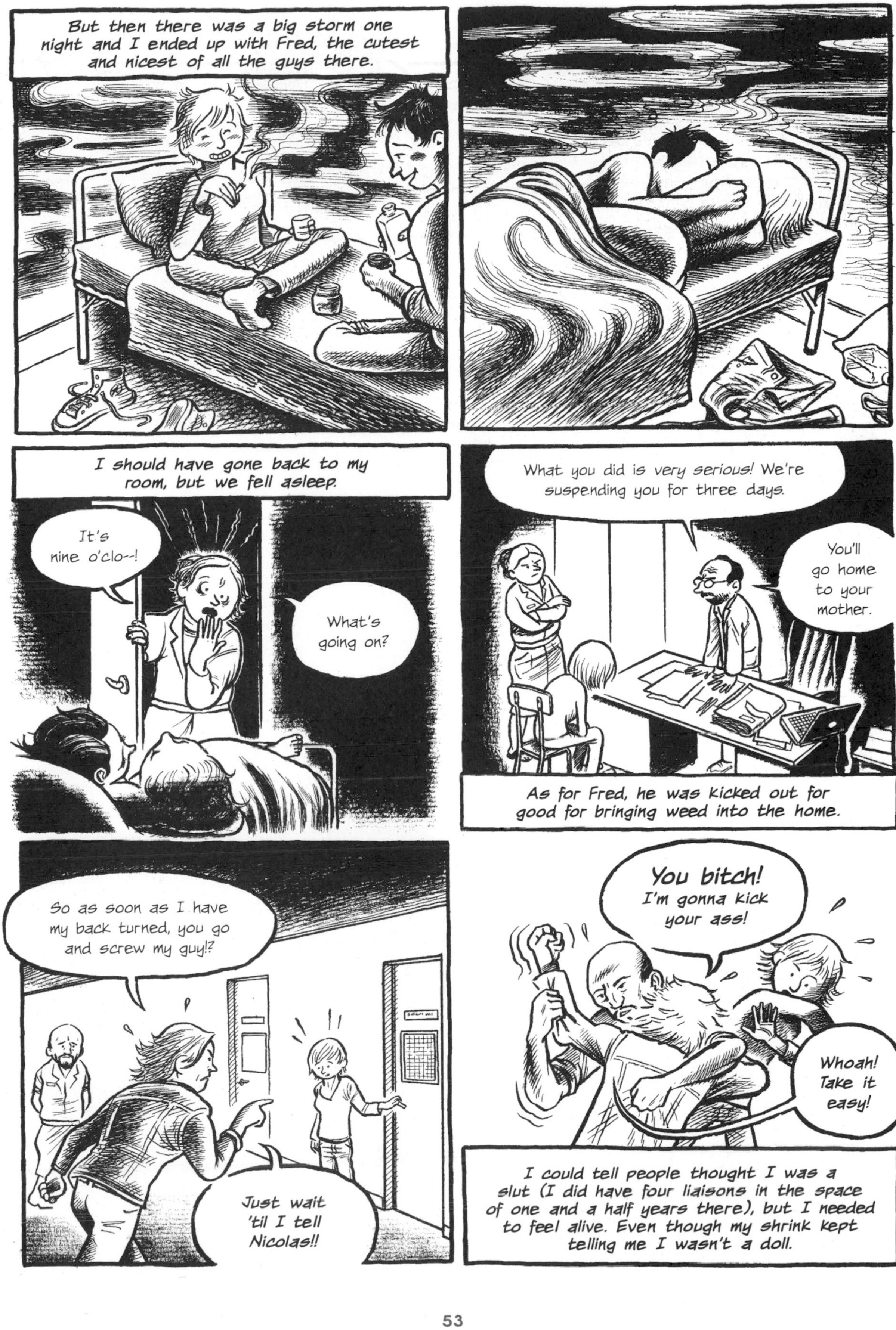

But then there was a big storm one night and I ended up with Fred, the cutest and nicest of all the guys there.
I should have gone back to my room, but we fell asleep.
It's nine o'clo--!
What's going on?
What you did is very serious! We're suspending you for three days.
You'll go home to your mother.
As for Fred, he was kicked out for good for bringing weed into the home.
So as soon as I have my back turned, you go and screw my guy!?
Just wait 'til I tell Nicolas!!
You bitch! I'm gonna kick your ass!
Whoah! Take it easy!
I could tell people thought I was a slut (I did have four liaisons in the space of one and a half years there), but I needed to feel alive. Even though my shrink kept telling me I wasn't a doll.

To cheer myself up, I would go shopping downtown several times a week.

Um... everything okay, Miss?

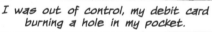

I was out of control, my debit card burning a hole in my pocket.

Can I help you find something?

I'll take that beige sweater and oh, that little jacket, too!

How much is the matching handbag?

Don't you want to try them on, Miss?

No need! I'll take it all!

That'll be 155 dollars...

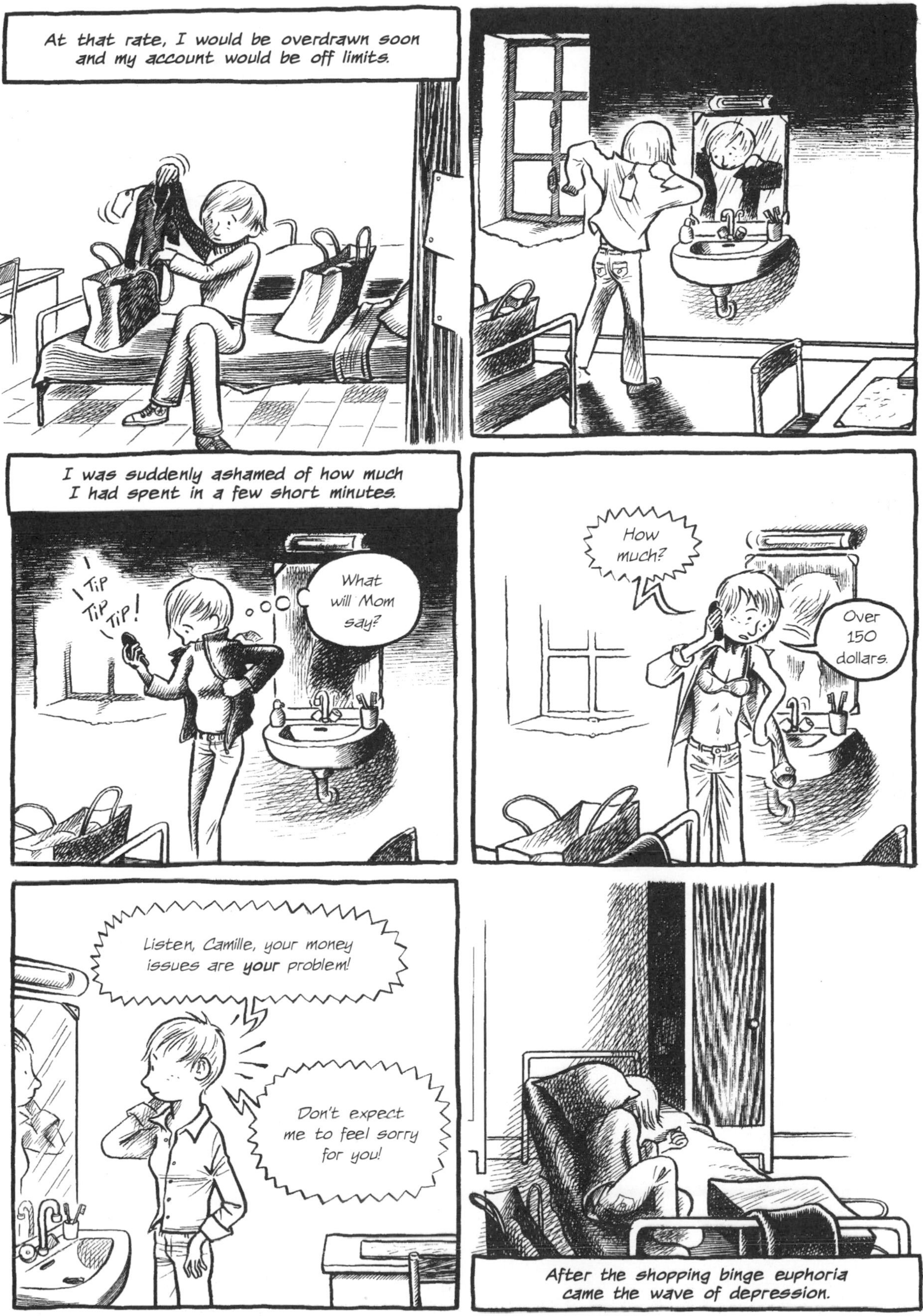
At that rate, I would be overdrawn soon and my account would be off limits.
I was suddenly ashamed of how much I had spent in a few short minutes.
Tip Tip Tip!
What will Mom say?
How much?
Over 150 dollars.
Listen, Camille, your money issues are **your** problem!
Don't expect me to feel sorry for you!
After the shopping binge euphoria came the wave of depression.

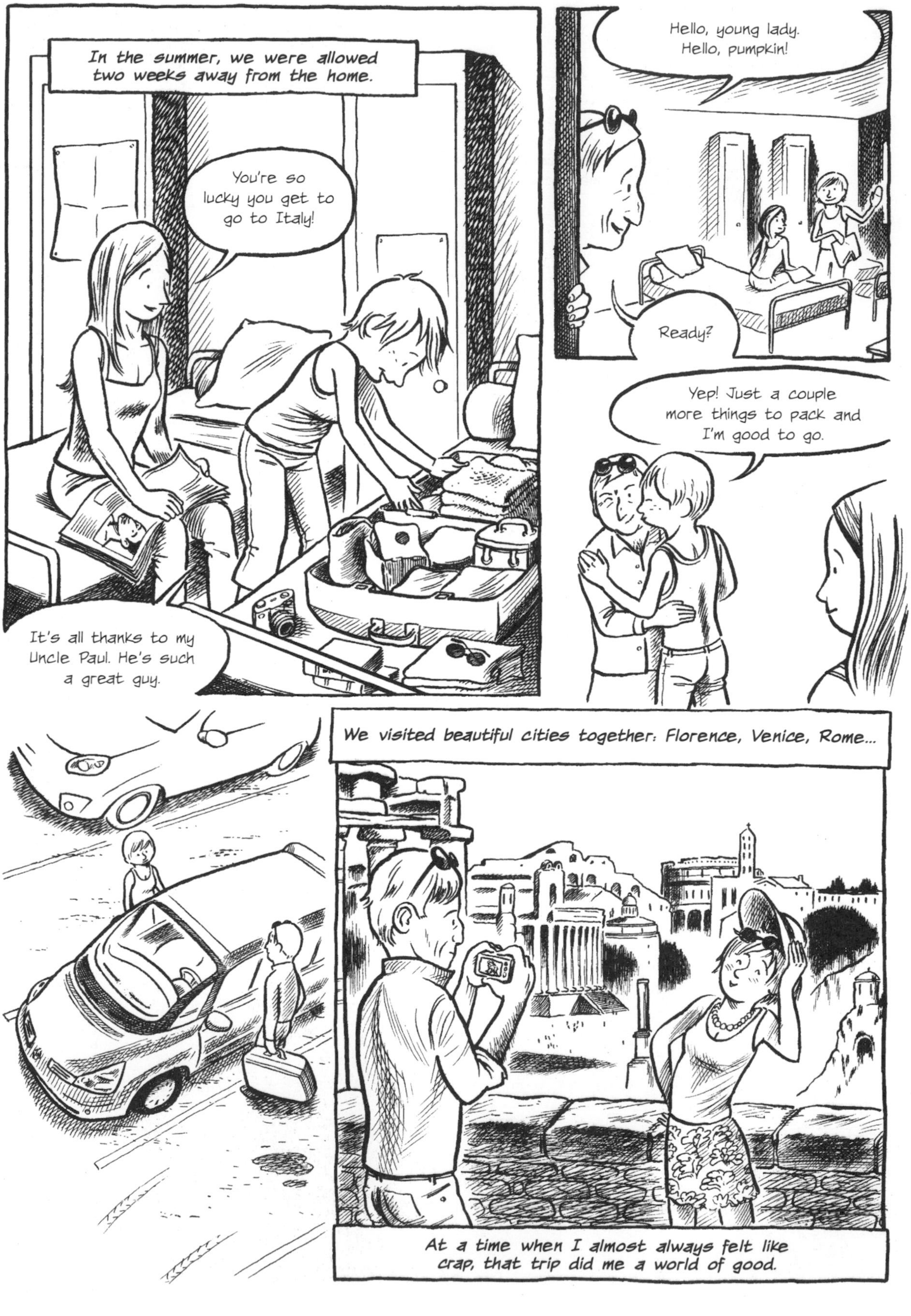
In the summer, we were allowed two weeks away from the home.
You're so lucky you get to go to Italy!
It's all thanks to my Uncle Paul. He's such a great guy.
Hello, young lady. Hello, pumpkin!
Ready?
Yep! Just a couple more things to pack and I'm good to go.
We visited beautiful cities together: Florence, Venice, Rome...
At a time when I almost always felt like crap, that trip did me a world of good.

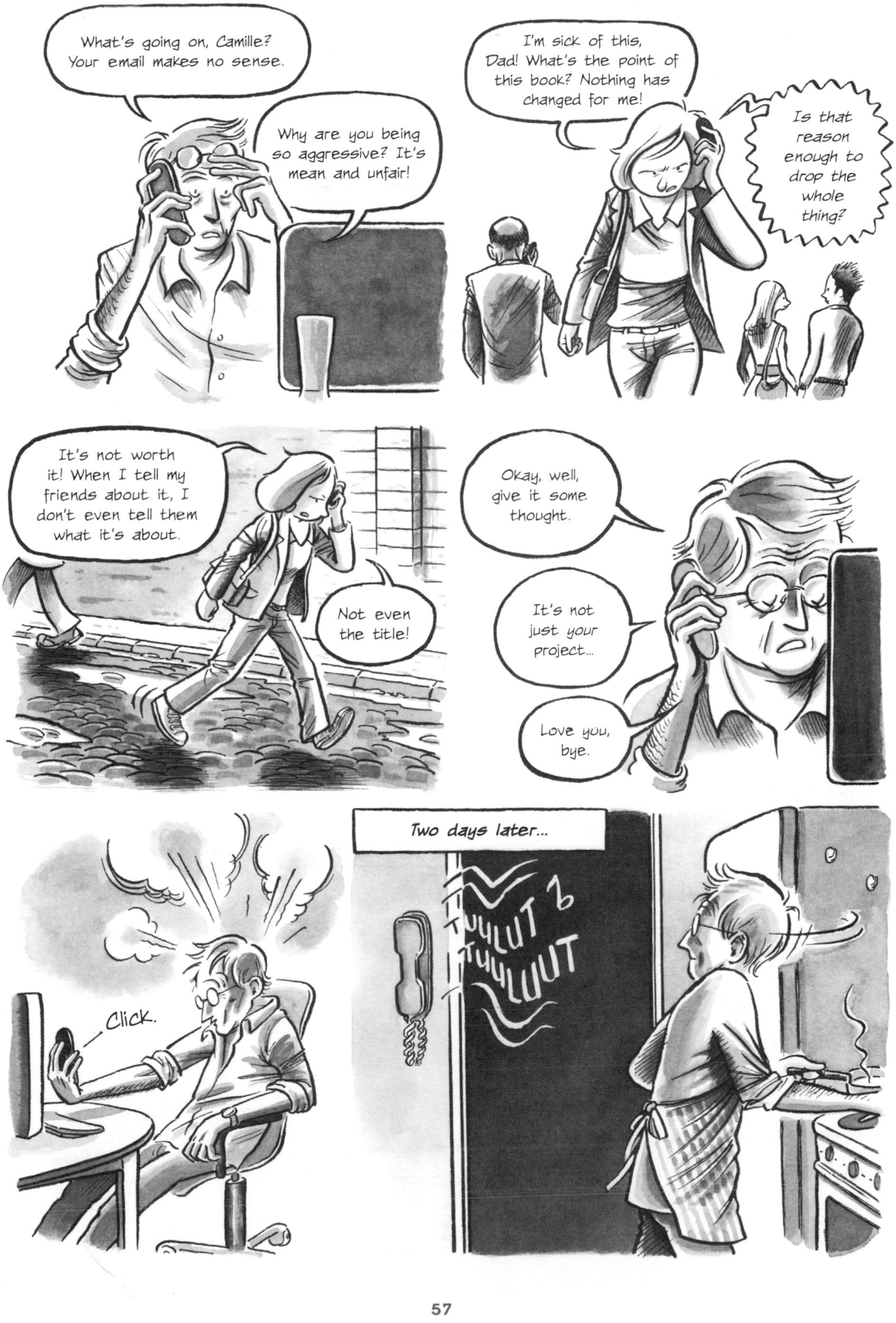
What's going on, Camille? Your email makes no sense.
Why are you being so aggressive? It's mean and unfair!
I'm sick of this, Dad! What's the point of this book? Nothing has changed for me!
Is that reason enough to drop the whole thing?
It's not worth it! When I tell my friends about it, I don't even tell them what it's about.
Not even the title!
Okay, well, give it some thought.
It's not just your project...
Love you, bye.
Click.
Two days later...
TUULUT TUULUUT

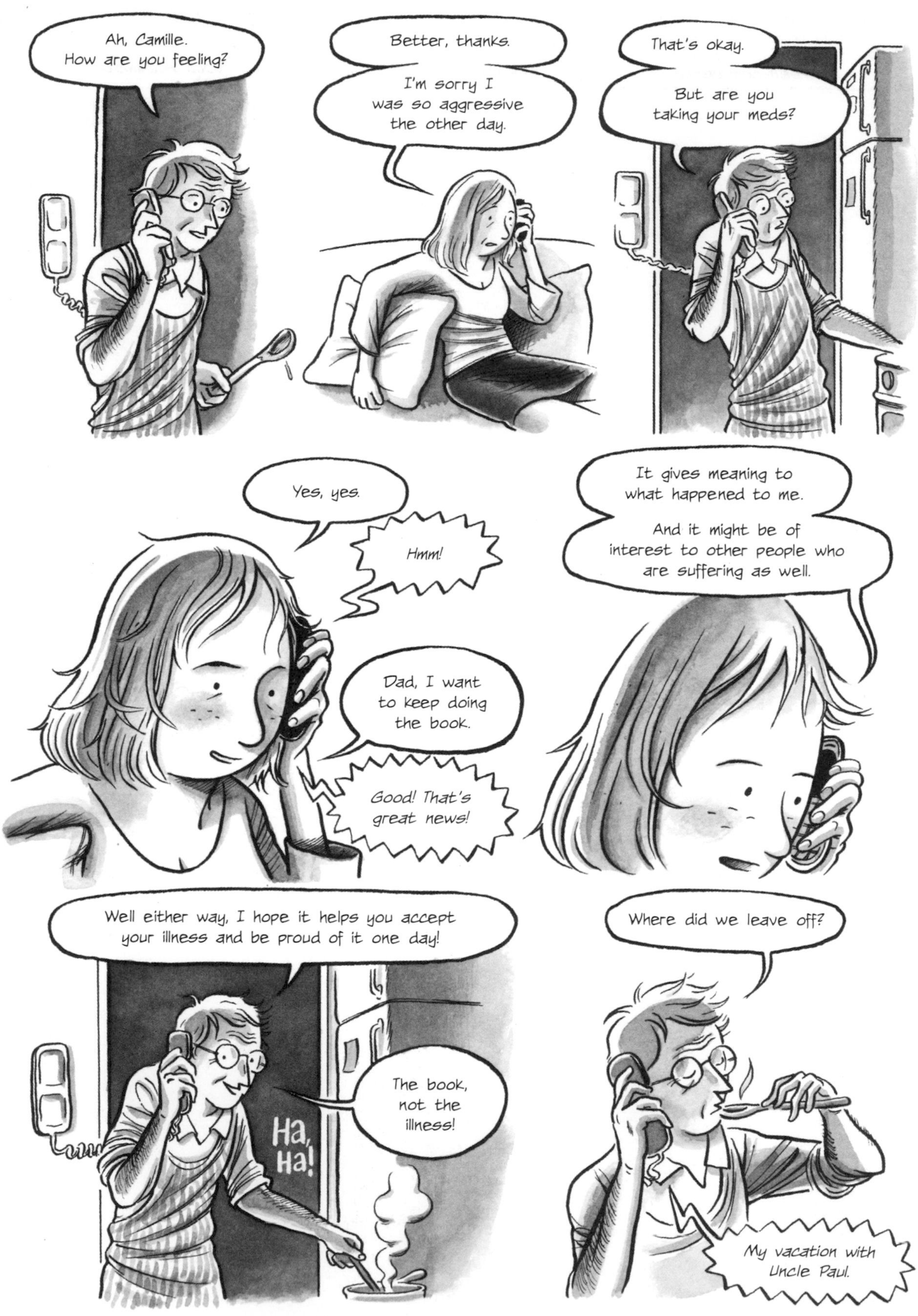
Ah, Camille.
How are you feeling?
Better, thanks.
I'm sorry I was so aggressive the other day.
That's okay.
But are you taking your meds?
Yes, yes.
Hmm!
Dad, I want to keep doing the book.
Good! That's great news!
It gives meaning to what happened to me.
And it might be of interest to other people who are suffering as well.
Well either way, I hope it helps you accept your illness and be proud of it one day!
The book, not the illness!
Ha, Ha!
Where did we leave off?
My vacation with Uncle Paul.

When I came back from Italy, I had recovered a little serenity and self-confidence.

With my mom's encouragement, I decided--just like my friend Clementine and others from law school--to take the entrance exam for the Center for Public Administration at Science Po* (CPAG).

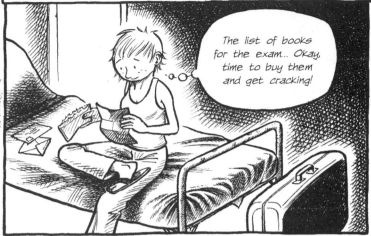

The list of books for the exam... Okay, time to buy them and get cracking!

We were allowed to spend every other weekend outside the home. Most of the time, I spent them with my mom and stepdad at the vacation home they time-shared with my dad and his wife during the summer.

Sorry, but I don't agree with what you're saying!

There was some tension between me and my stepdad.

Because you just don't get the argument, period!

No, not "period"! Why do you get to decide when the discussion is over?

Because you're **wrong**!

And maybe you should try to figure out why you act this way with me.

*Prestigious institute of higher education.

59

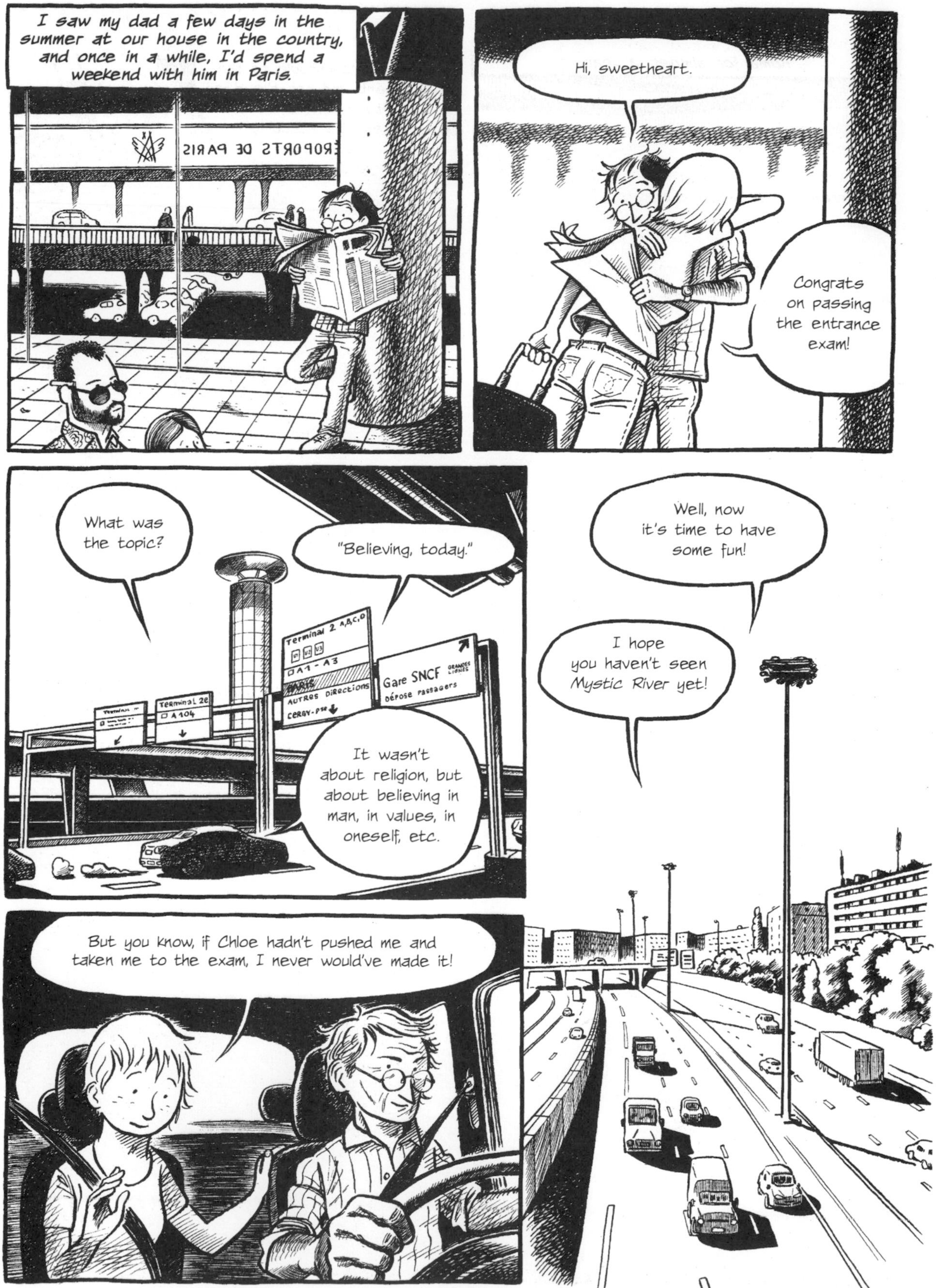
I saw my dad a few days in the summer at our house in the country, and once in a while, I'd spend a weekend with him in Paris.
EROPORTS DE PARIS
Hi, sweetheart.
Congrats on passing the entrance exam!
What was the topic?
"Believing, today."
Terminal 2 A,B,C,D
A1 - A3
AUTRES DIRECTIONS
CERGY-PSE
Gare SNCF GRANDES LIGNES
Dépose passagers
Terminal 2E
A104
It wasn't about religion, but about believing in man, in values, in oneself, etc.
Well, now it's time to have some fun!
I hope you haven't seen Mystic River yet!
But you know, if Chloe hadn't pushed me and taken me to the exam, I never would've made it!

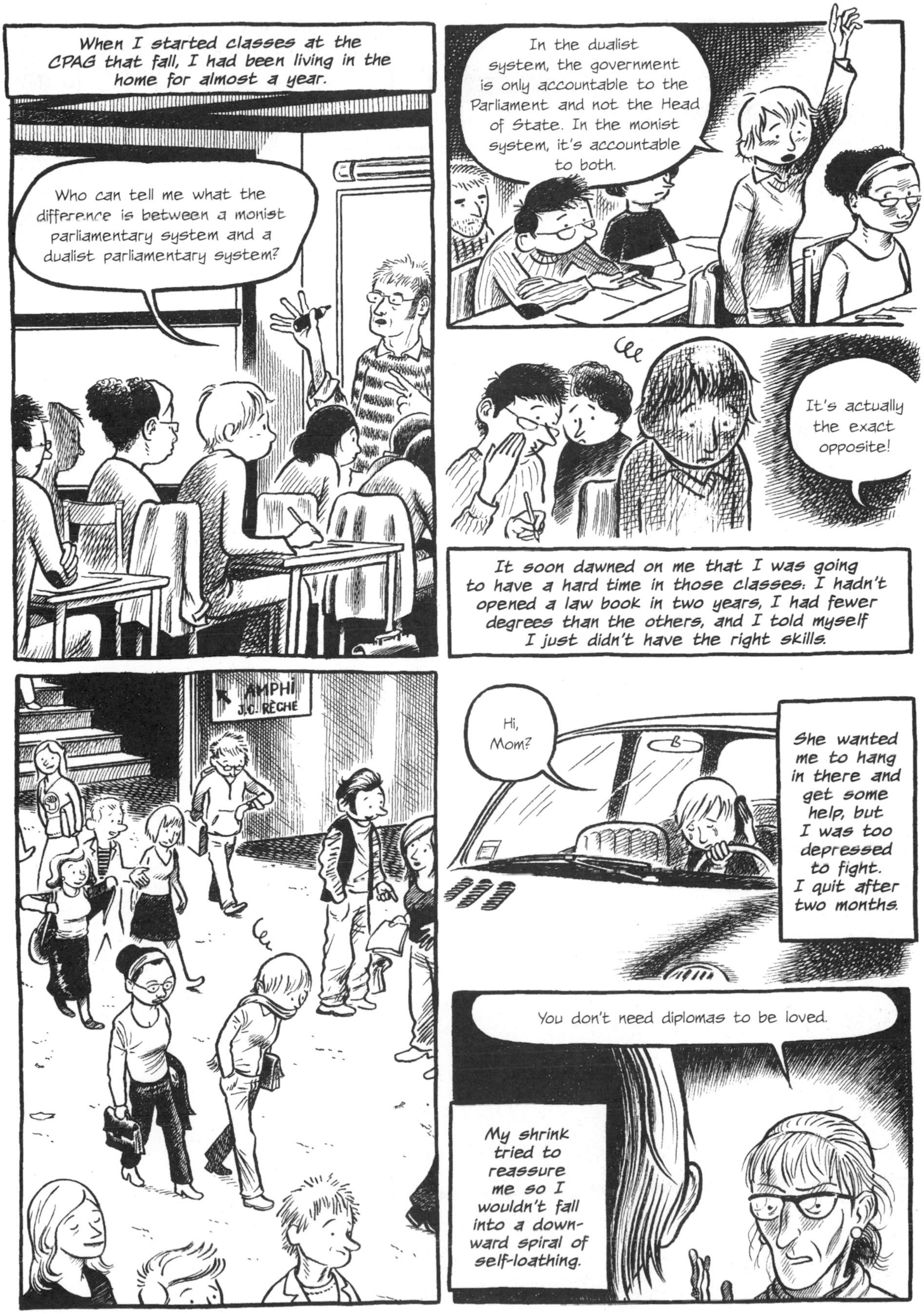
When I started classes at the CPAG that fall, I had been living in the home for almost a year.
Who can tell me what the difference is between a monist parliamentary system and a dualist parliamentary system?
In the dualist system, the government is only accountable to the Parliament and not the Head of State. In the monist system, it's accountable to both.
It's actually the exact opposite!
It soon dawned on me that I was going to have a hard time in those classes: I hadn't opened a law book in two years, I had fewer degrees than the others, and I told myself I just didn't have the right skills.
AMPHI
J.C. RÈCHE
Hi, Mom?
She wanted me to hang in there and get some help, but I was too depressed to fight. I quit after two months.
You don't need diplomas to be loved.
My shrink tried to reassure me so I wouldn't fall into a downward spiral of self-loathing.

I just stayed in my room, mulling over my latest failure.

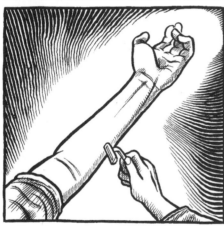

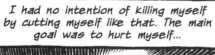

I had no intention of killing myself by cutting myself like that. The main goal was to hurt myself...

...but also to draw attention to my despair.

Oh, no! You're at it again!

Come on, let's get this disinfected.

I sacrificed myself like that several times during my stay at the home.

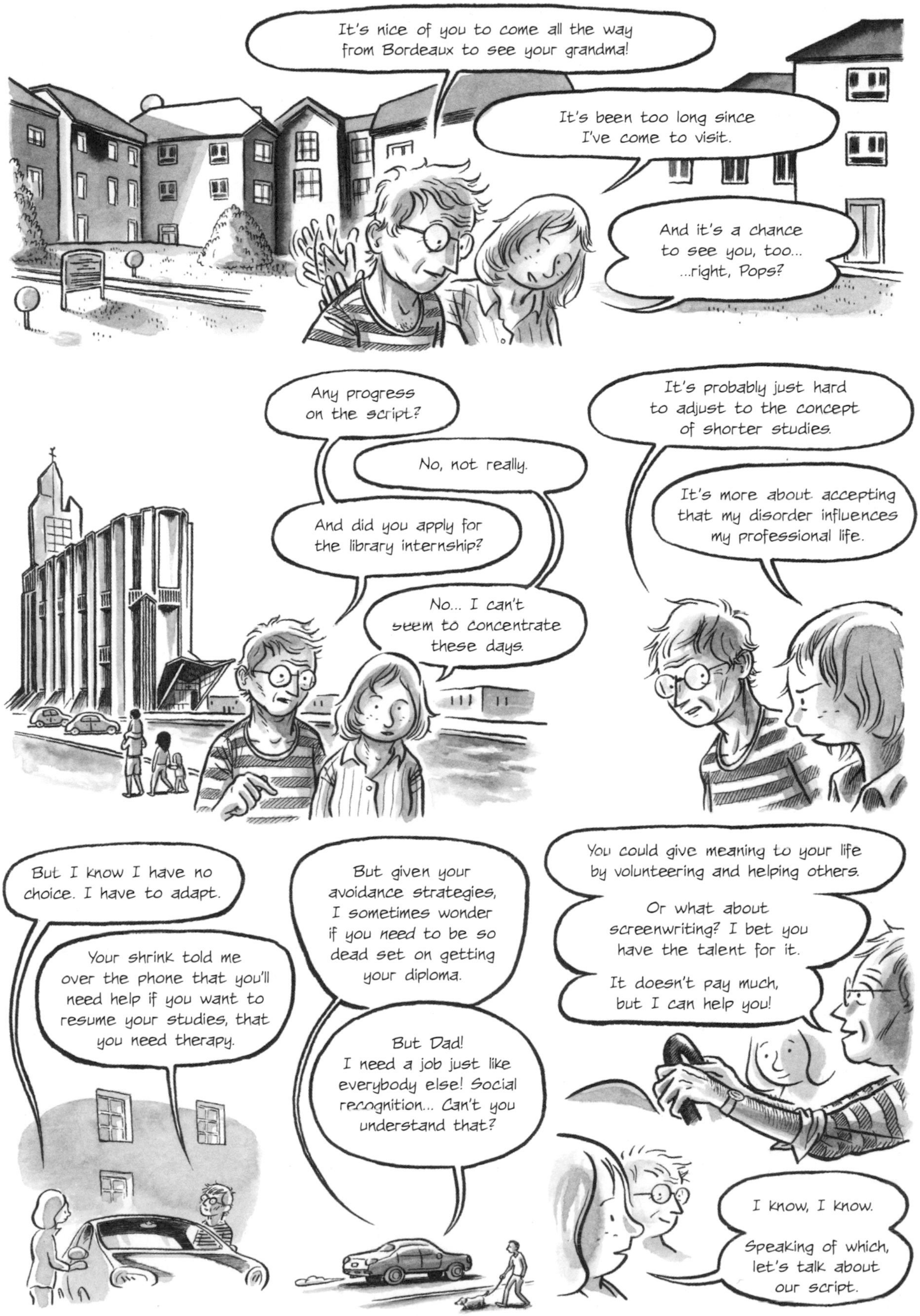
It's nice of you to come all the way from Bordeaux to see your grandma!
It's been too long since I've come to visit.
And it's a chance to see you, too... ...right, Pops?
Any progress on the script?
No, not really.
And did you apply for the library internship?
No... I can't seem to concentrate these days.
It's probably just hard to adjust to the concept of shorter studies.
It's more about accepting that my disorder influences my professional life.
But I know I have no choice. I have to adapt.
Your shrink told me over the phone that you'll need help if you want to resume your studies, that you need therapy.
But given your avoidance strategies, I sometimes wonder if you need to be so dead set on getting your diploma.
But Dad! I need a job just like everybody else! Social recognition... Can't you understand that?
You could give meaning to your life by volunteering and helping others.
Or what about screenwriting? I bet you have the talent for it.
It doesn't pay much, but I can help you!
I know, I know.
Speaking of which, let's talk about our script.

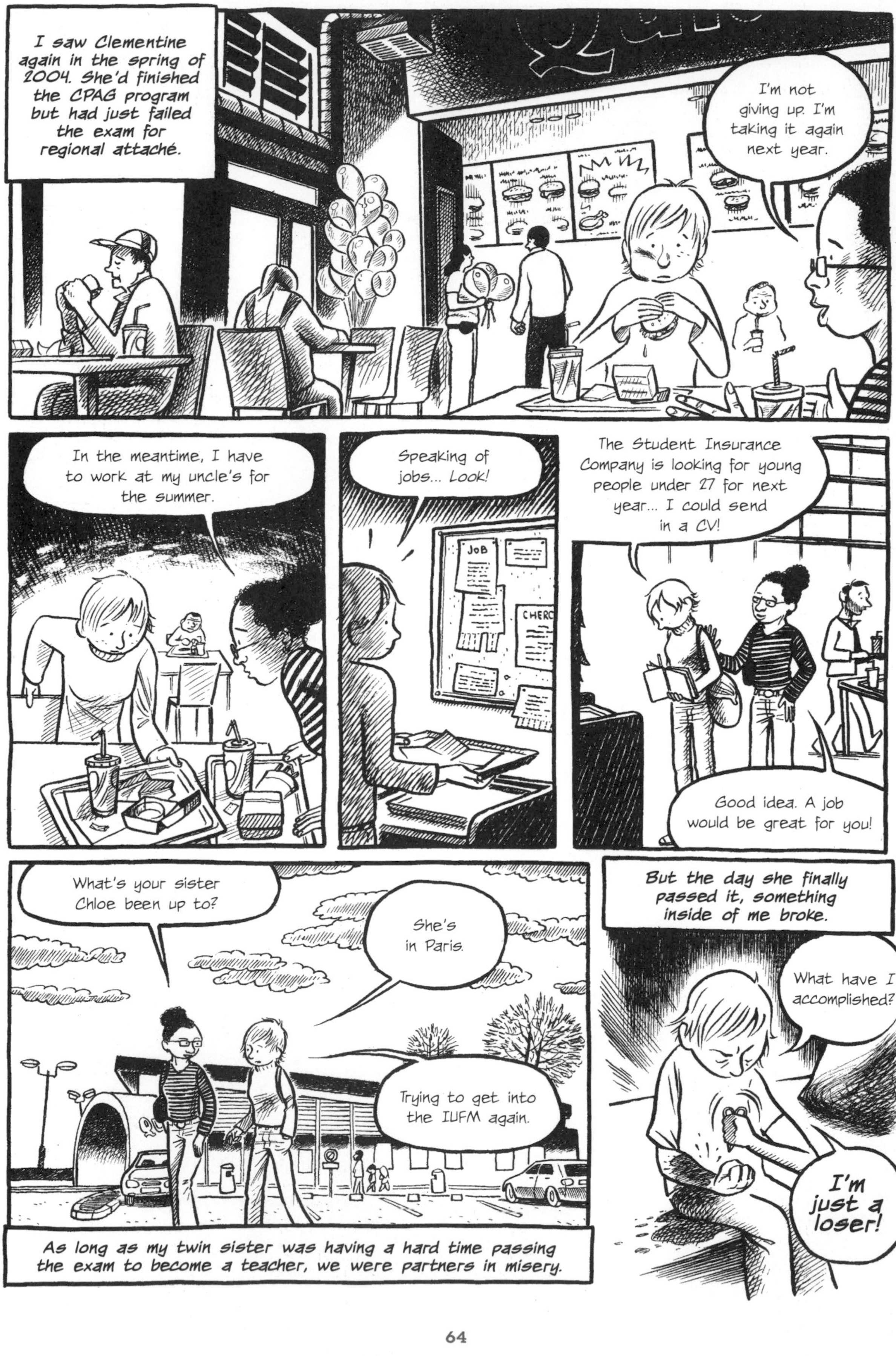
I saw Clementine again in the spring of 2004. She'd finished the CPAG program but had just failed the exam for regional attaché.
I'm not giving up. I'm taking it again next year.
In the meantime, I have to work at my uncle's for the summer.
Speaking of jobs... Look!
JOB
CHERC
The Student Insurance Company is looking for young people under 27 for next year... I could send in a CV!
Good idea. A job would be great for you!
What's your sister Chloe been up to?
She's in Paris.
Trying to get into the IUFM again.
As long as my twin sister was having a hard time passing the exam to become a teacher, we were partners in misery.
But the day she finally passed it, something inside of me broke.
What have I accomplished?
I'm just a loser!

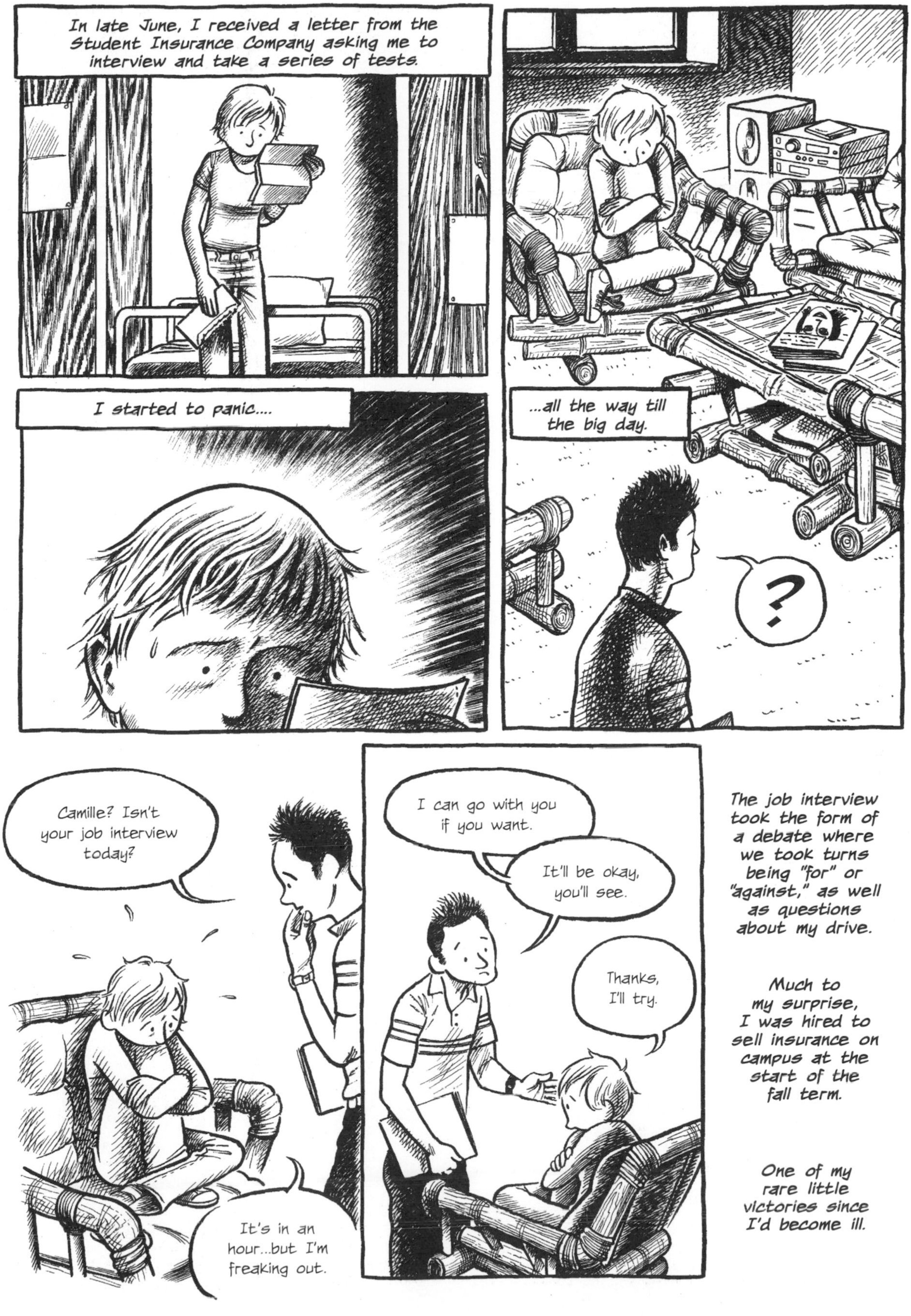
In late June, I received a letter from the Student Insurance Company asking me to interview and take a series of tests.
I started to panic....
...all the way till the big day.
?
Camille? Isn't your job interview today?
It's in an hour...but I'm freaking out.
I can go with you if you want.
It'll be okay, you'll see.
Thanks, I'll try.
The job interview took the form of a debate where we took turns being "for" or "against," as well as questions about my drive.
Much to my surprise, I was hired to sell insurance on campus at the start of the fall term.
One of my rare little victories since I'd become ill.

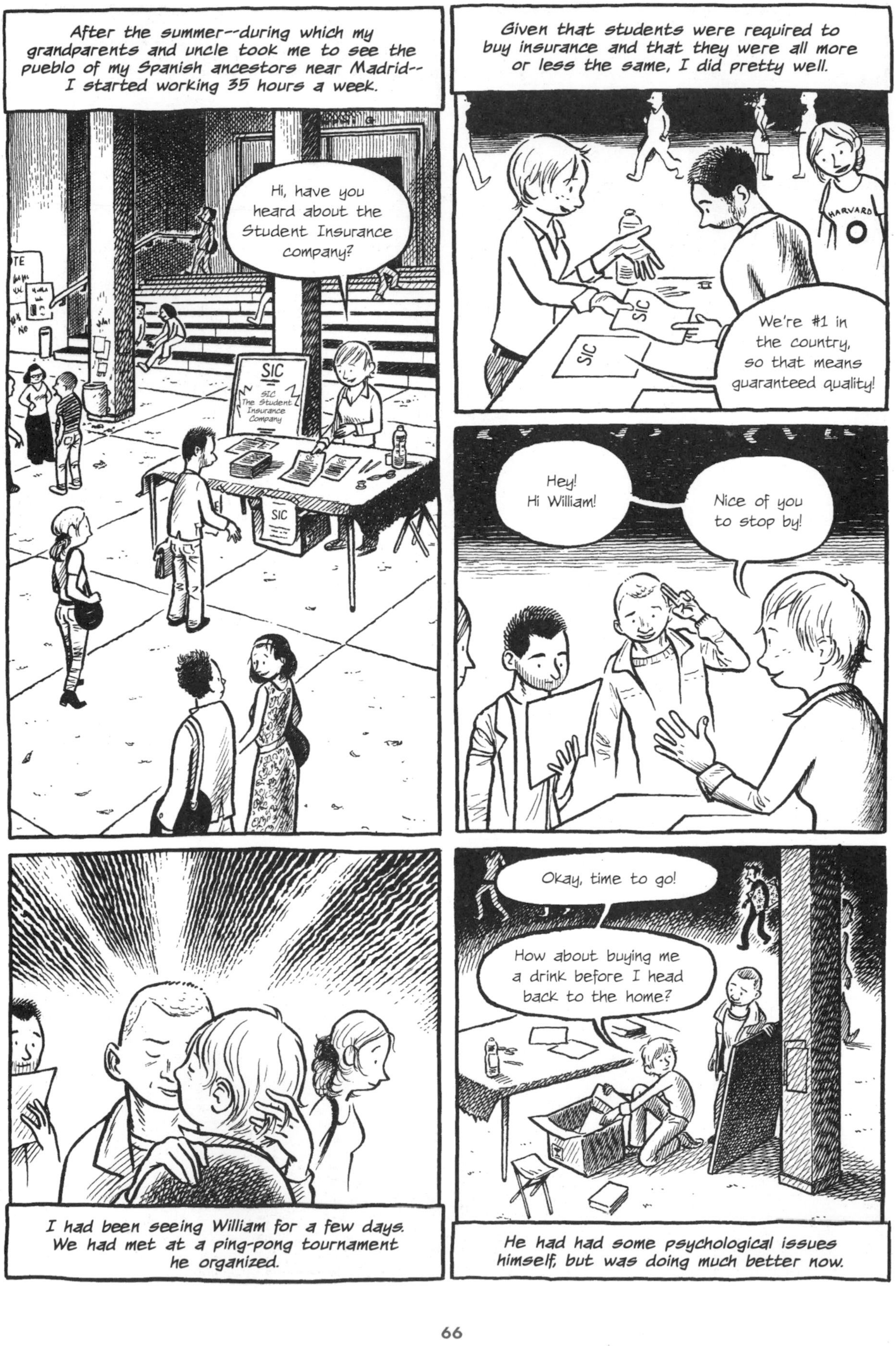
After the summer--during which my grandparents and uncle took me to see the pueblo of my Spanish ancestors near Madrid--I started working 35 hours a week.
Hi, have you heard about the Student Insurance company?
SIC
SIC The Student Insurance Company
Given that students were required to buy insurance and that they were all more or less the same, I did pretty well.
HARVARD
We're #1 in the country, so that means guaranteed quality!
Hey! Hi William!
Nice of you to stop by!
I had been seeing William for a few days. We had met at a ping-pong tournament he organized.
Okay, time to go!
How about buying me a drink before I head back to the home?
He had had some psychological issues himself, but was doing much better now.

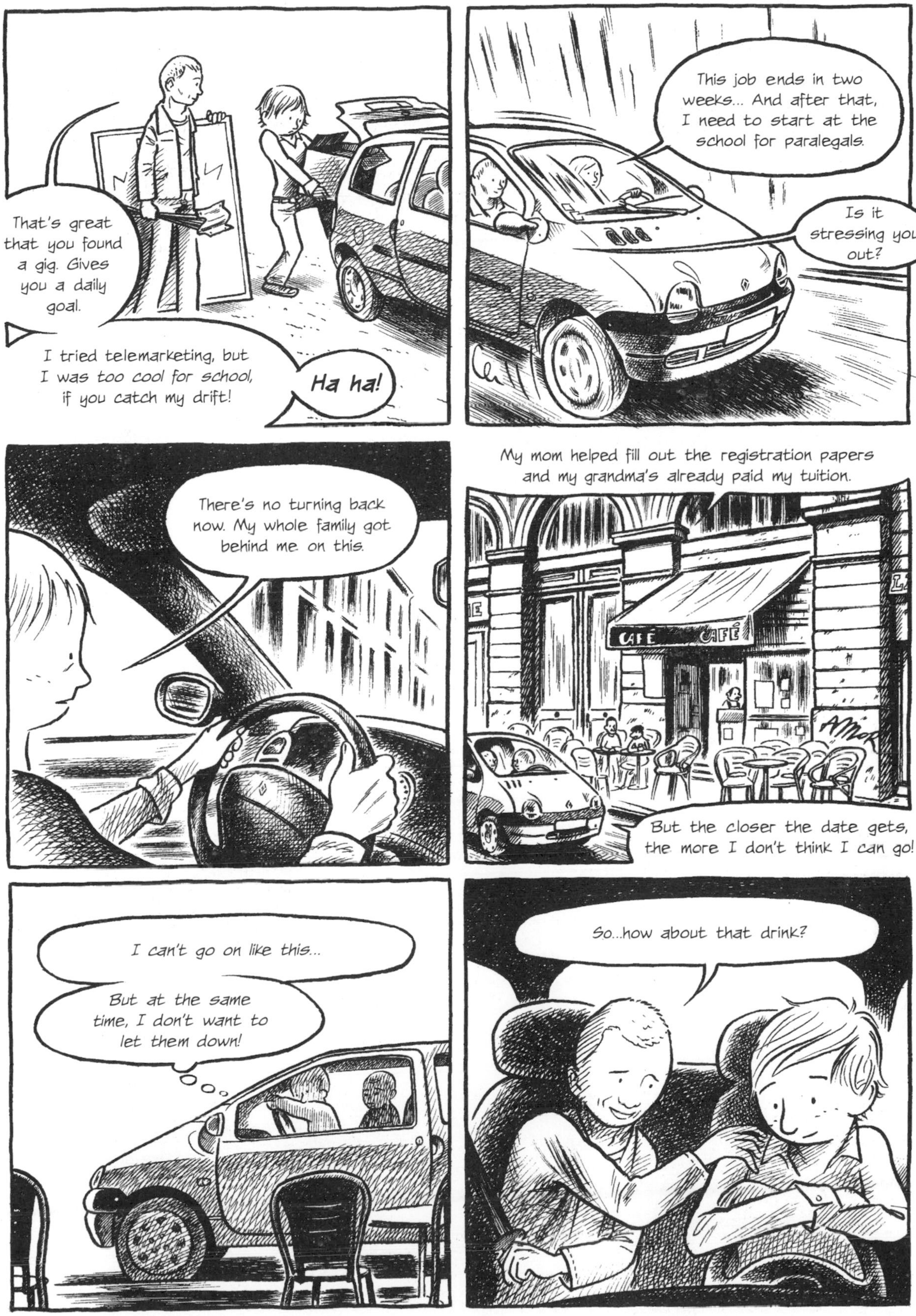
That's great that you found a gig. Gives you a daily goal.
I tried telemarketing, but I was too cool for school, if you catch my drift!
Ha ha!
This job ends in two weeks... And after that, I need to start at the school for paralegals.
Is it stressing you out?
There's no turning back now. My whole family got behind me on this.
My mom helped fill out the registration papers and my grandma's already paid my tuition.
CAFÉ
CAFÉ
But the closer the date gets, the more I don't think I can go!
I can't go on like this...
But at the same time, I don't want to let them down!
So...how about that drink?

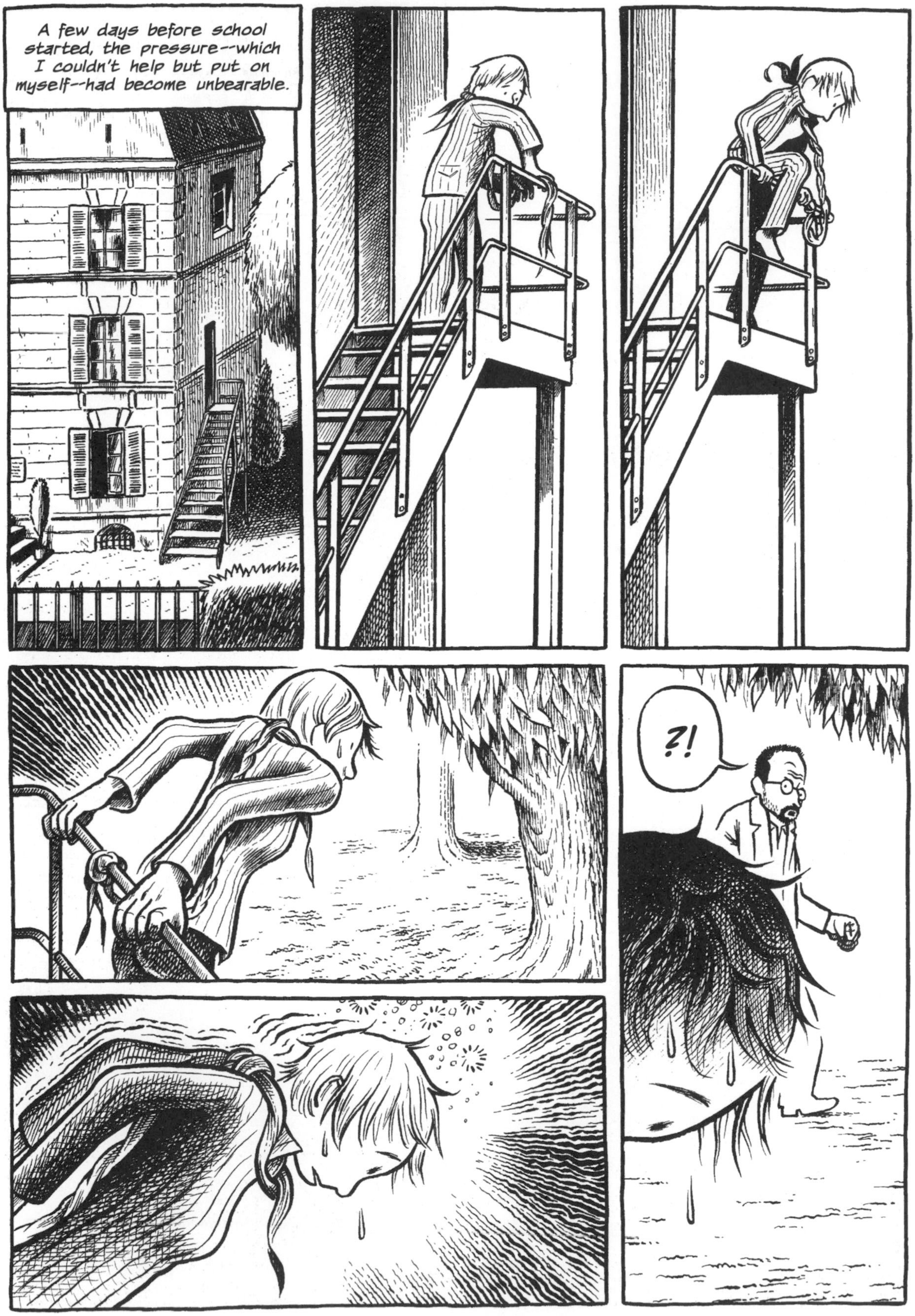
A few days before school started, the pressure--which I couldn't help but put on myself--had become unbearable.
?!

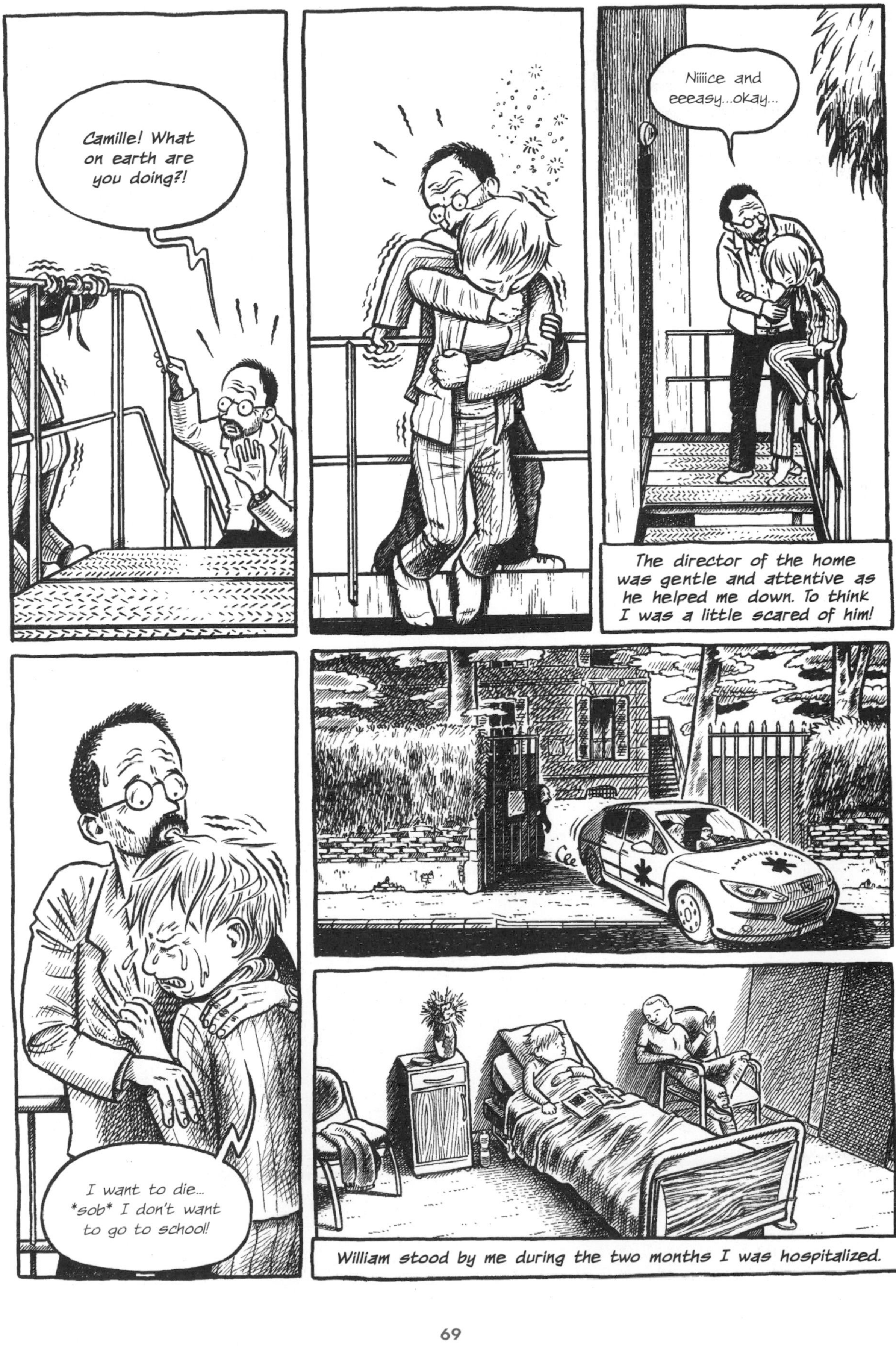
Camille! What on earth are you doing?!
Niiiice and eeeasy...okay...
The director of the home was gentle and attentive as he helped me down. To think I was a little scared of him!
I want to die... *sob* I don't want to go to school!
William stood by me during the two months I was hospitalized.

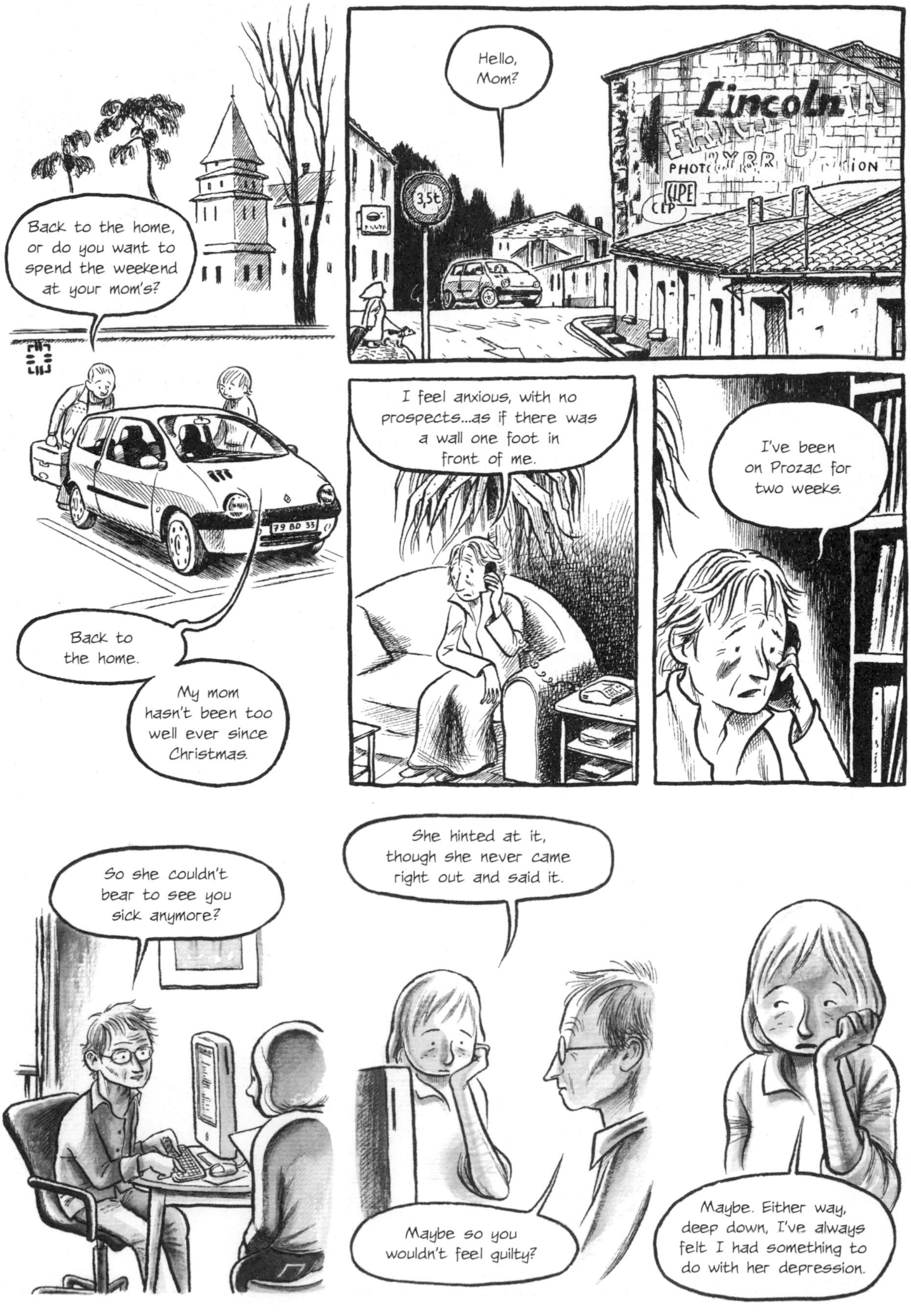

Back to the home, or do you want to spend the weekend at your mom's?
Back to the home.
My mom hasn't been too well ever since Christmas.
Hello, Mom?
I feel anxious, with no prospects...as if there was a wall one foot in front of me.
I've been on Prozac for two weeks.
So she couldn't bear to see you sick anymore?
She hinted at it, though she never came right out and said it.
Maybe so you wouldn't feel guilty?
Maybe. Either way, deep down, I've always felt I had something to do with her depression.

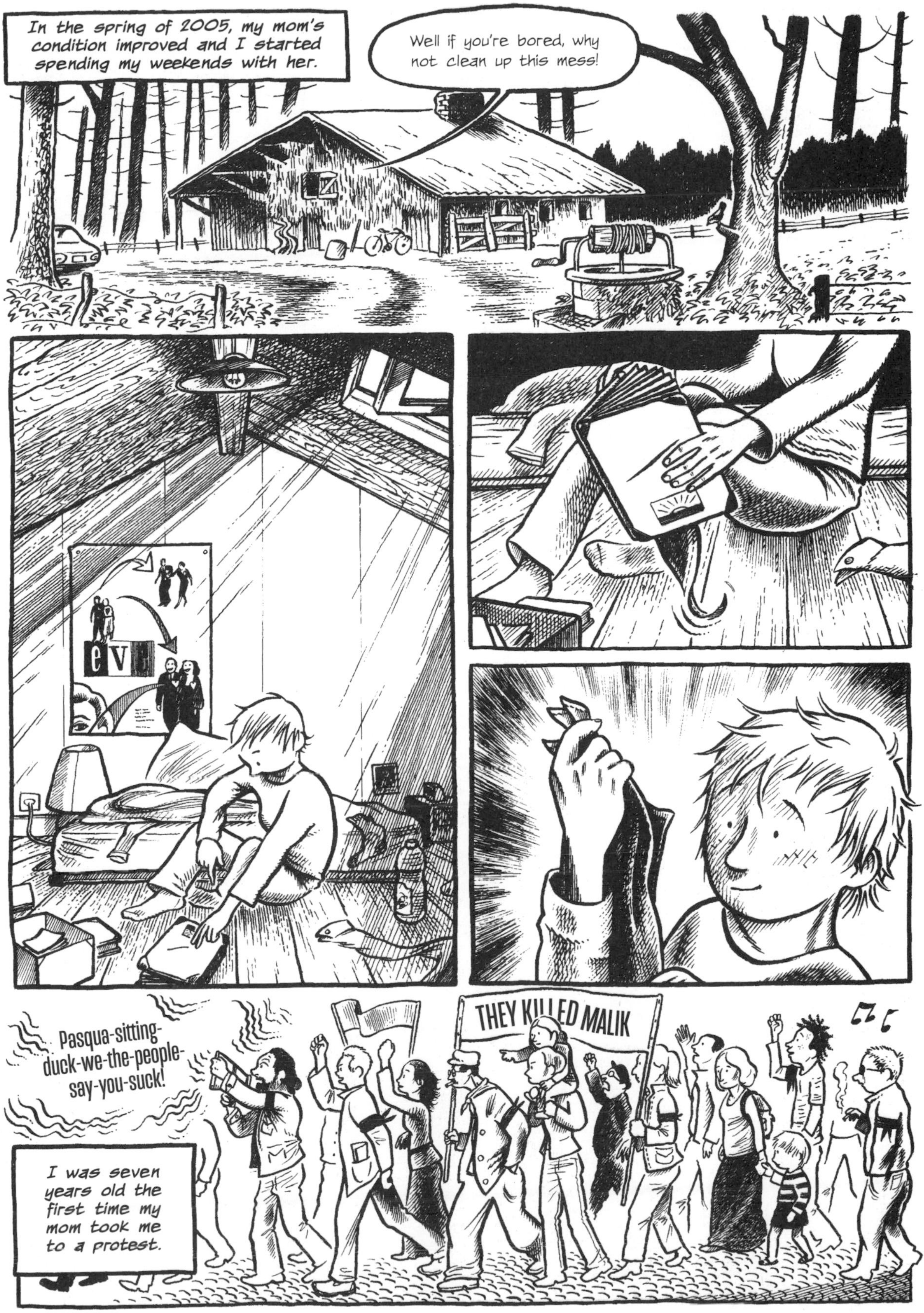
In the spring of 2005, my mom's condition improved and I started spending my weekends with her.
Well if you're bored, why not clean up this mess!
eve
Pasqua-sitting-duck-we-the-people-say-you-suck!
THEY KILLED MALIK
I was seven years old the first time my mom took me to a protest.

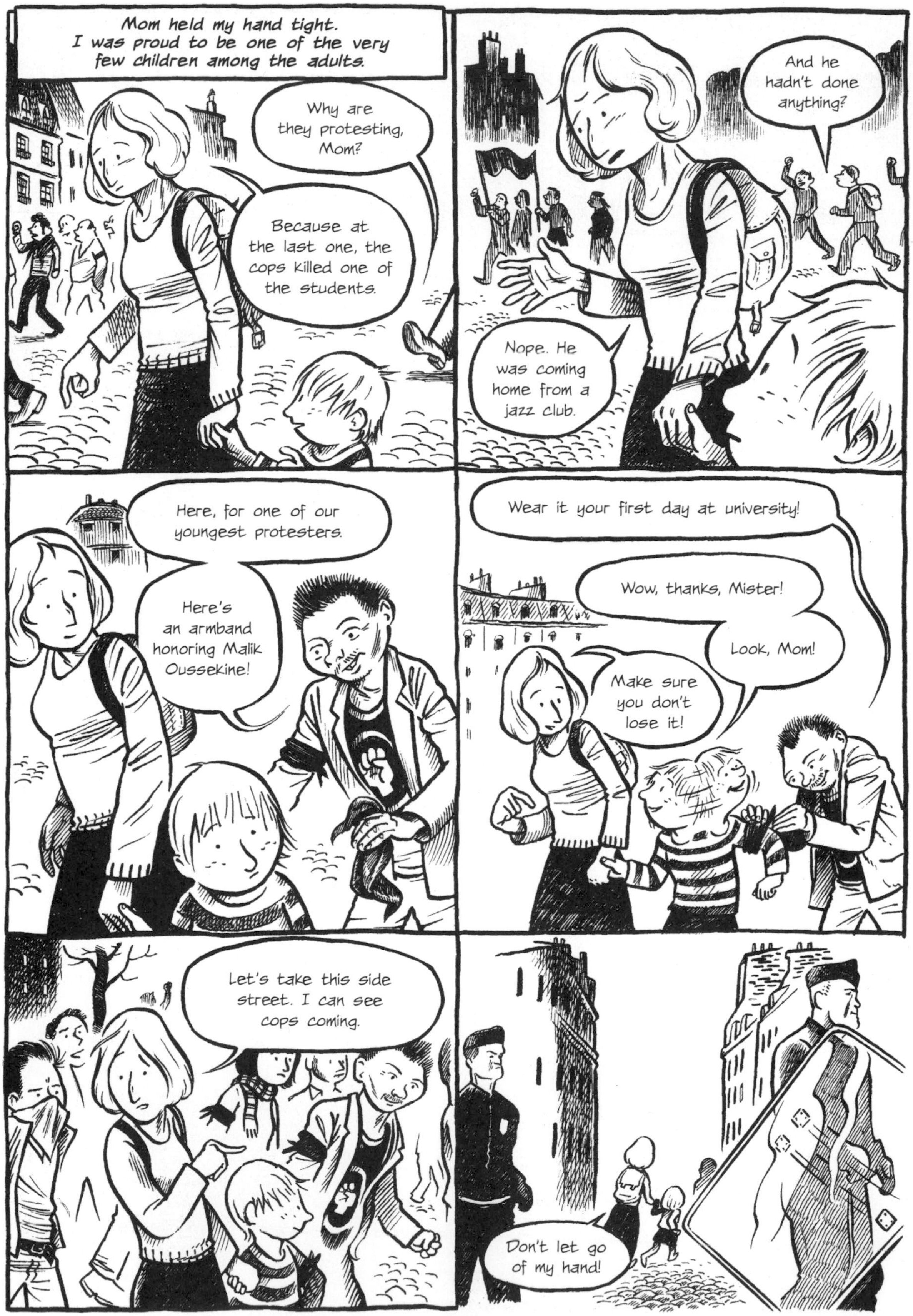
Mom held my hand tight. I was proud to be one of the very few children among the adults.
Why are they protesting, Mom?
Because at the last one, the cops killed one of the students.
And he hadn't done anything?
Nope. He was coming home from a jazz club.
Here, for one of our youngest protesters.
Here's an armband honoring Malik Oussekine!
Wear it your first day at university!
Wow, thanks, Mister!
Look, Mom!
Make sure you don't lose it!
Let's take this side street. I can see cops coming.
Don't let go of my hand!

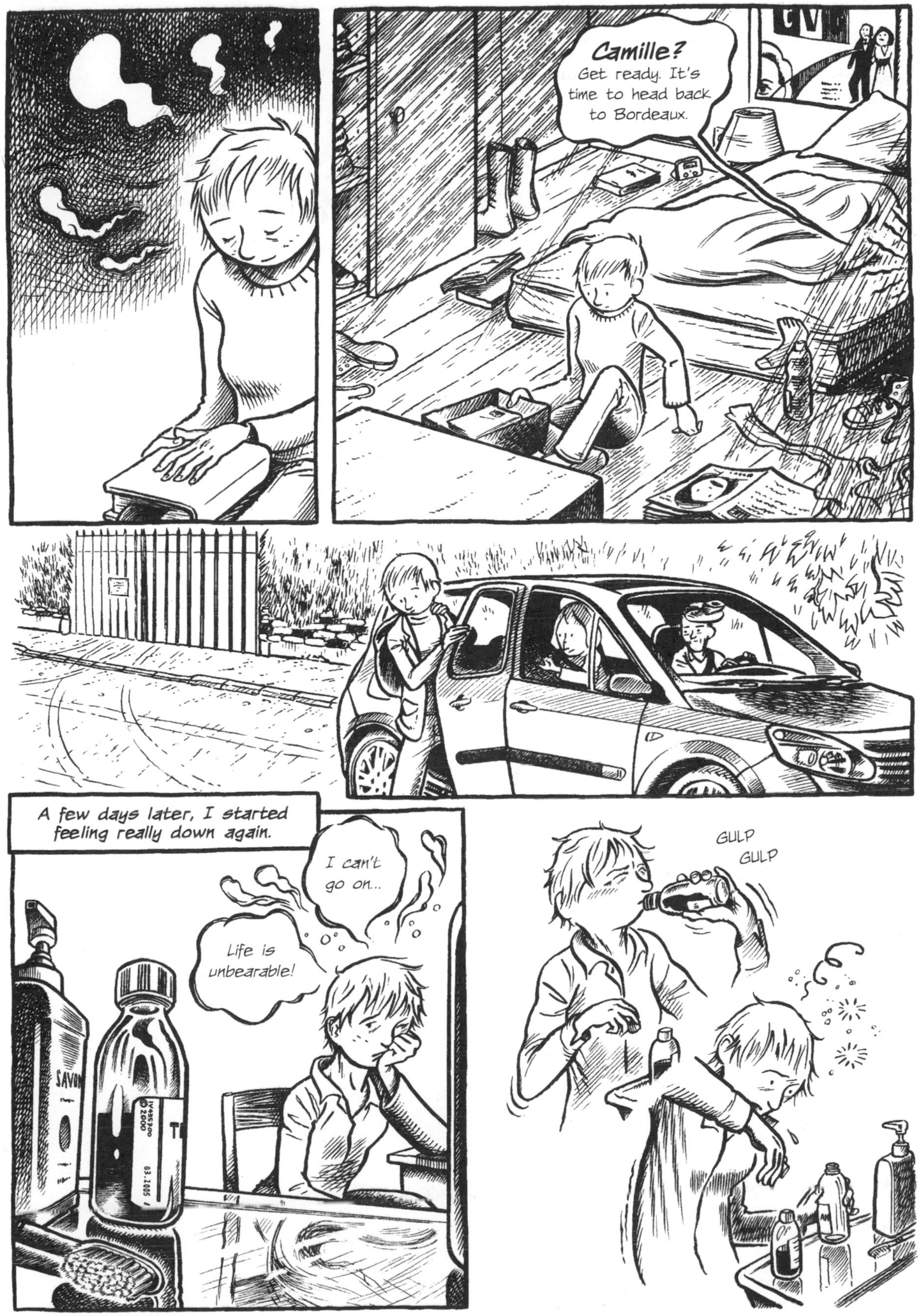
Camille?
Get ready. It's time to head back to Bordeaux.
A few days later, I started feeling really down again.
I can't go on...
Life is unbearable!
SAVON
03.2005
GULP
GULP

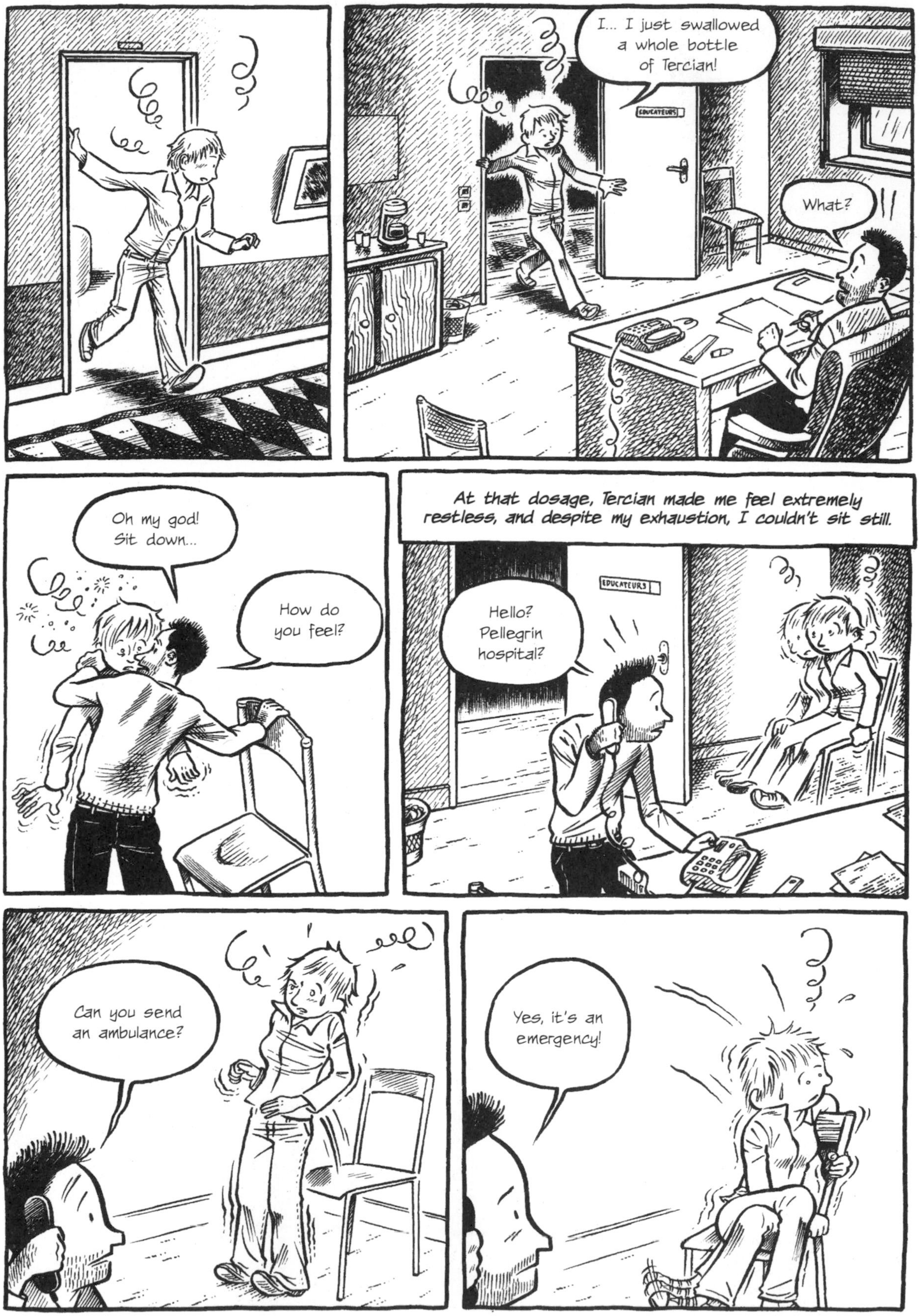
I... I just swallowed a whole bottle of Tercian!
EDUCATEURS
What?
Oh my god! Sit down...
How do you feel?
At that dosage, Tercian made me feel extremely restless, and despite my exhaustion, I couldn't sit still.
EDUCATEURS
Hello? Pellegrin hospital?
Can you send an ambulance?
Yes, it's an emergency!

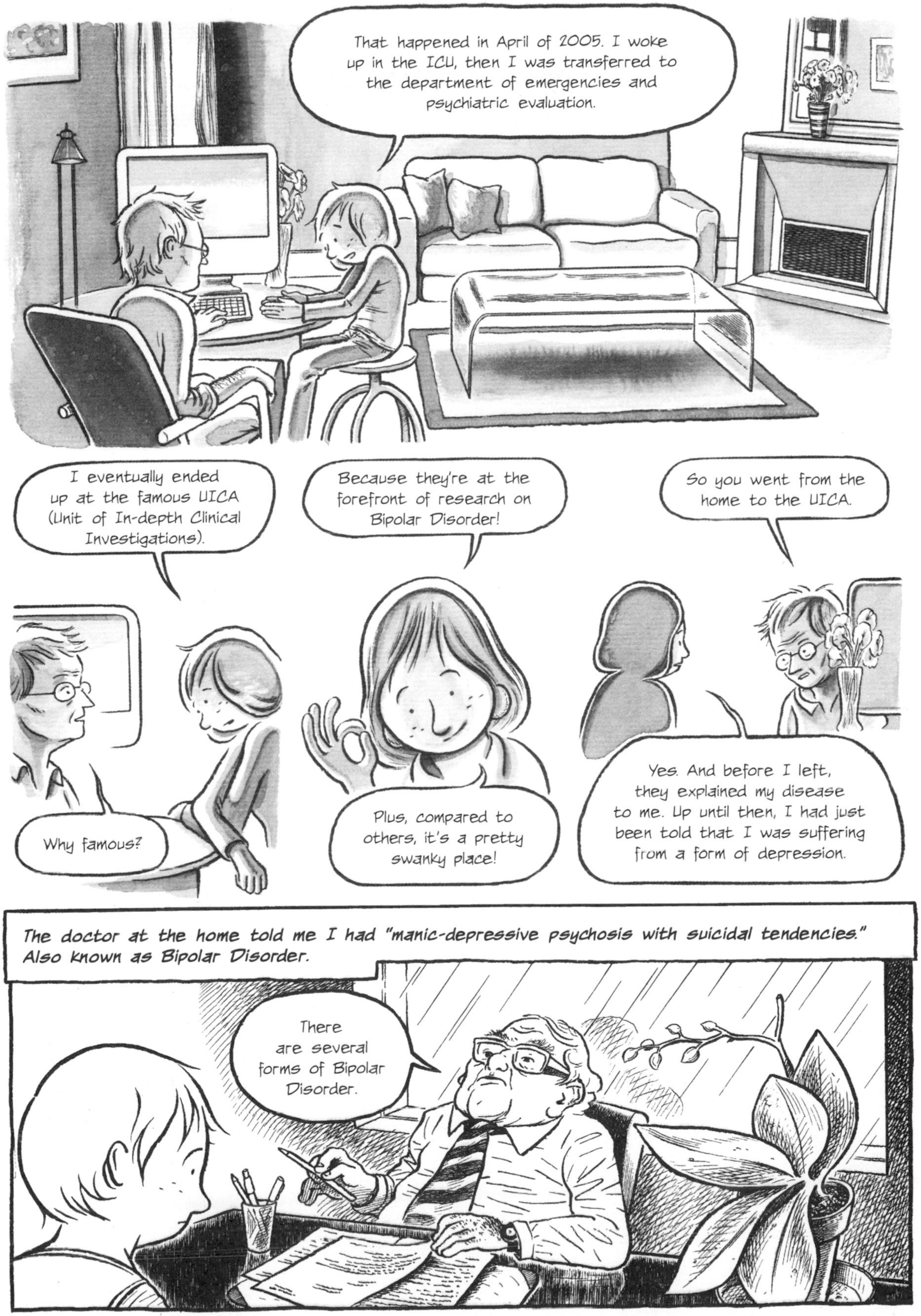

That happened in April of 2005. I woke up in the ICU, then I was transferred to the department of emergencies and psychiatric evaluation.
I eventually ended up at the famous UICA (Unit of In-depth Clinical Investigations).
Why famous?
Because they're at the forefront of research on Bipolar Disorder!
Plus, compared to others, it's a pretty swanky place!
So you went from the home to the UICA.
Yes. And before I left, they explained my disease to me. Up until then, I had just been told that I was suffering from a form of depression.
The doctor at the home told me I had "manic-depressive psychosis with suicidal tendencies." Also known as Bipolar Disorder.
There are several forms of Bipolar Disorder.

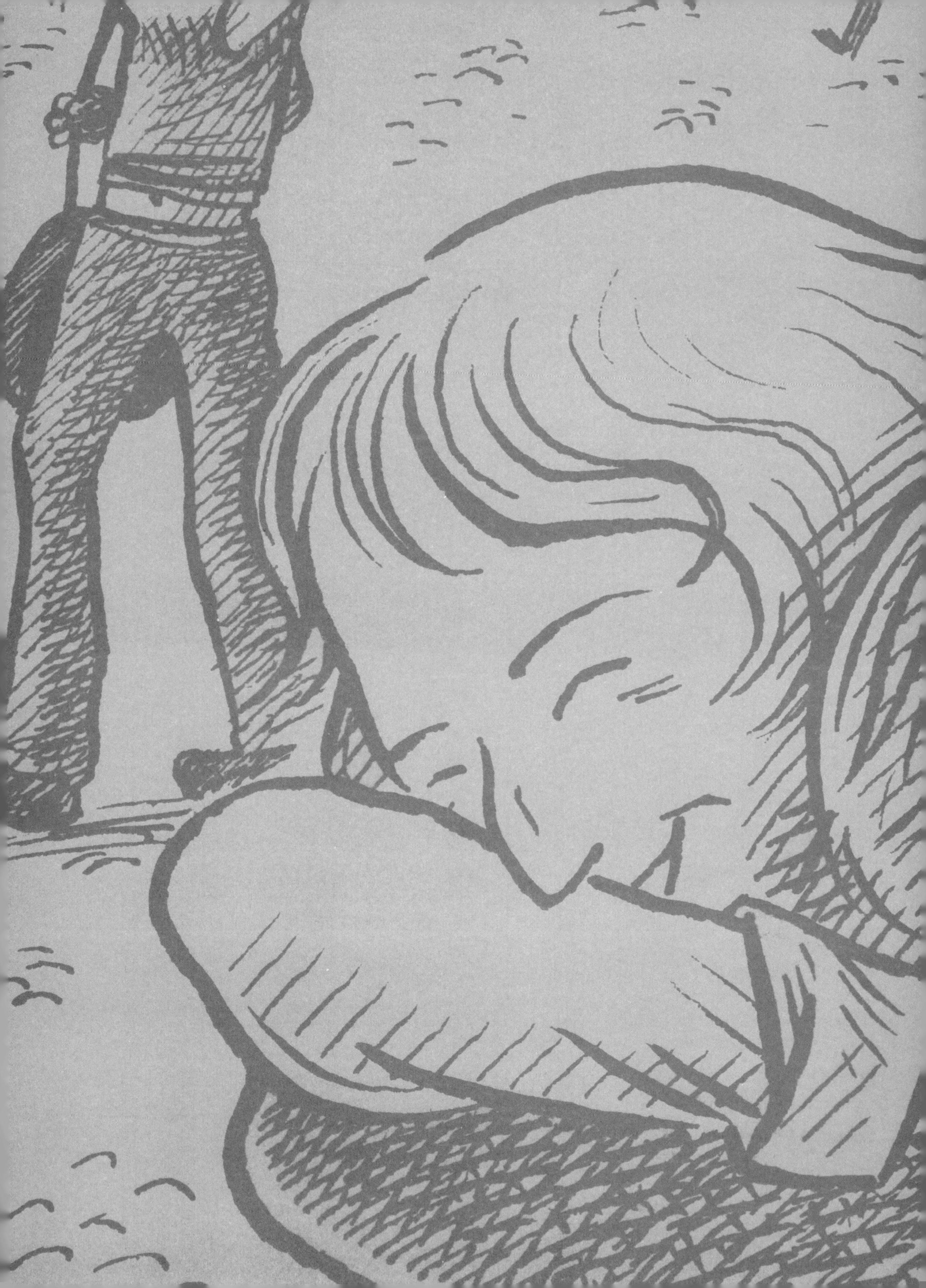

.5.
“*She’s Falling Apart*”
Lisa Loeb

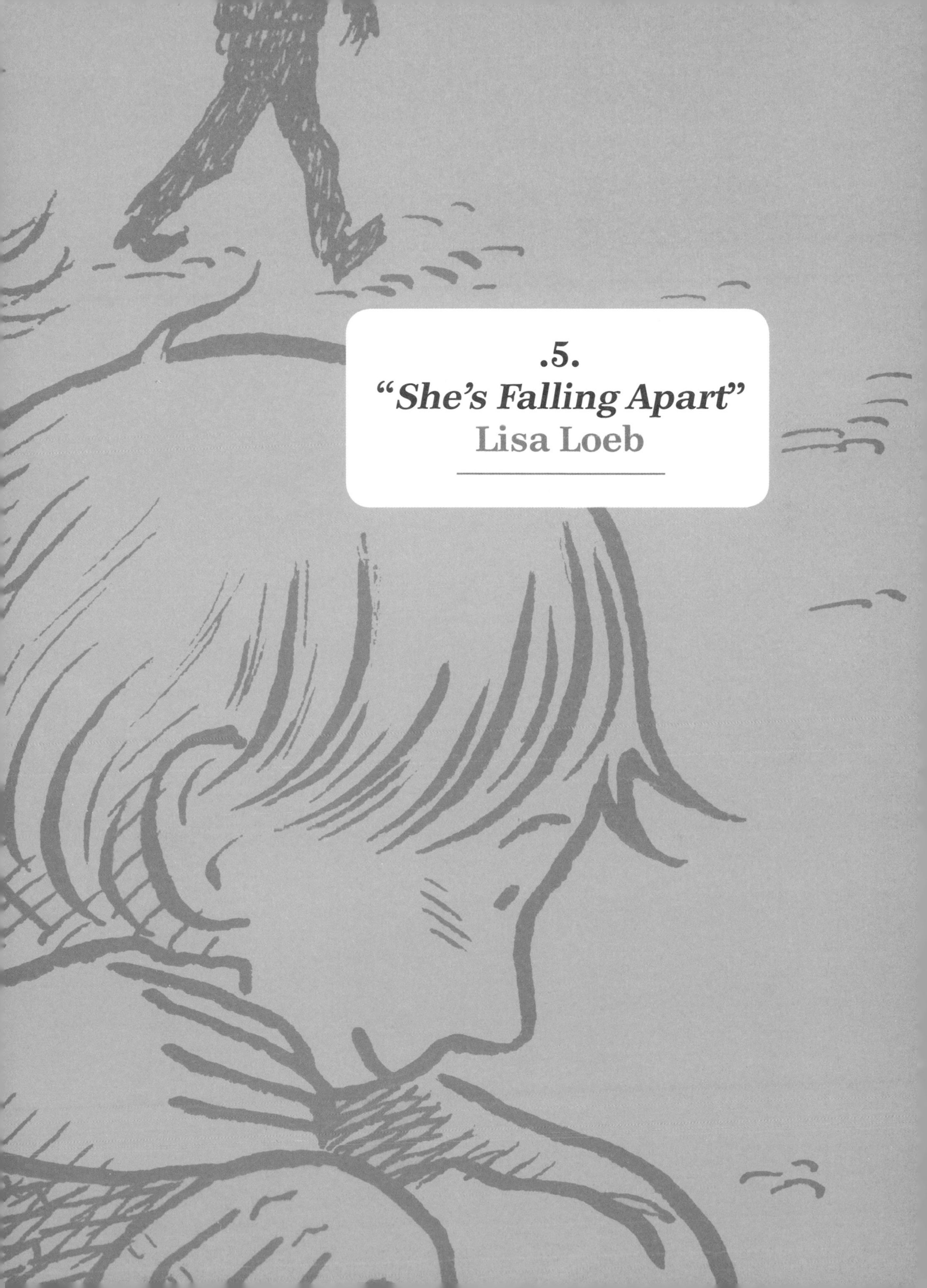

There are depressive episodes, which is when your mood crashes and you feel overall exhaustion...

Then mania, which is an abnormally elevated mood for at least one week, with no control over behavior, thoughts or emotions...

...and then there's hypomania, which is a milder manic episode in terms of the intensity and duration of the symptoms.

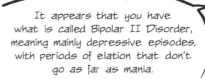

There are also several sub-categories...

It appears that you have what is called Bipolar II Disorder, meaning mainly depressive episodes, with periods of elation that don't go as far as mania.

Now I knew what my condition was called: Bipolar Disorder.

What is this medication?

A new drug the doctor prescribed.

It's a lithium-based mood stabilizer. It has a direct effect on a person's mood.

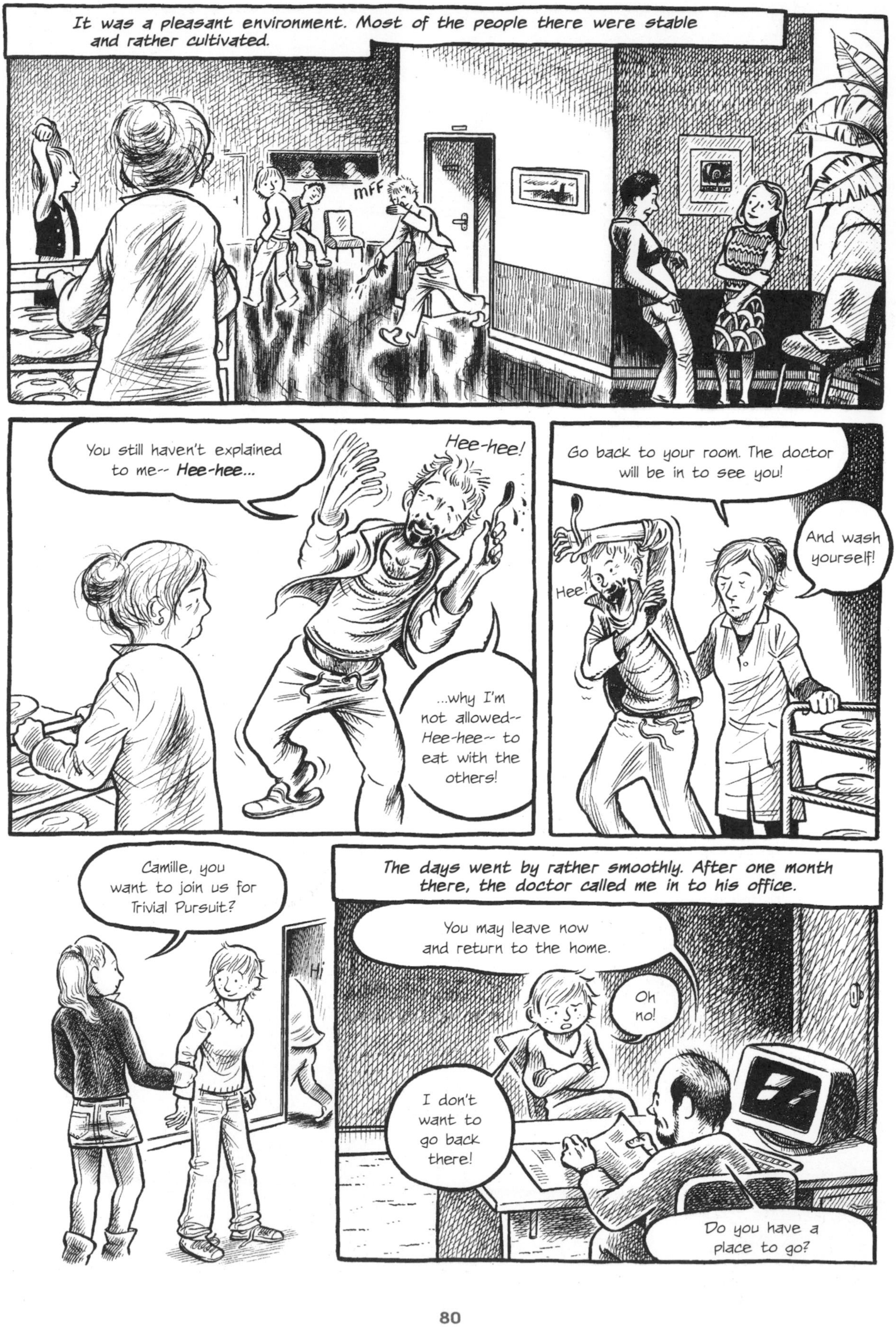
It was a pleasant environment. Most of the people there were stable and rather cultivated.
MFF
You still haven't explained to me-- **Hee-hee...**
Hee-hee!
...why I'm not allowed-- Hee-hee-- to eat with the others!
Go back to your room. The doctor will be in to see you!
Hee!
And wash yourself!
Camille, you want to join us for Trivial Pursuit?
Hi
The days went by rather smoothly. After one month there, the doctor called me in to his office.
You may leave now and return to the home.
Oh no!
I don't want to go back there!
Do you have a place to go?

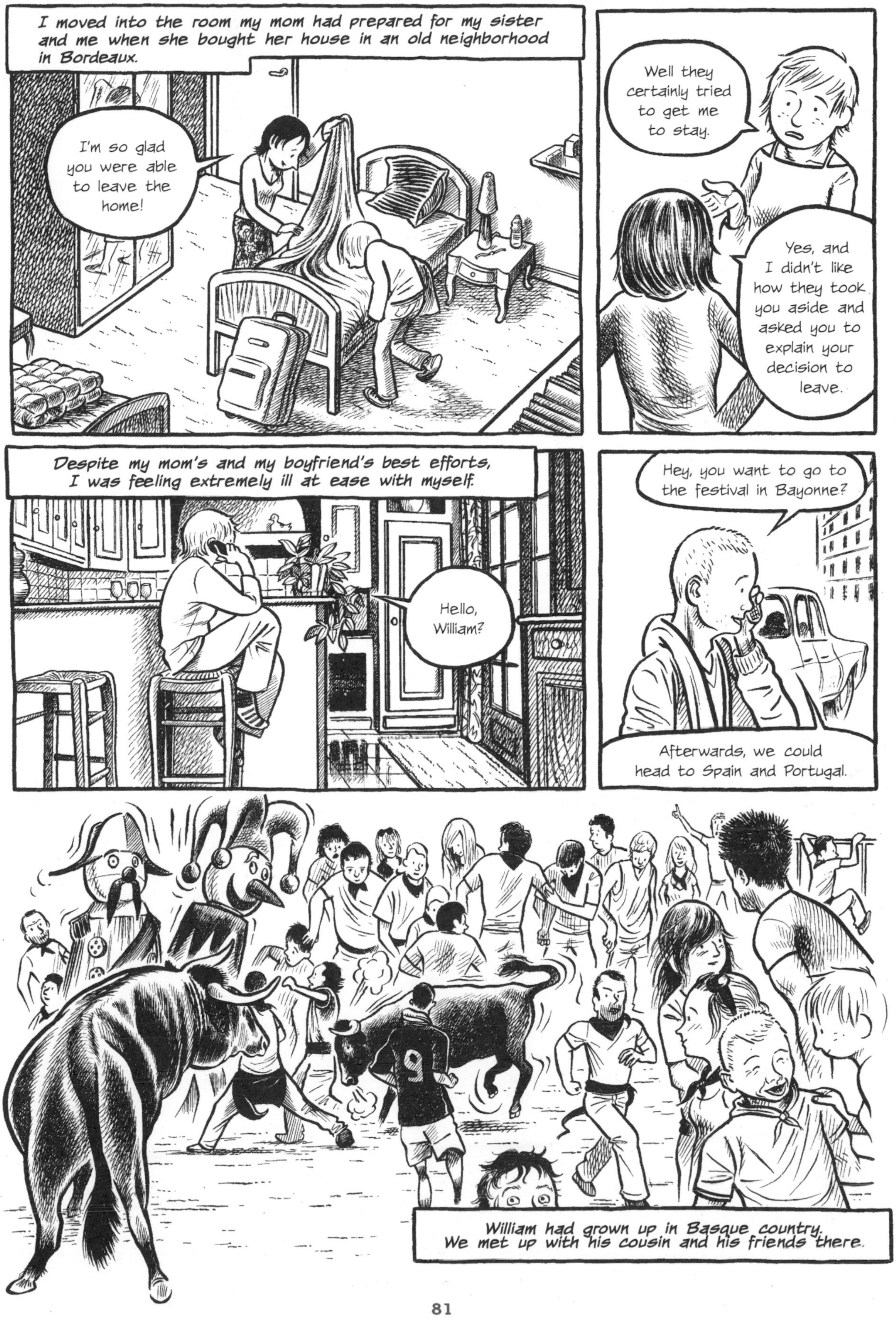
I moved into the room my mom had prepared for my sister and me when she bought her house in an old neighborhood in Bordeaux.
I'm so glad you were able to leave the home!
Well they certainly tried to get me to stay.
Yes, and I didn't like how they took you aside and asked you to explain your decision to leave.
Despite my mom's and my boyfriend's best efforts, I was feeling extremely ill at ease with myself.
Hello, William?
Hey, you want to go to the festival in Bayonne?
Afterwards, we could head to Spain and Portugal.
William had grown up in Basque country. We met up with his cousin and his friends there.

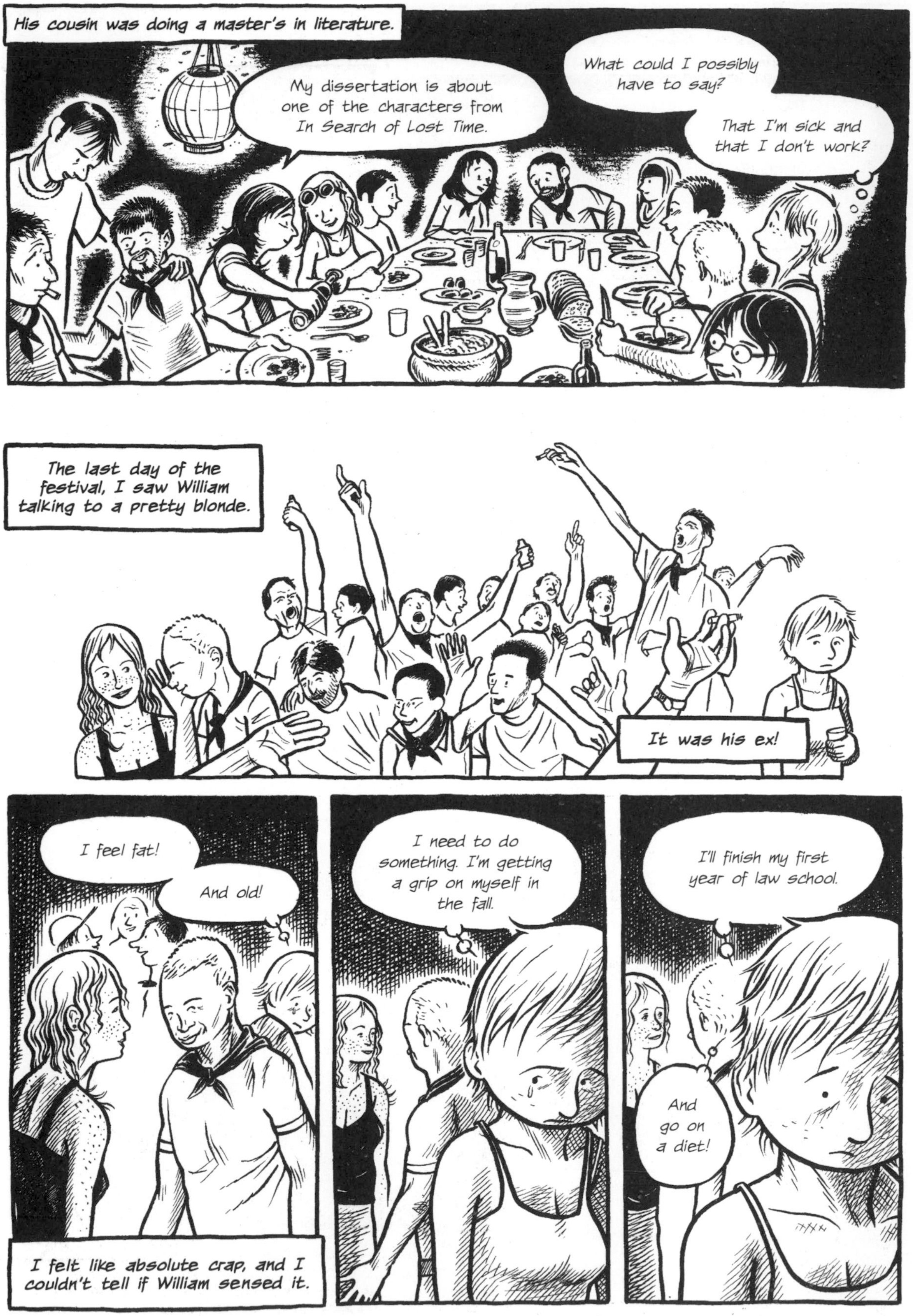
His cousin was doing a master's in literature.
My dissertation is about one of the characters from In Search of Lost Time.
What could I possibly have to say?
That I'm sick and that I don't work?
The last day of the festival, I saw William talking to a pretty blonde.
It was his ex!
I feel fat!
And old!
I felt like absolute crap, and I couldn't tell if William sensed it.
I need to do something. I'm getting a grip on myself in the fall.
I'll finish my first year of law school.
And go on a diet!

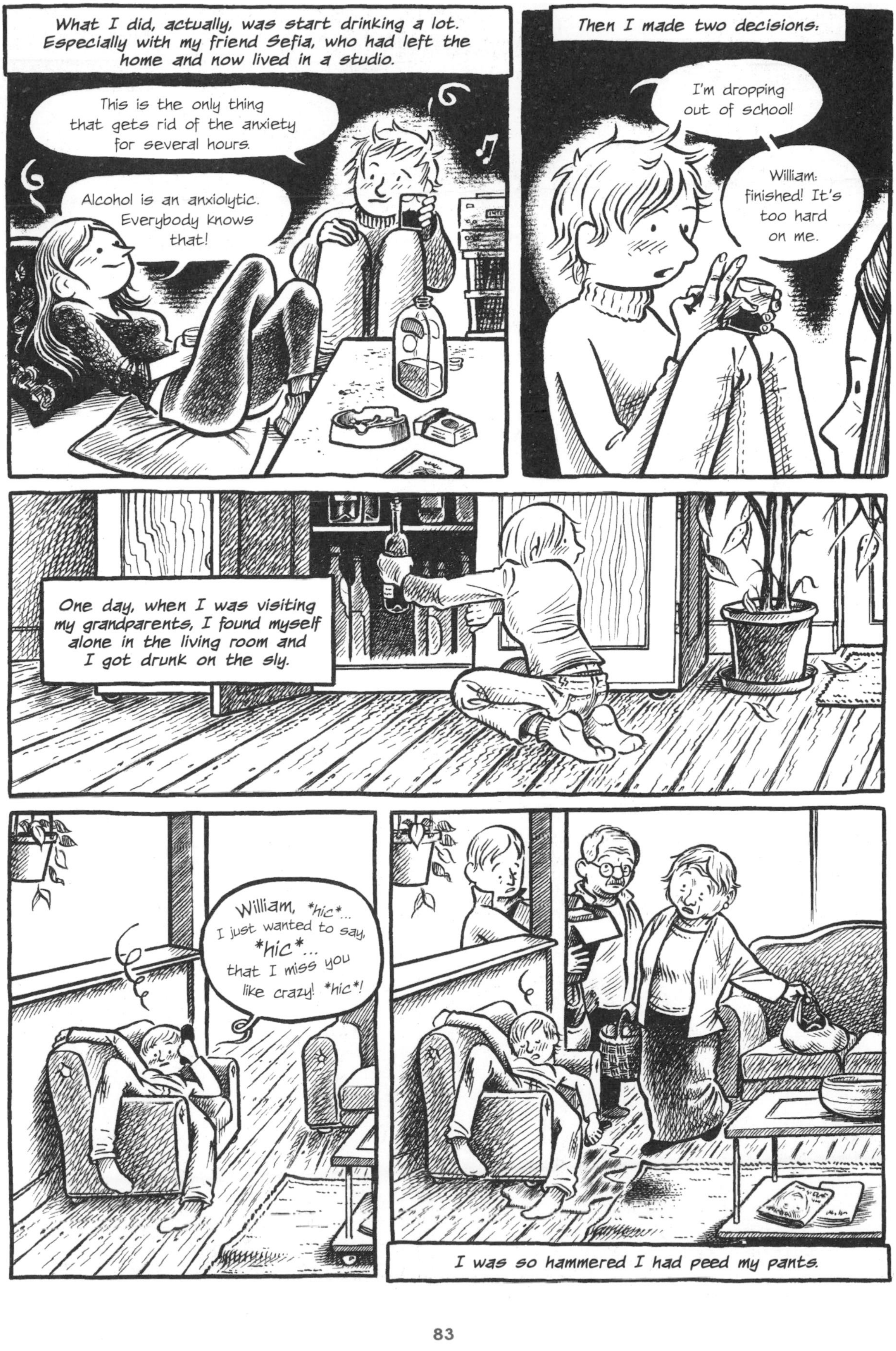

What I did, actually, was start drinking a lot. Especially with my friend Sefia, who had left the home and now lived in a studio.
This is the only thing that gets rid of the anxiety for several hours.
Alcohol is an anxiolytic. Everybody knows that!
Then I made two decisions:
I'm dropping out of school!
William: finished! It's too hard on me.
One day, when I was visiting my grandparents, I found myself alone in the living room and I got drunk on the sly.
William, *hic*... I just wanted to say, *hic*... that I miss you like crazy! *hic*!
I was so hammered I had peed my pants.

So that's when you went back to the Medical Center?

Yes, in March of 2006. I was in a state of severe depression.

They gave me another drug on top of the lithium: Lamictal.

I'll write the rest of the dialogue and send it to you.

Take your time. I have colors to finish for Delcourt*.

If you don't find a parking space, just drop me off out front.

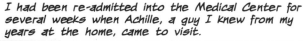

I had been re-admitted into the Medical Center for several weeks when Achille, a guy I knew from my years at the home, came to visit.

Wow, you look like you've lost some weight.

You look great!

Thanks Achille, that's sweet.

Some friends of mine are having a party. You want to go?

Okay, but I need to be back before dinner.

I'm not sure I'm allowed to leave the unit.

No worries, it's nearby!

*French comics publisher.

84

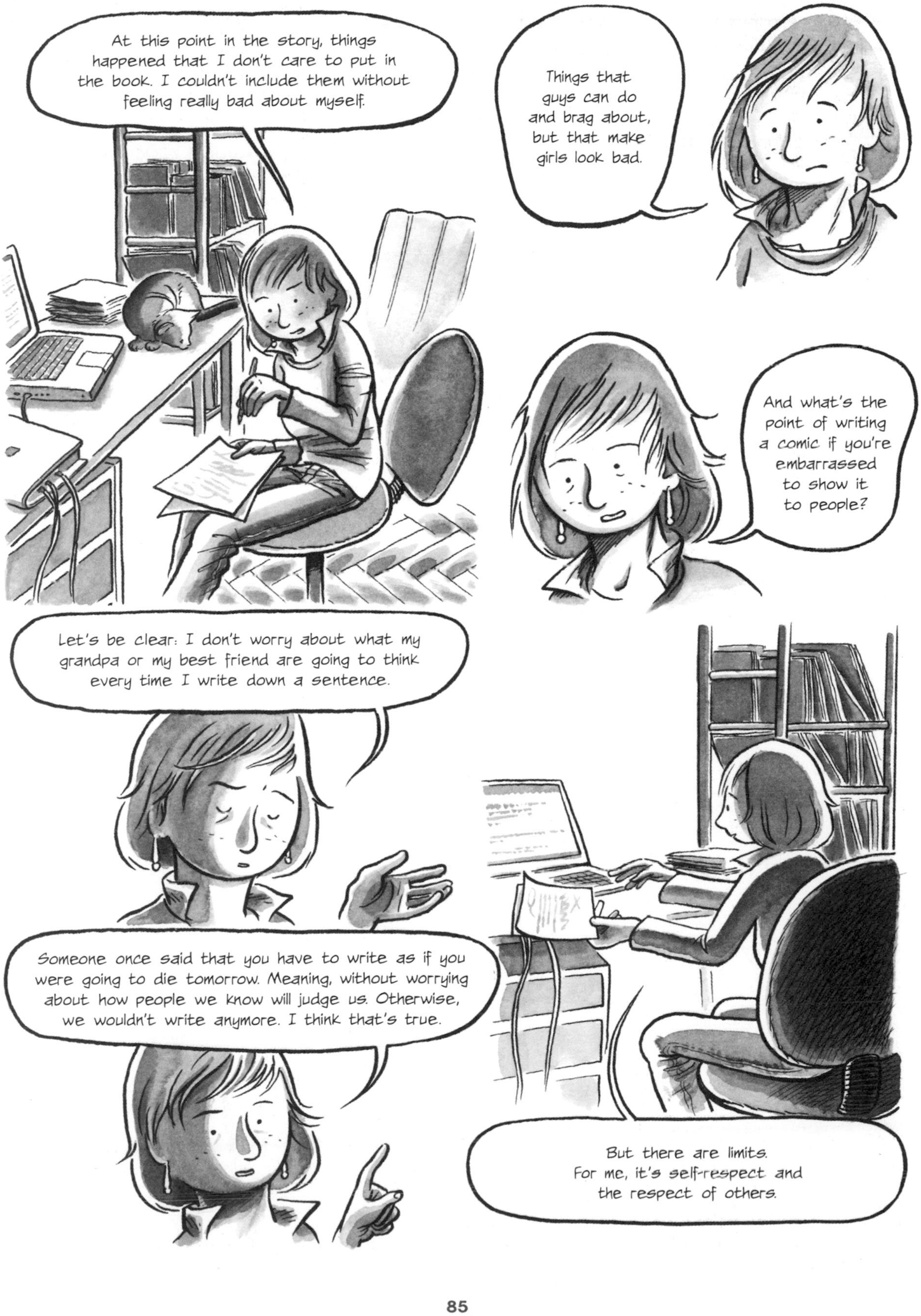

At this point in the story, things happened that I don't care to put in the book. I couldn't include them without feeling really bad about myself.
Things that guys can do and brag about, but that make girls look bad.
And what's the point of writing a comic if you're embarrassed to show it to people?
Let's be clear: I don't worry about what my grandpa or my best friend are going to think every time I write down a sentence.
Someone once said that you have to write as if you were going to die tomorrow. Meaning, without worrying about how people we know will judge us. Otherwise, we wouldn't write anymore. I think that's true.
But there are limits. For me, it's self-respect and the respect of others.

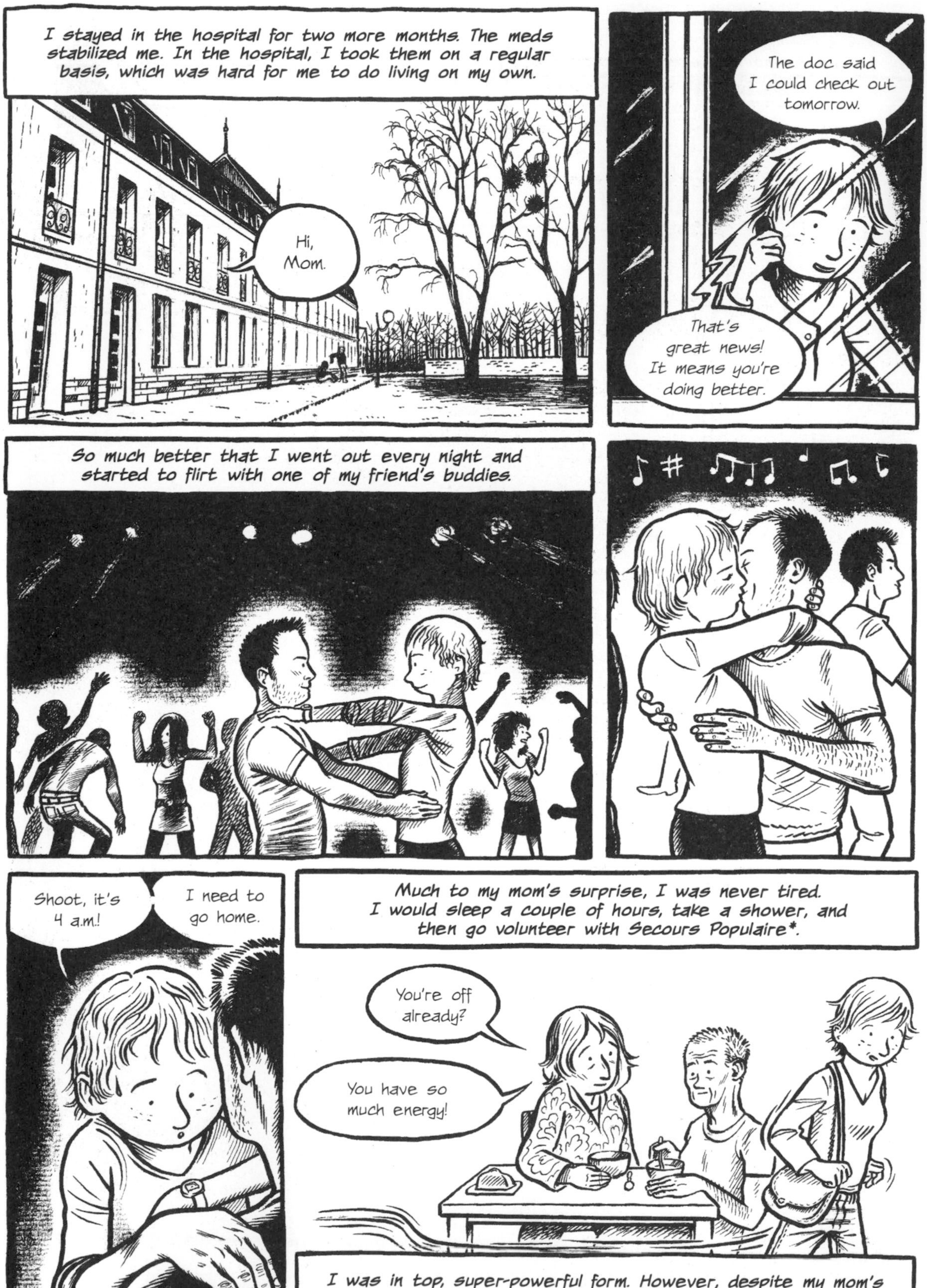
I stayed in the hospital for two more months. The meds stabilized me. In the hospital, I took them on a regular basis, which was hard for me to do living on my own.
Hi, Mom.
The doc said I could check out tomorrow.
That's great news! It means you're doing better.
So much better that I went out every night and started to flirt with one of my friend's buddies.
Shoot, it's 4 a.m.!
I need to go home.
Much to my mom's surprise, I was never tired. I would sleep a couple of hours, take a shower, and then go volunteer with Secours Populaire*.
You're off already?
You have so much energy!
I was in top, super-powerful form. However, despite my mom's diligence, I was taking my meds with less and less regularity.

*A French non-profit that fights against poverty, hunger, social injustice and more.

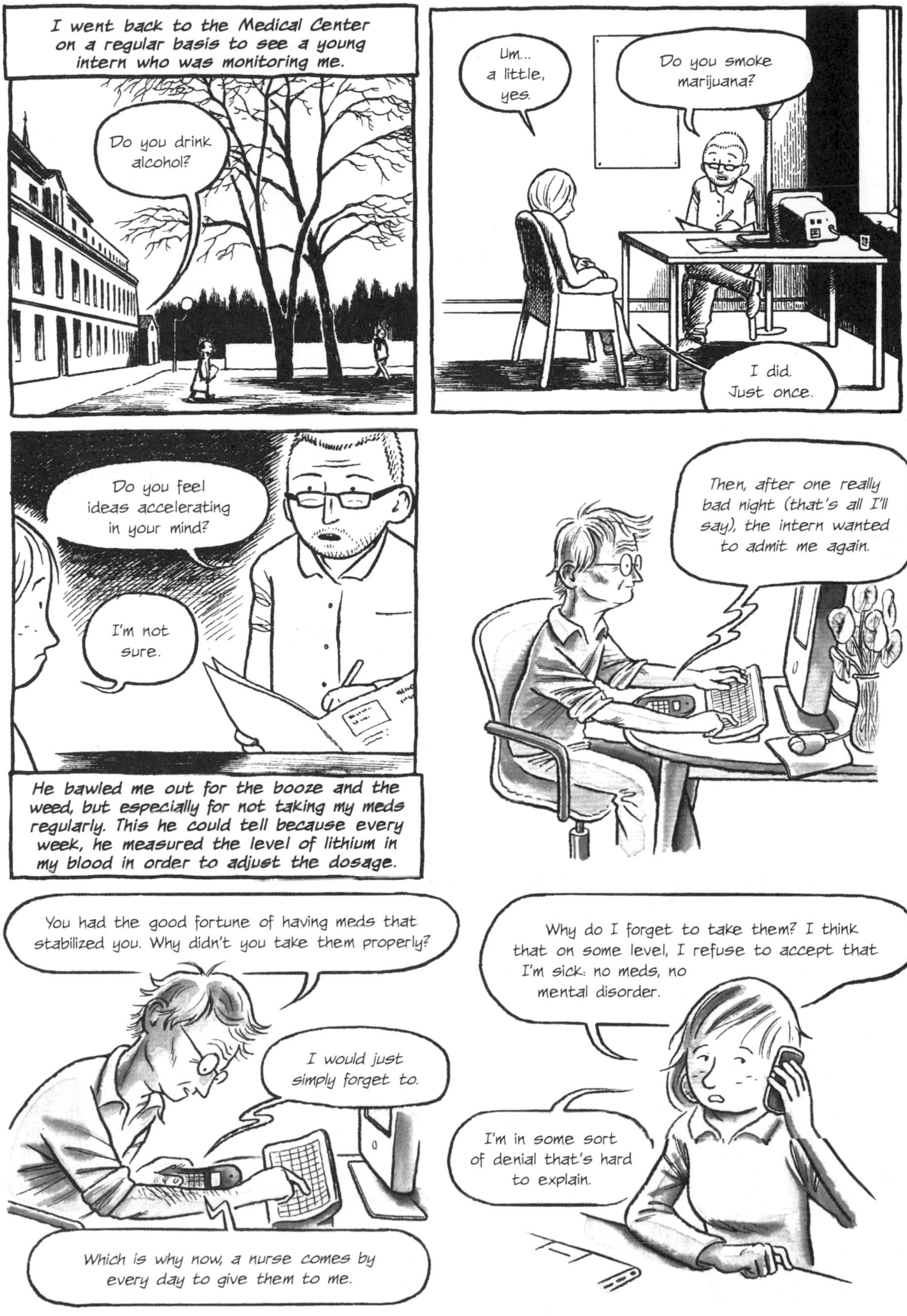
I went back to the Medical Center on a regular basis to see a young intern who was monitoring me.
Do you drink alcohol?
Do you smoke marijuana?
Um... a little, yes.
I did. Just once.
Do you feel ideas accelerating in your mind?
I'm not sure.
He bawled me out for the booze and the weed, but especially for not taking my meds regularly. This he could tell because every week, he measured the level of lithium in my blood in order to adjust the dosage.
Then, after one really bad night (that's all I'll say), the intern wanted to admit me again.
You had the good fortune of having meds that stabilized you. Why didn't you take them properly?
I would just simply forget to.
Which is why now, a nurse comes by every day to give them to me.
Why do I forget to take them? I think that on some level, I refuse to accept that I'm sick: no meds, no mental disorder.
I'm in some sort of denial that's hard to explain.

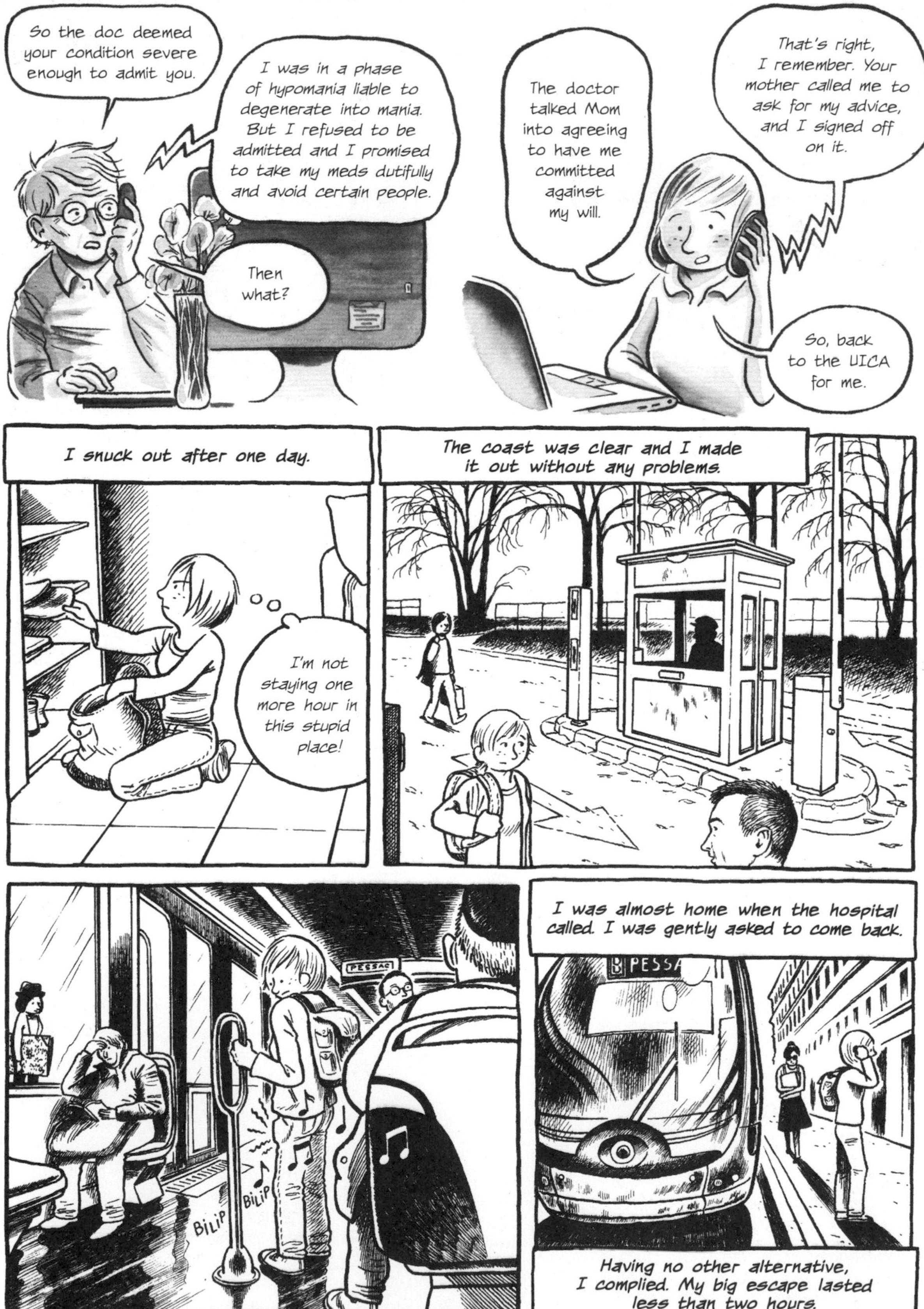
So the doc deemed your condition severe enough to admit you.
I was in a phase of hypomania liable to degenerate into mania. But I refused to be admitted and I promised to take my meds dutifully and avoid certain people.
Then what?
The doctor talked Mom into agreeing to have me committed against my will.
That's right, I remember. Your mother called me to ask for my advice, and I signed off on it.
So, back to the UICA for me.
I snuck out after one day.
I'm not staying one more hour in this stupid place!
The coast was clear and I made it out without any problems.
PESSAC
BILIP
BILIP
I was almost home when the hospital called. I was gently asked to come back.
PESSA
Having no other alternative, I complied. My big escape lasted less than two hours.

Because the Center is an open facility and you violated the rules, we're transferring you to North 2!

Nooo!!

North 2 was punishment: a rather dilapidated, secure unit that took in the worst cases.

Checking in was the usual protocol: no visitors, no outings, no phone.

And yet I don't feel anything. Not depressed, not anything. And with the whack jobs in here, it's going to be hell!

Being hospitalized did have the advantage of immediately lowering my euphoric behavior, even though that was linked more to an aspect of my personality than to my disorder (at least that's what the intern who was treating me said).

As soon as I was allowed visitors, my father and my stepmom came to see me.

So how are you?

I can't stand being locked up in here with nothing to do, when I feel totally fine!

I lost my job at Secours Populaire, I lost my new boyfriend...

It's enough to make me crazy for real!

Can't you find something to do?

Like what? I can't concentrate enough to read and there are no activities. All I can do is keep a diary where I write down everything I do.

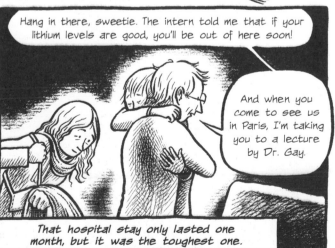

Hang in there, sweetie. The intern told me that if your lithium levels are good, you'll be out of here soon!

And when you come to see us in Paris, I'm taking you to a lecture by Dr. Gay.

That hospital stay only lasted one month, but it was the toughest one.

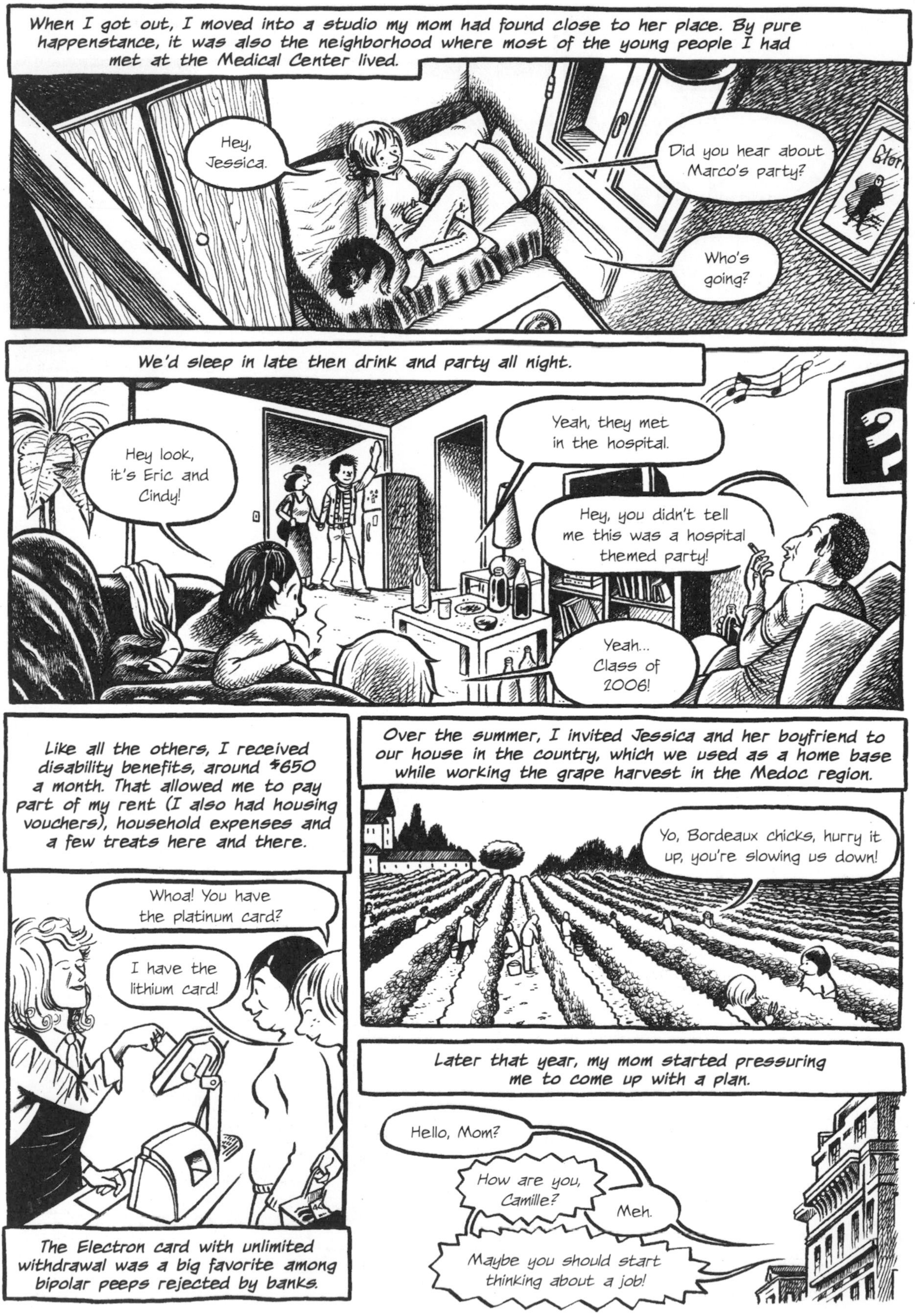

When I got out, I moved into a studio my mom had found close to her place. By pure happenstance, it was also the neighborhood where most of the young people I had met at the Medical Center lived.
Hey, Jessica.
Did you hear about Marco's party?
Who's going?
We'd sleep in late then drink and party all night.
Hey look, it's Eric and Cindy!
Yeah, they met in the hospital.
Hey, you didn't tell me this was a hospital themed party!
Yeah... Class of 2006!
Like all the others, I received disability benefits, around $650 a month. That allowed me to pay part of my rent (I also had housing vouchers), household expenses and a few treats here and there.
Whoa! You have the platinum card?
I have the lithium card!
The Electron card with unlimited withdrawal was a big favorite among bipolar peeps rejected by banks.
Over the summer, I invited Jessica and her boyfriend to our house in the country, which we used as a home base while working the grape harvest in the Medoc region.
Yo, Bordeaux chicks, hurry it up, you're slowing us down!
Later that year, my mom started pressuring me to come up with a plan.
Hello, Mom?
How are you, Camille?
Meh.
Maybe you should start thinking about a job!

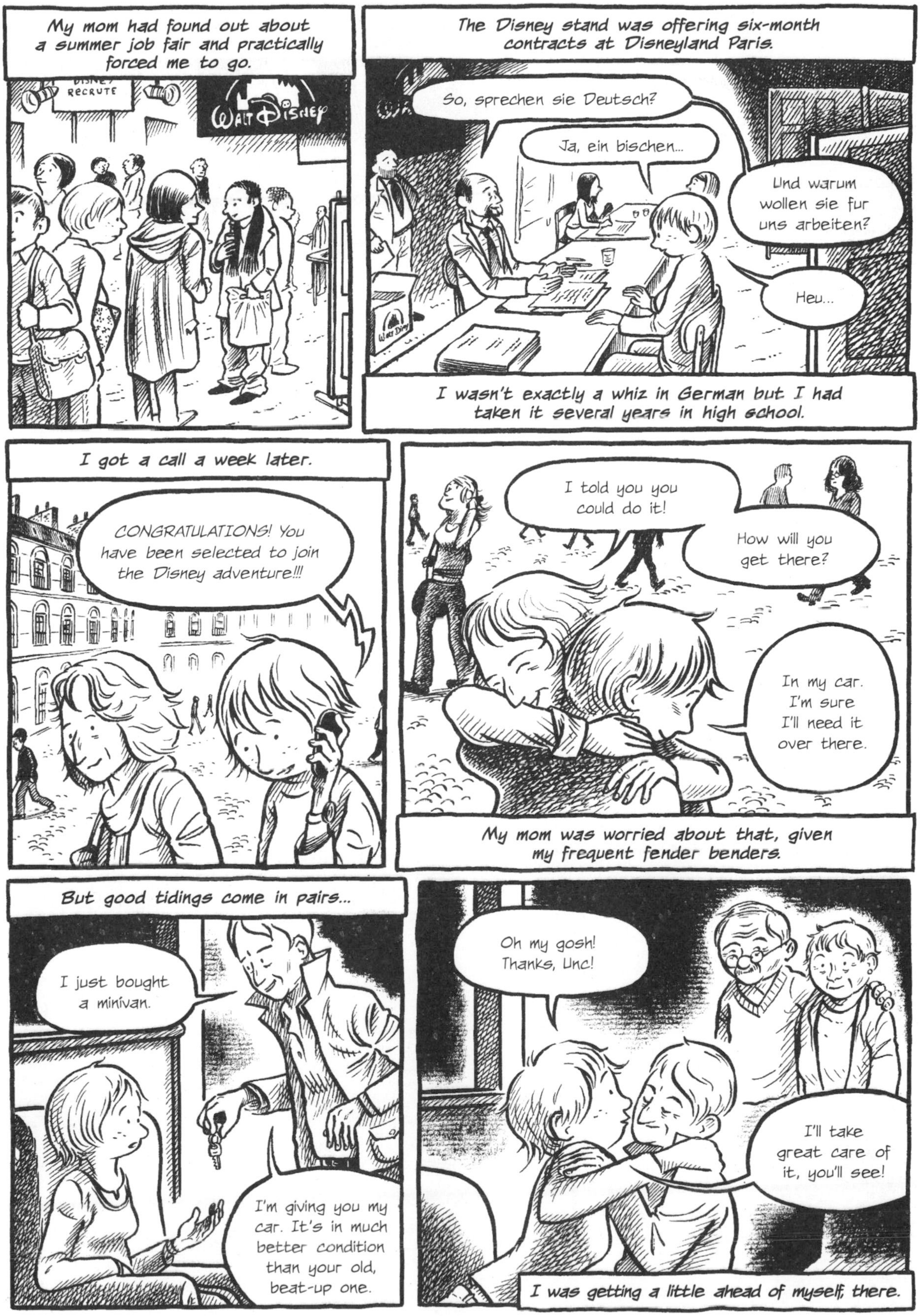

My mom had found out about a summer job fair and practically forced me to go.
DISNEY RECRUTE
WALT DISNEY
The Disney stand was offering six-month contracts at Disneyland Paris.
So, sprechen sie Deutsch?
Ja, ein bischen...
Und warum wollen sie fur uns arbeiten?
Heu...
I wasn't exactly a whiz in German but I had taken it several years in high school.
I got a call a week later.
CONGRATULATIONS! You have been selected to join the Disney adventure!!!
I told you you could do it!
How will you get there?
In my car. I'm sure I'll need it over there.
My mom was worried about that, given my frequent fender benders.
But good tidings come in pairs...
I just bought a minivan.
I'm giving you my car. It's in much better condition than your old, beat-up one.
Oh my gosh! Thanks, Unc!
I'll take great care of it, you'll see!
I was getting a little ahead of myself, there.

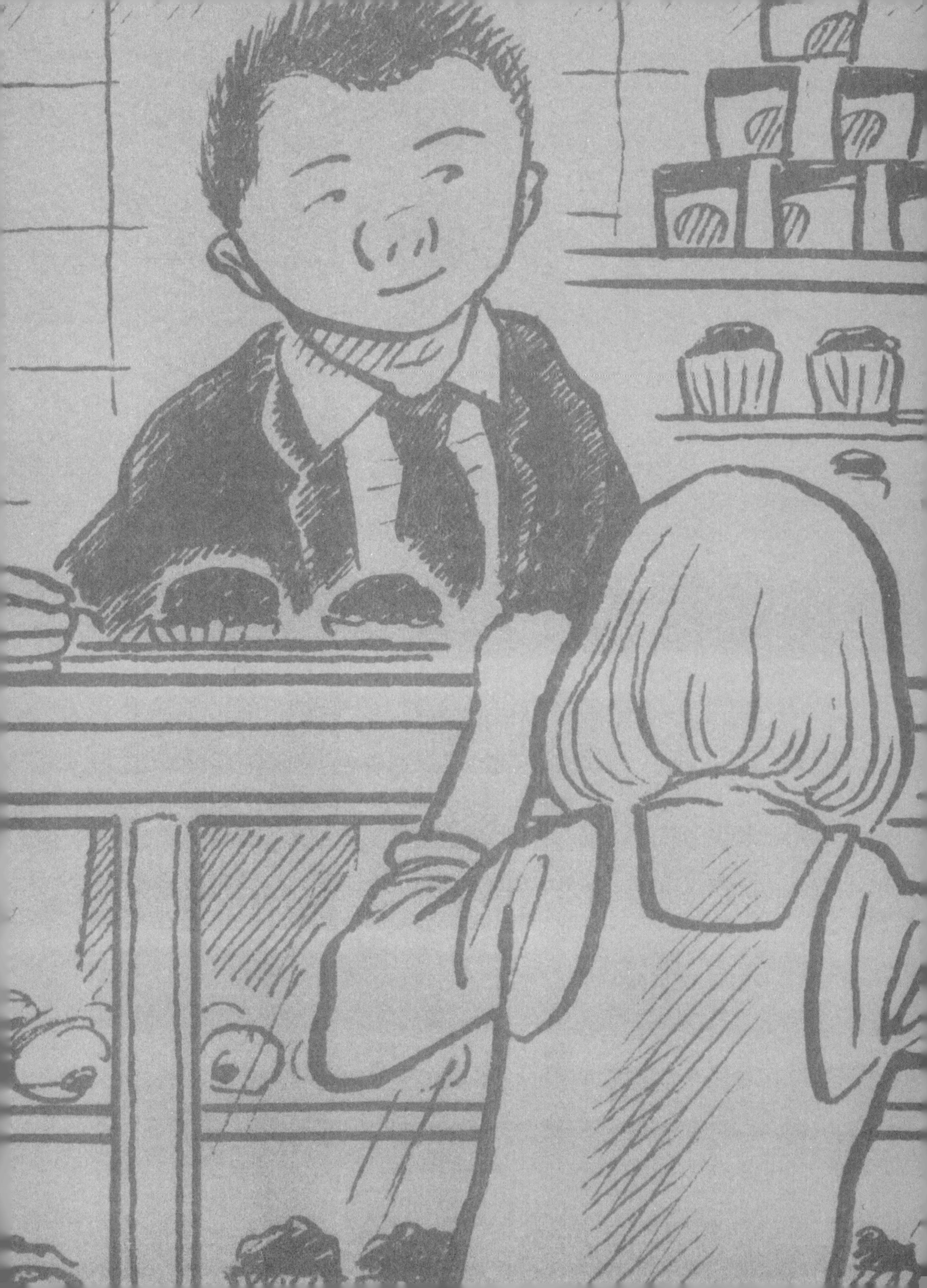

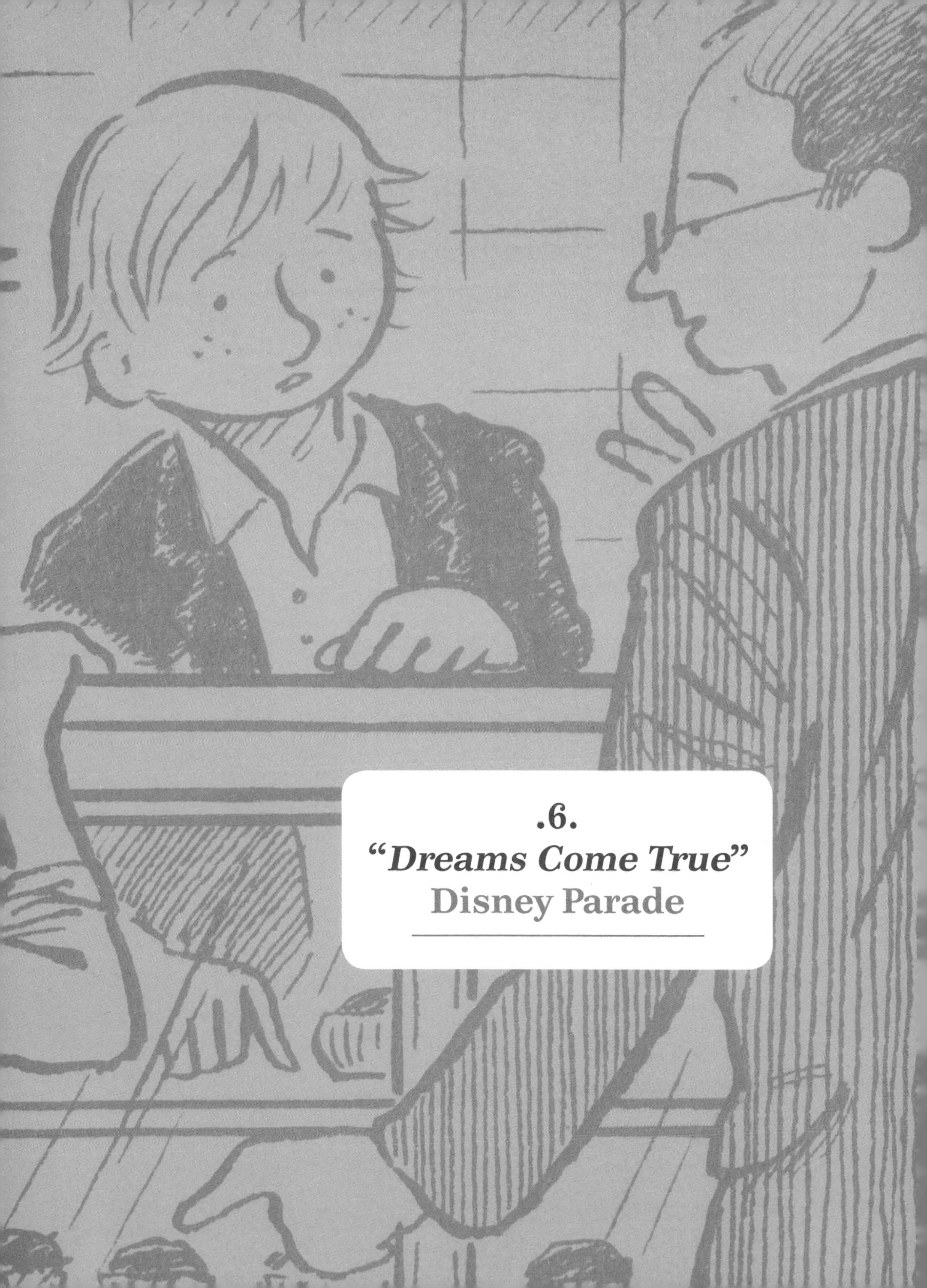

.6.
"Dreams Come True"
Disney Parade

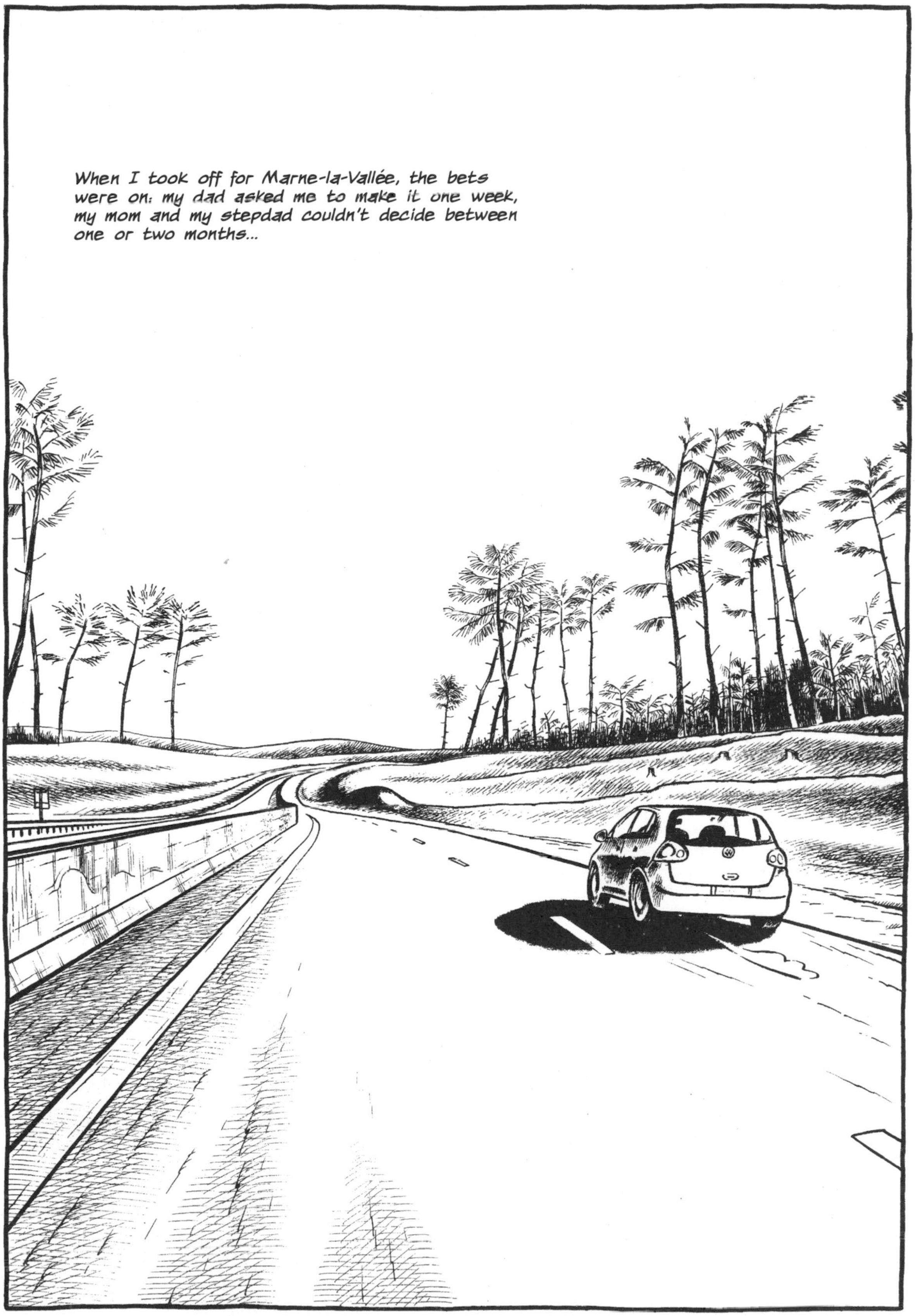
When I took off for Marne-la-Vallée, the bets were on: my dad asked me to make it one week, my mom and my stepdad couldn't decide between one or two months...

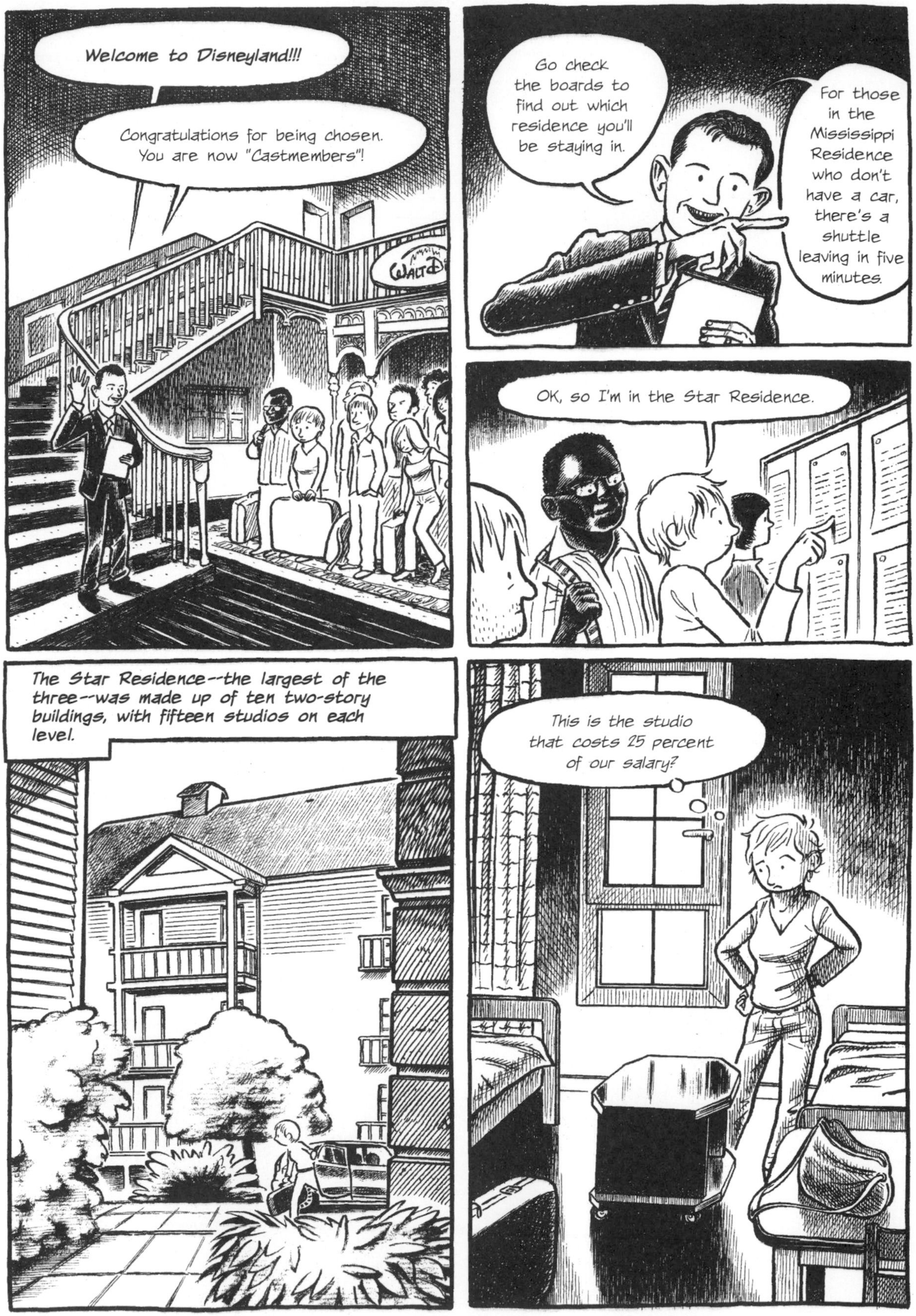
Welcome to Disneyland!!!
Congratulations for being chosen. You are now "Castmembers"!
WALT DI
Go check the boards to find out which residence you'll be staying in.
For those in the Mississippi Residence who don't have a car, there's a shuttle leaving in five minutes.
OK, so I'm in the Star Residence.
The Star Residence--the largest of the three--was made up of ten two-story buildings, with fifteen studios on each level.
This is the studio that costs 25 percent of our salary?

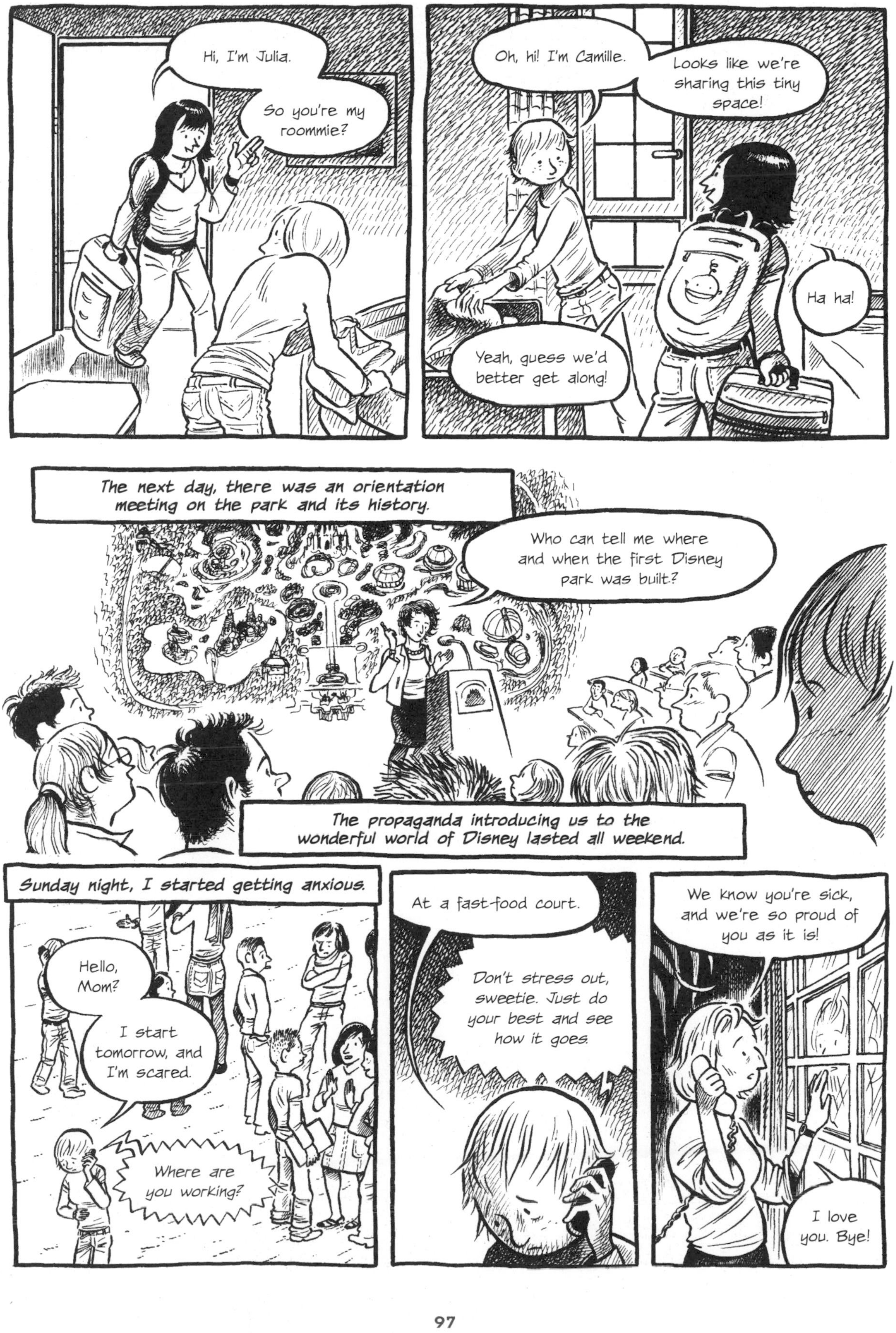
Hi, I'm Julia.
So you're my roommie?
Oh, hi! I'm Camille.
Looks like we're sharing this tiny space!
Yeah, guess we'd better get along!
Ha ha!
The next day, there was an orientation meeting on the park and its history.
Who can tell me where and when the first Disney park was built?
The propaganda introducing us to the wonderful world of Disney lasted all weekend.
Sunday night, I started getting anxious.
Hello, Mom?
I start tomorrow, and I'm scared.
Where are you working?
At a fast-food court.
Don't stress out, sweetie. Just do your best and see how it goes.
We know you're sick, and we're so proud of you as it is!
I love you. Bye!

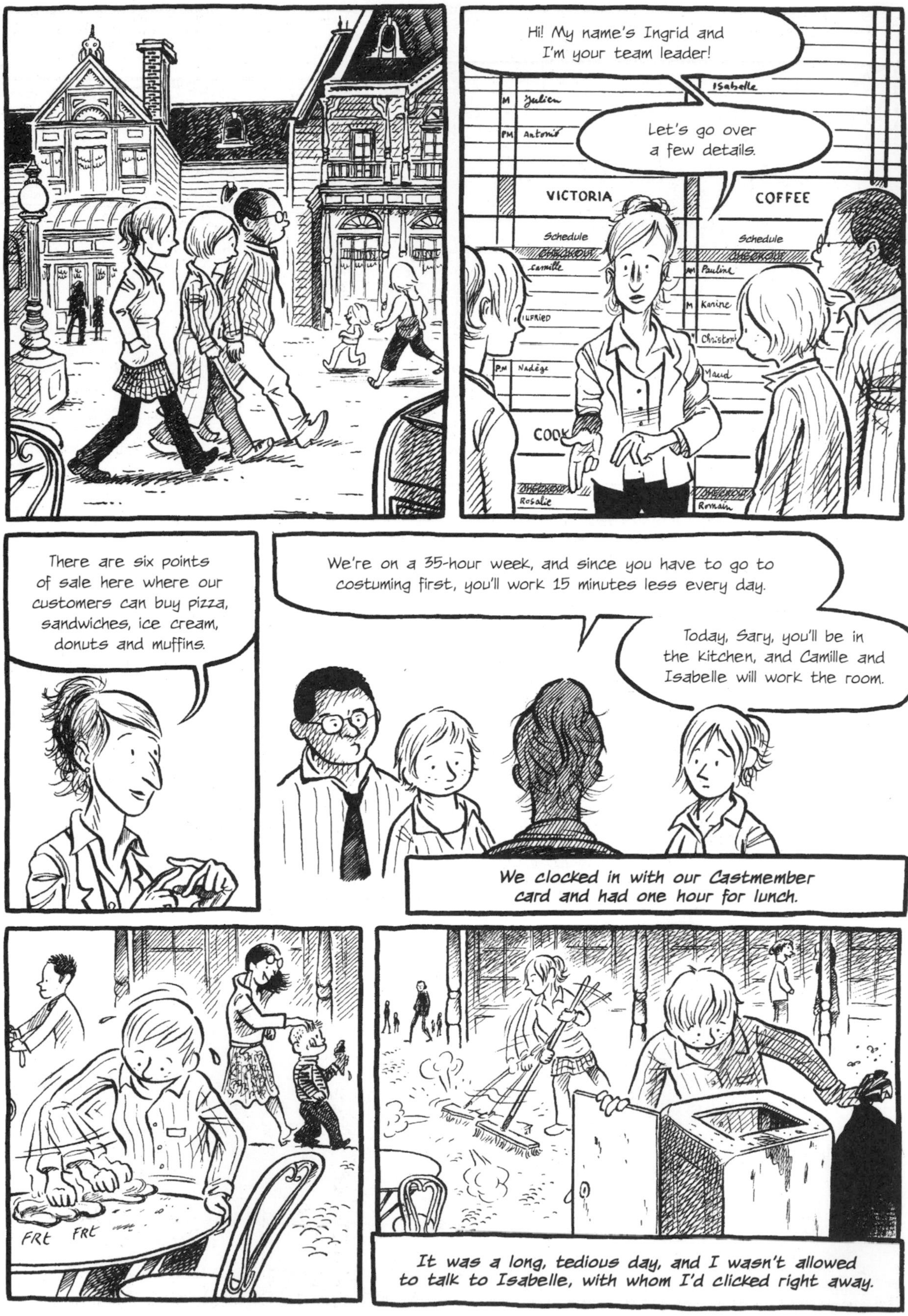

Hi! My name's Ingrid and I'm your team leader!
Let's go over a few details.
VICTORIA
COFFEE
There are six points of sale here where our customers can buy pizza, sandwiches, ice cream, donuts and muffins.
We're on a 35-hour week, and since you have to go to costuming first, you'll work 15 minutes less every day.
Today, Sary, you'll be in the kitchen, and Camille and Isabelle will work the room.
We clocked in with our Castmember card and had one hour for lunch.
FRt FRt
It was a long, tedious day, and I wasn't allowed to talk to Isabelle, with whom I'd clicked right away.

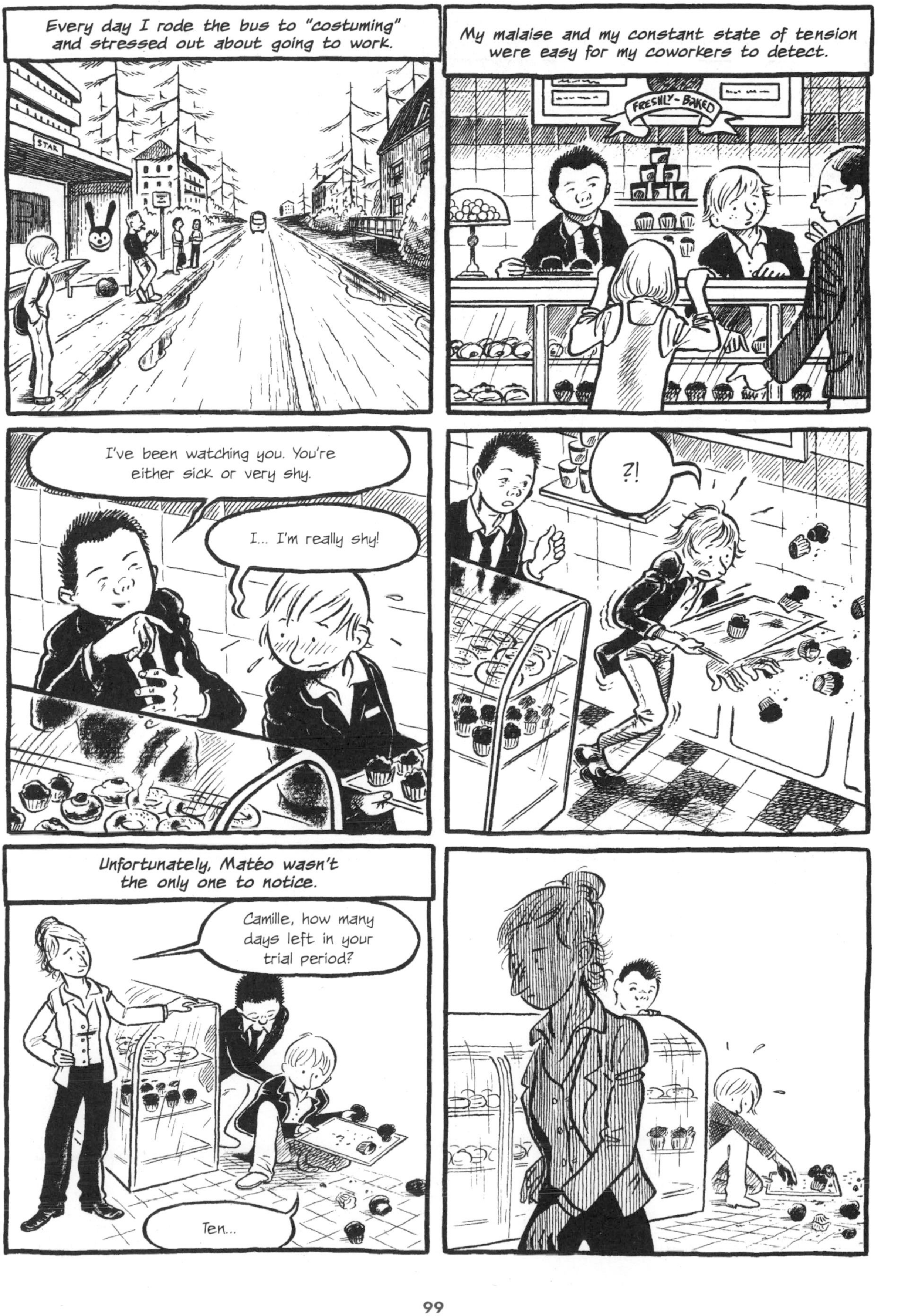

Every day I rode the bus to "costuming" and stressed out about going to work.
STAR
My malaise and my constant state of tension were easy for my coworkers to detect.
FRESHLY-BAKED
I've been watching you. You're either sick or very shy.
I... I'm really shy!
?!
Unfortunately, Matéo wasn't the only one to notice.
Camille, how many days left in your trial period?
Ten...

A few days later, another team leader made a remark.

Hey, Camille! Hurry it up a bit, you're too slow!

I couldn't stand the pressure. Two days before my trial period ended, I went to see the manager.

MANAGER

Knock knock

Come in!

I know you're going to fire me, so I'd might as well leave now!

Just so you know, it's because I have a disorder!

I had no intention of firing you.

What's your disorder?

I'm bipolar.

What's that?

It's the new word for manic-depressive.

Depressive, ah... Calm down, and don't worry.

Get to work. You're staying here.

Despite his support, I was still highly anxious. I requested the most humble jobs, with no register or contact with customers.

COFFEE

Schedule

AM Camille

M Sany

PM Fara
Isabelle

Sadie

Schedule

AM Eric

M David

PM Fred

Whew! I'm on cleaning duty again!

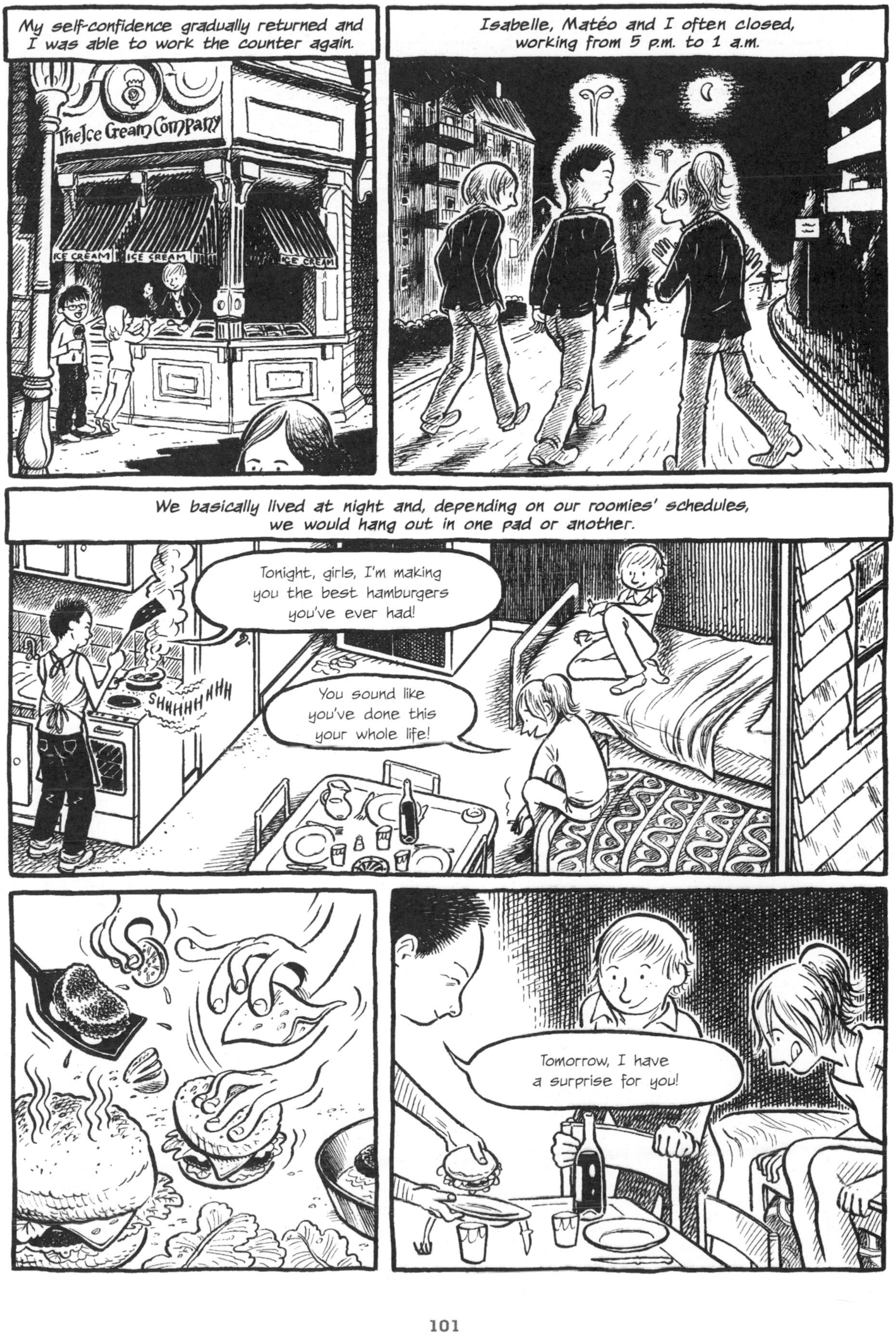
My self-confidence gradually returned and I was able to work the counter again.
The Ice Cream Company
ICE CREAM
ICE CREAM
ICE CREAM
Isabelle, Matéo and I often closed, working from 5 p.m. to 1 a.m.
We basically lived at night and, depending on our roomies' schedules, we would hang out in one pad or another.
Tonight, girls, I'm making you the best hamburgers you've ever had!
SHHHHHHHHH
You sound like you've done this your whole life!
Tomorrow, I have a surprise for you!

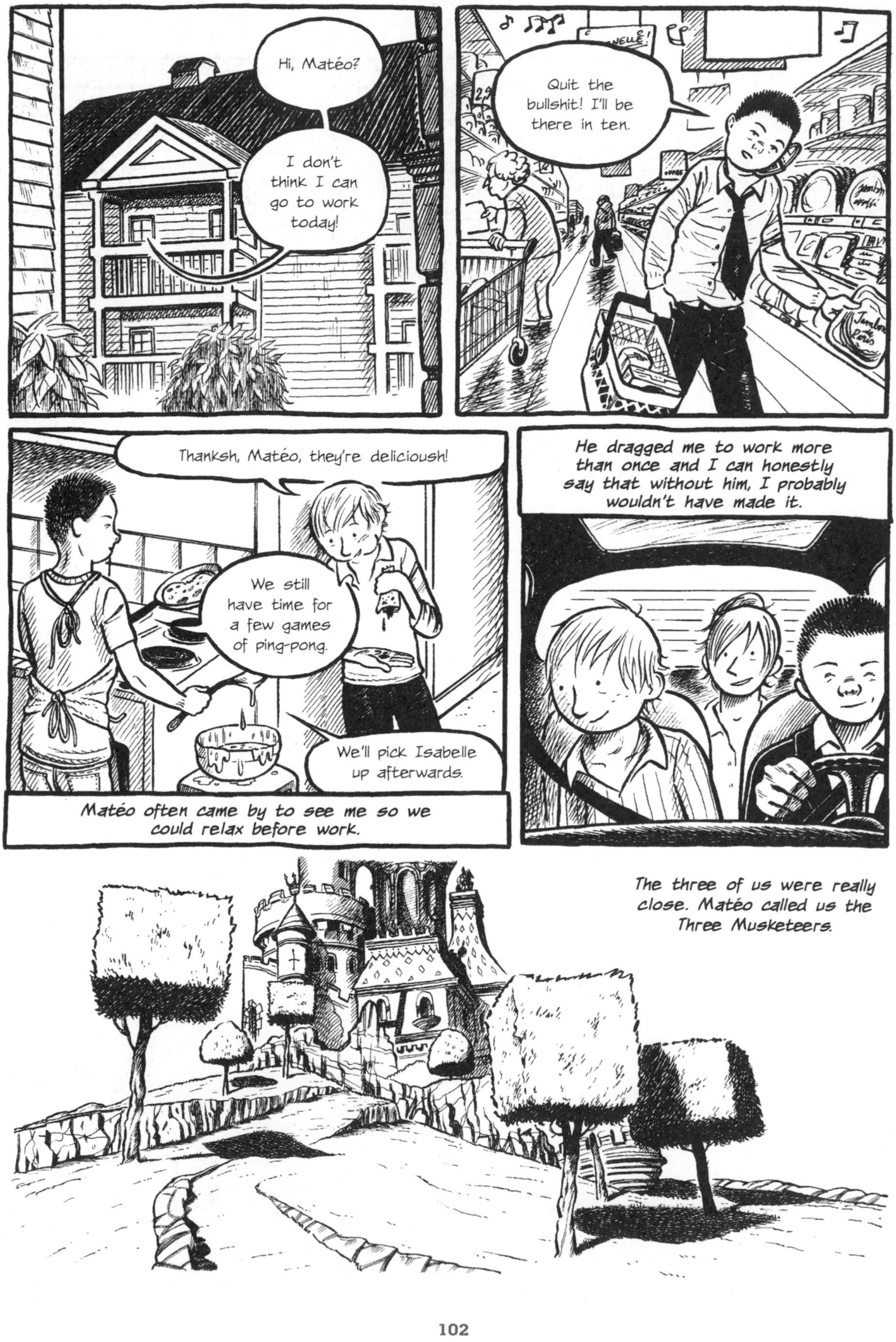
Hi, Matéo?
I don't think I can go to work today!
Quit the bullshit! I'll be there in ten.
Thanksh, Matéo, they're delicioush!
We still have time for a few games of ping-pong.
We'll pick Isabelle up afterwards.
Matéo often came by to see me so we could relax before work.
He dragged me to work more than once and I can honestly say that without him, I probably wouldn't have made it.
The three of us were really close. Matéo called us the Three Musketeers.

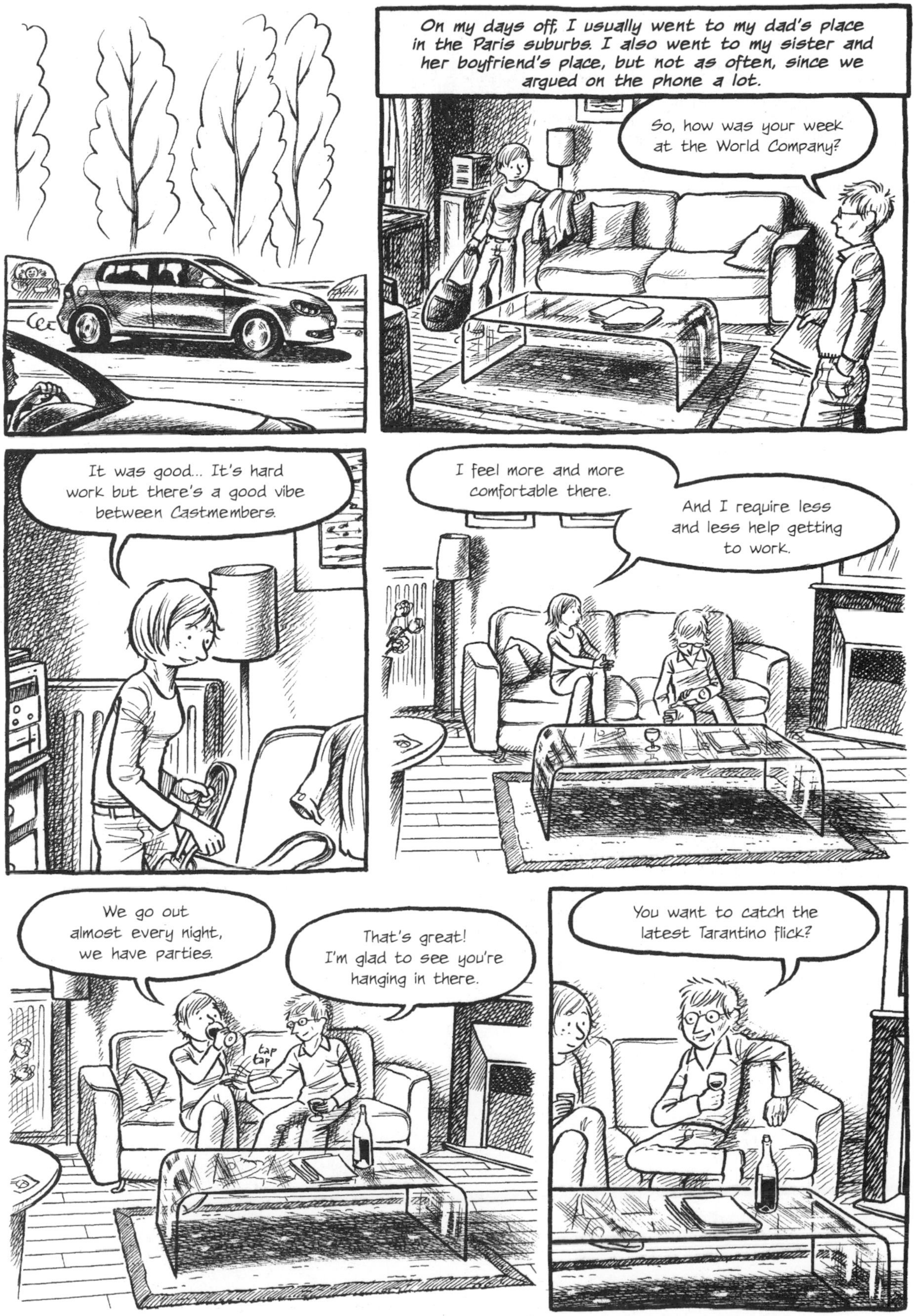

On my days off, I usually went to my dad's place in the Paris suburbs. I also went to my sister and her boyfriend's place, but not as often, since we argued on the phone a lot.
So, how was your week at the World Company?
It was good... It's hard work but there's a good vibe between Castmembers.
I feel more and more comfortable there.
And I require less and less help getting to work.
We go out almost every night, we have parties.
tap tap
That's great! I'm glad to see you're hanging in there.
You want to catch the latest Tarantino flick?

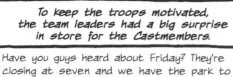

To keep the troops motivated, the team leaders had a big surprise in store for the Castmembers.

Have you guys heard about Friday? They're closing at seven and we have the park to ourselves!

And Mariah Carey's giving a private concert!

No way!

Way! And there will be stands with free champagne!

Yesss!

I called my mom every day, and when things were bad, even more.

Hi, Mom.

I'm stressing about tomorrow.

Are you sure you took all your meds?

Well actually, I'm missing one.

Hurry up and go see a GP and get a prescription.

And call your father. Now that he's close by, he can take care of you.

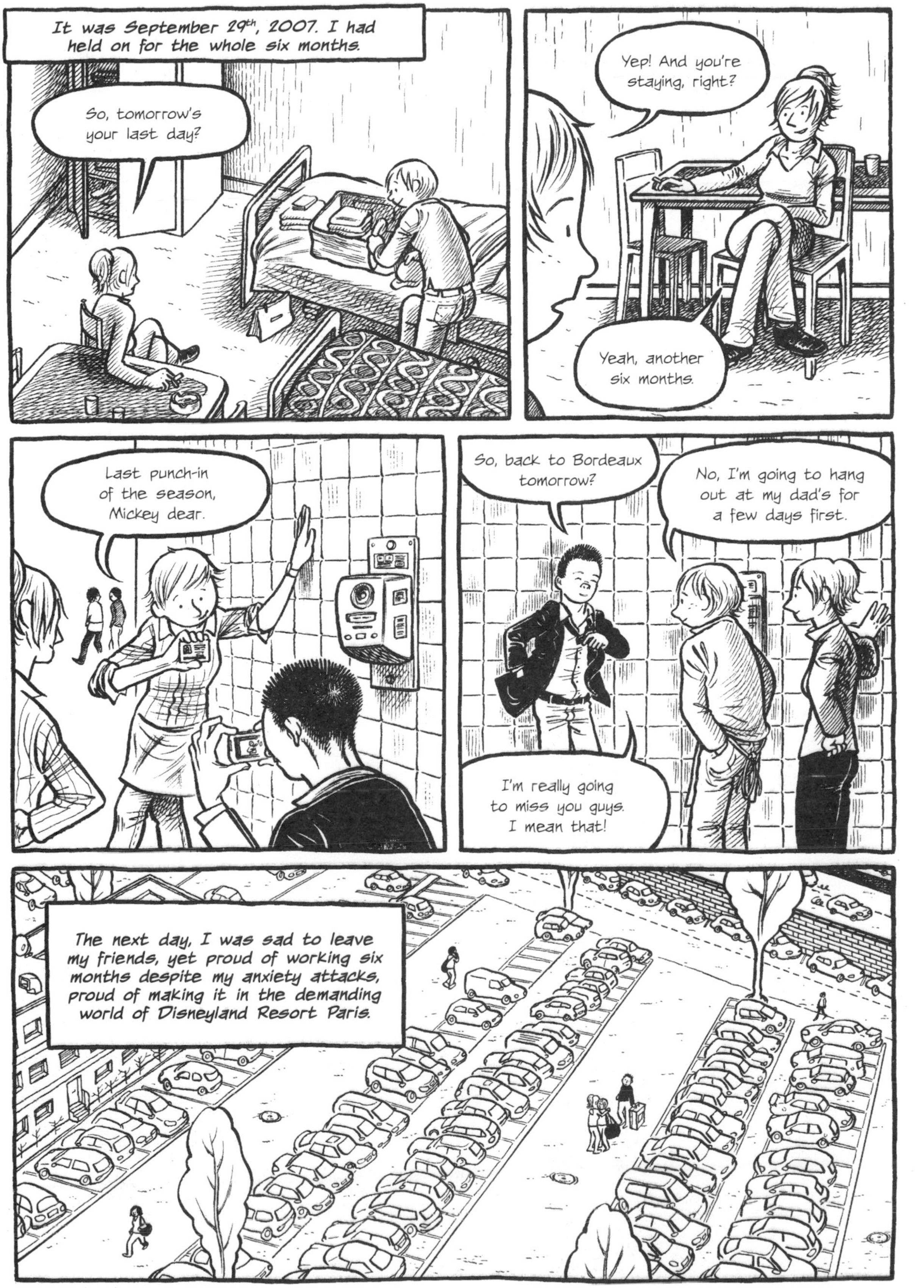
It was September 29th, 2007. I had held on for the whole six months.
So, tomorrow's your last day?
Yep! And you're staying, right?
Yeah, another six months.
Last punch-in of the season, Mickey dear.
So, back to Bordeaux tomorrow?
No, I'm going to hang out at my dad's for a few days first.
I'm really going to miss you guys. I mean that!
The next day, I was sad to leave my friends, yet proud of working six months despite my anxiety attacks, proud of making it in the demanding world of Disneyland Resort Paris.

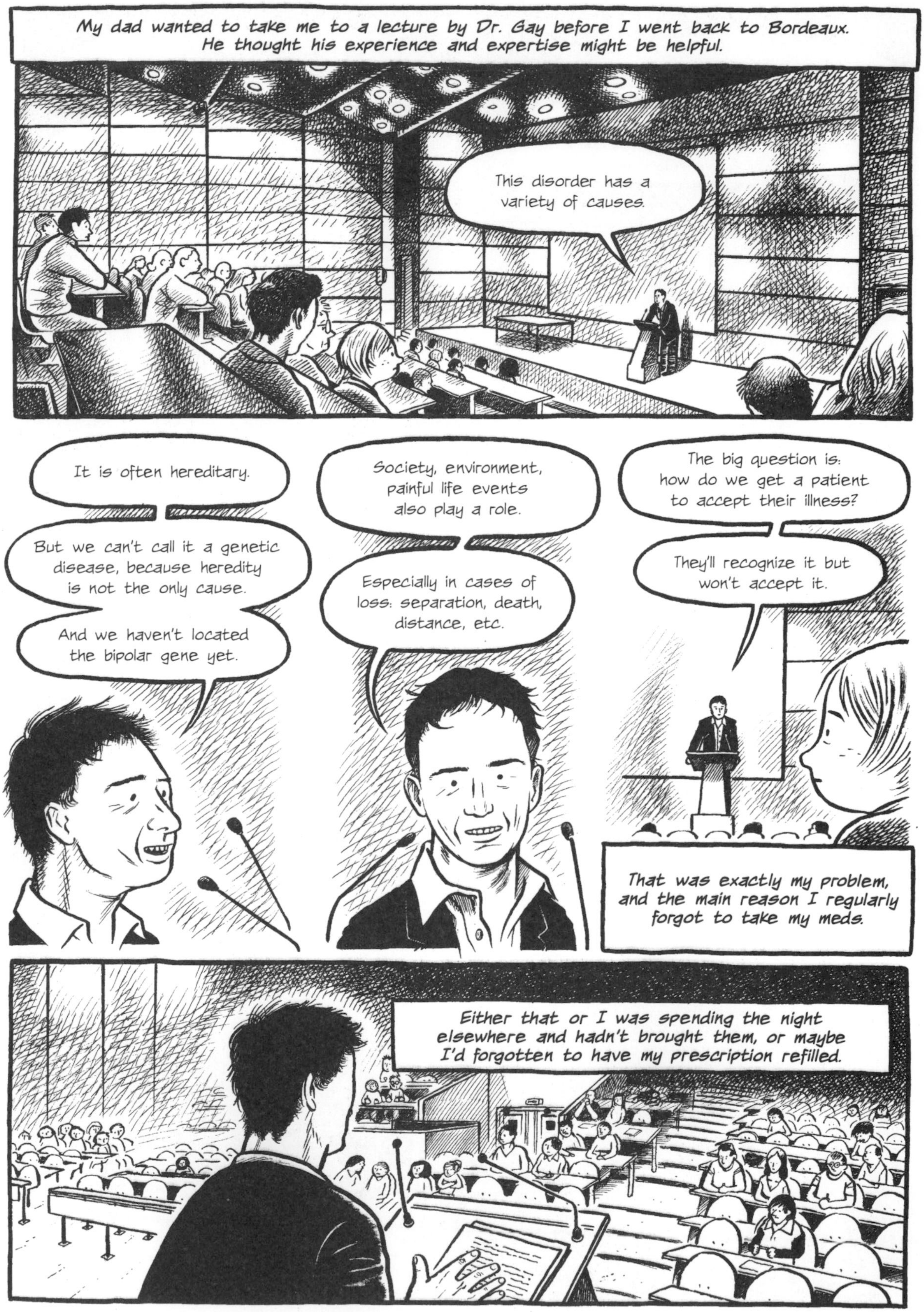
My dad wanted to take me to a lecture by Dr. Gay before I went back to Bordeaux. He thought his experience and expertise might be helpful.
This disorder has a variety of causes.
It is often hereditary.
But we can't call it a genetic disease, because heredity is not the only cause.
And we haven't located the bipolar gene yet.
Society, environment, painful life events also play a role.
Especially in cases of loss: separation, death, distance, etc.
The big question is: how do we get a patient to accept their illness?
They'll recognize it but won't accept it.
That was exactly my problem, and the main reason I regularly forgot to take my meds.
Either that or I was spending the night elsewhere and hadn't brought them, or maybe I'd forgotten to have my prescription refilled.

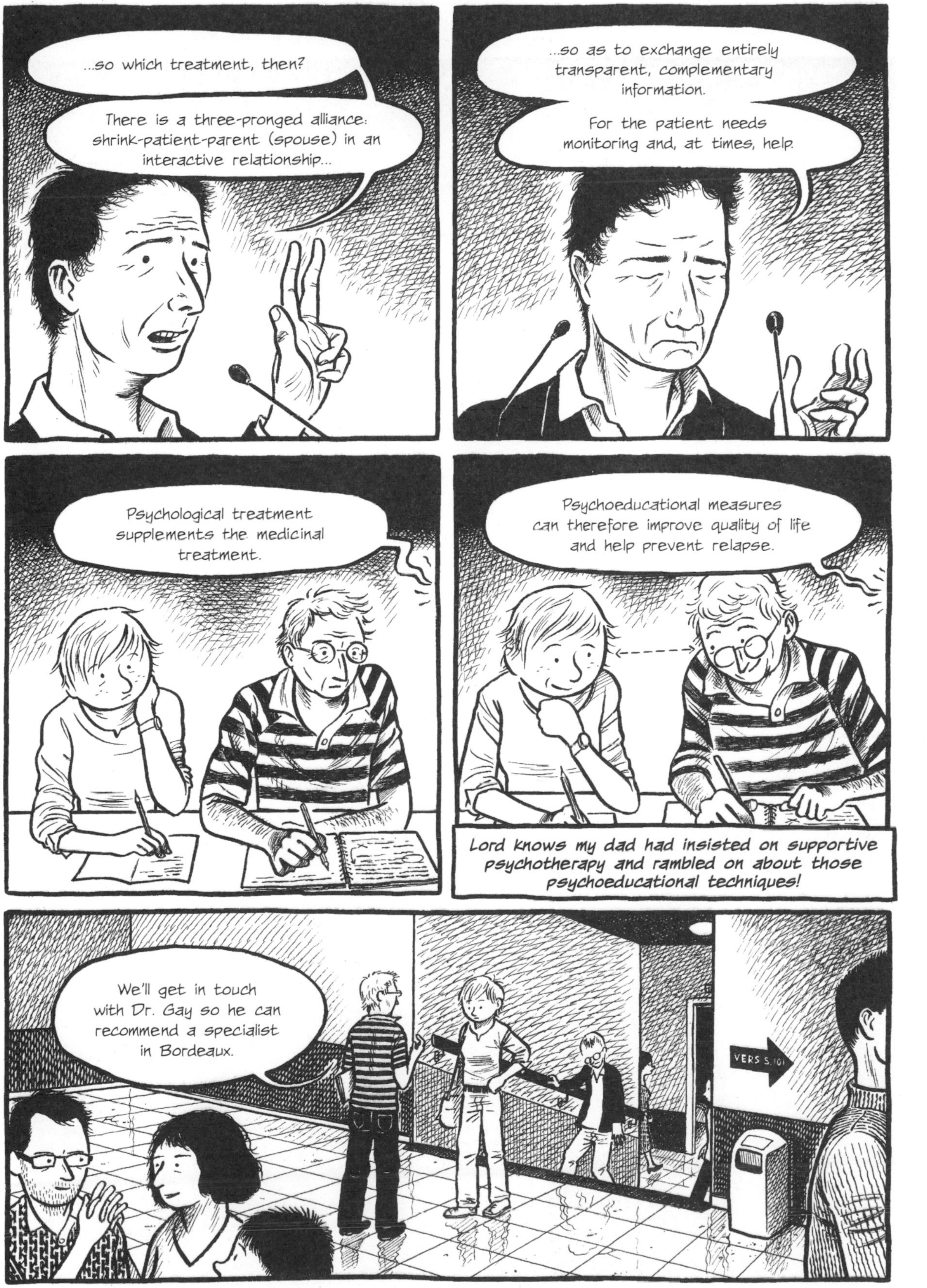
...so which treatment, then?
There is a three-pronged alliance: shrink-patient-parent (spouse) in an interactive relationship...
...so as to exchange entirely transparent, complementary information.
For the patient needs monitoring and, at times, help.
Psychological treatment supplements the medicinal treatment.
Psychoeducational measures can therefore improve quality of life and help prevent relapse.
Lord knows my dad had insisted on supportive psychotherapy and rambled on about those psychoeducational techniques!
We'll get in touch with Dr. Gay so he can recommend a specialist in Bordeaux.
VERS S.101

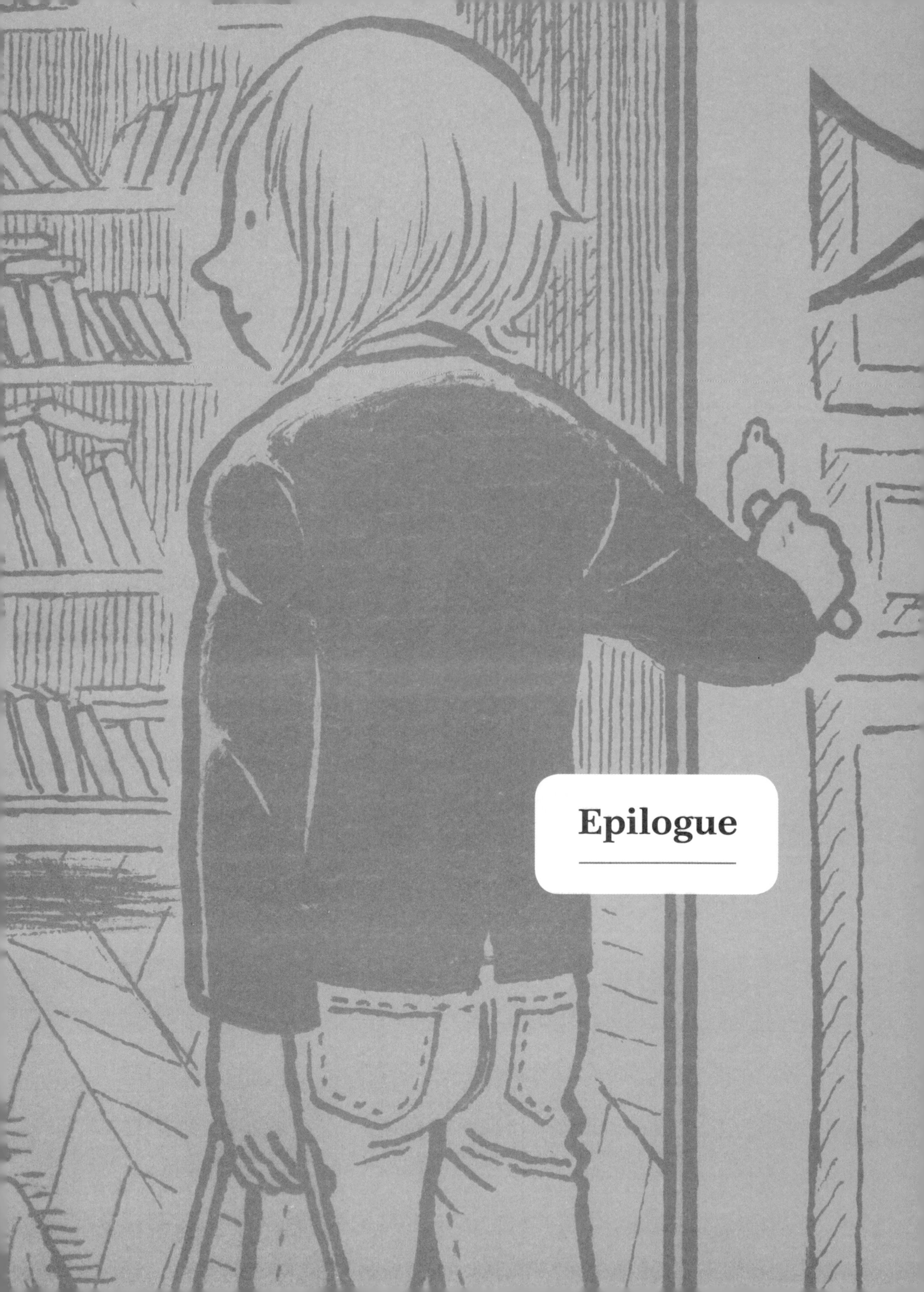

Epilogue

Hi, Mom!
I'll be there in ten minutes!
And guess what? I've decided to start therapy.
I have an appointment next week.
BZZZ
La Centrale
Good morning, Doctor.
My name is Camille. I've come here because I need help... I have Bipolar Disorder...

Emilie Guillon Patrice Guillon Sébastien Samson Août 2010

Behind the Scenes

Sebastien Samson shares some of his sketches for *States of Mind*, a peek into the book's creative process.

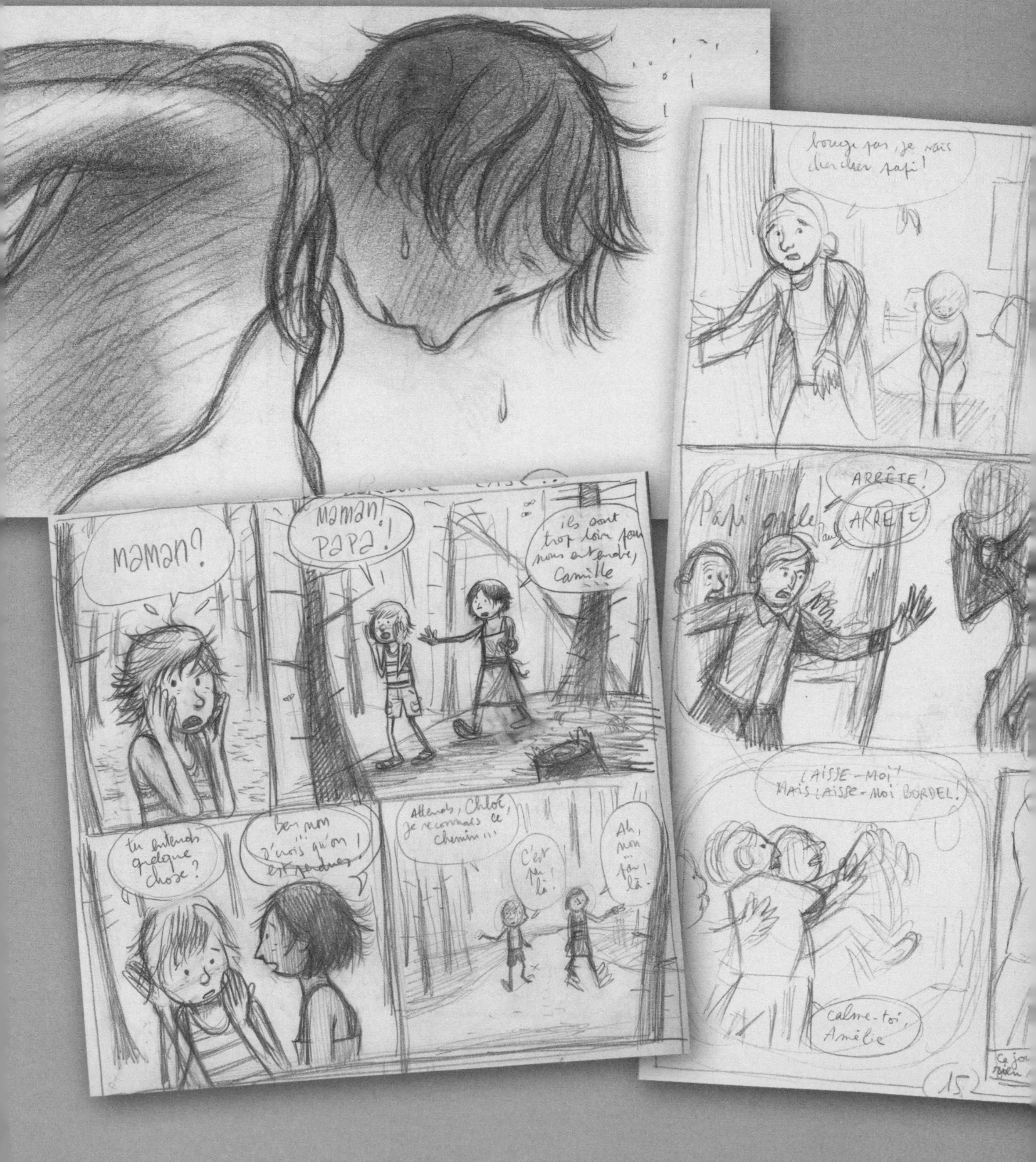
MAMAN?
MAMAN! PAPA!
ils sont trop loin pour nous entendre, Camille
tu entends quelque chose?
Ben non ... j'crois qu'on est perdues!
Attends, Chloé, je reconnais ce chemin...
C'est par là!
Ah, non ... par là.
bouge pas, je vais chercher papi!
ARRÊTE!
ARRÊTE
LAISSE-MOI! MAIS LAISSE-MOI BORDEL!
Calme-toi, Amélie
15

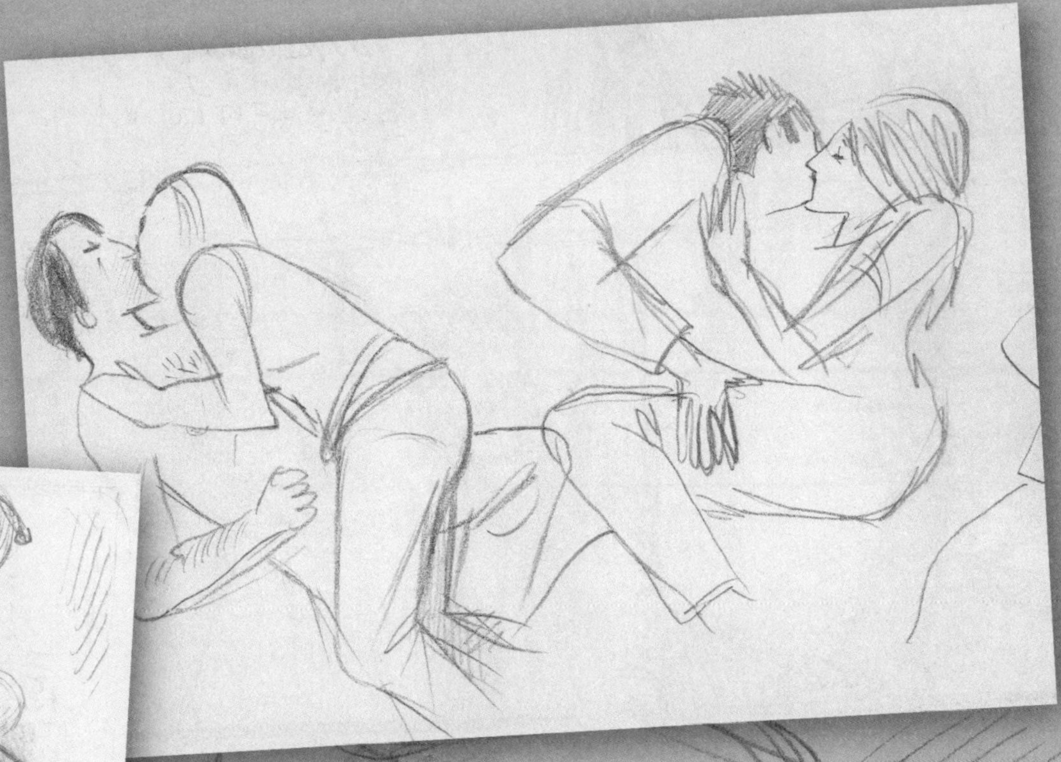

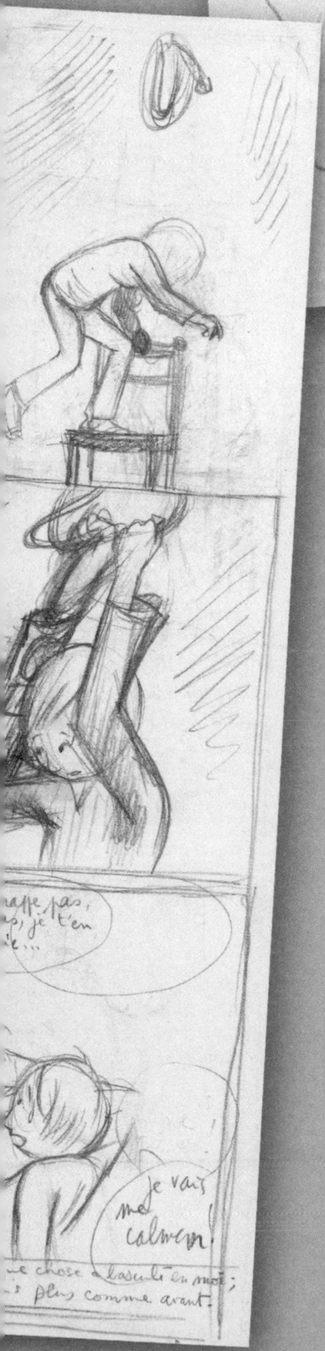
je vais me calmer!
plus comme avant.

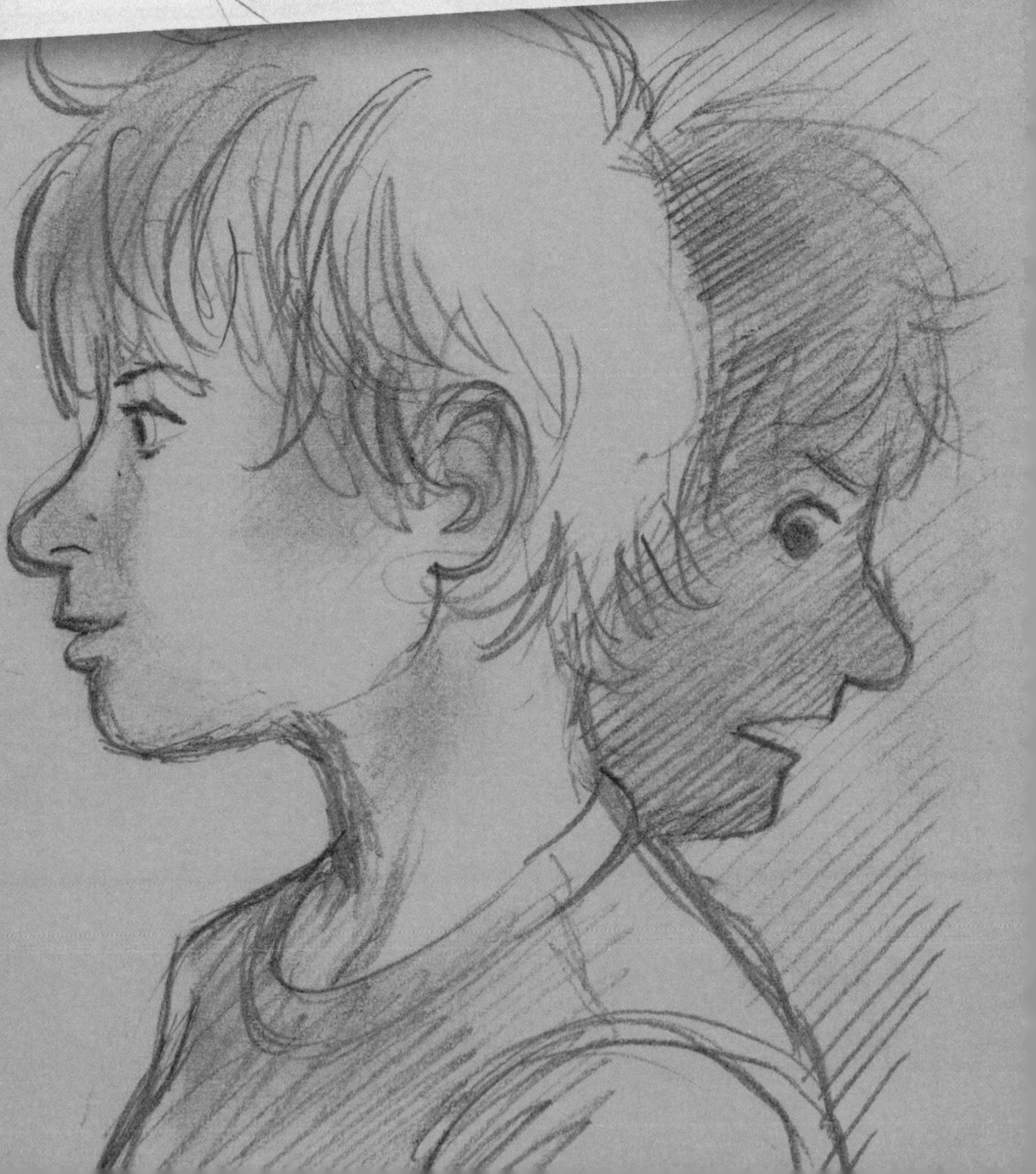

If you or someone
you know is in crisis
—whether they are
considering suicide or not—
please call the toll-free Lifeline
at **800-273-TALK (8255)**,
or text **NAMI to 741-741**
to speak with a trained
crisis counselor 24/7.

For non-emergency inquiries
and mental health resources, contact
1-800-950-NAMI (6264),
the National Alliance
on Mental Health.

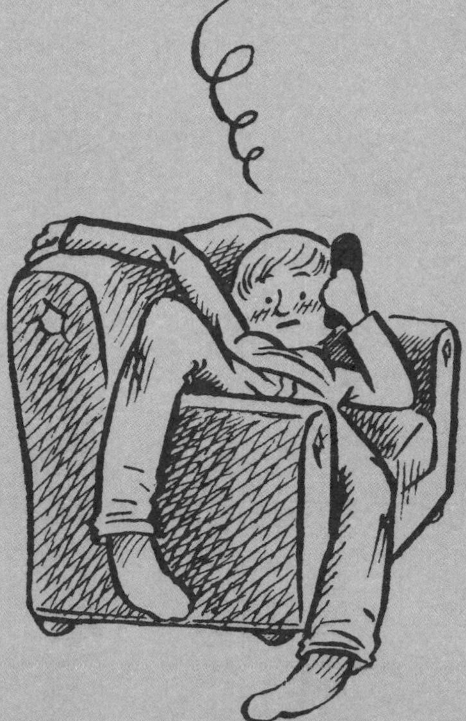

www.nami.org